DANGER IN THE DARKNESS

A ROSEMARY MOUNTAIN MYSTERY

BOOK THREE

NICOLE GARDNER

Chapter One

Daphne

If there's any such thing as a perfect moment, this must be it. I smiled, content, as I snuggled deeper into Emerson's arms. We were curled up on my sofa, sharing a blanket, as we watched the fire flickering in the stone fireplace. The world was quiet, and so were we.

Even Thor, Emerson's German shepherd, was curled up peacefully on the floor in front of the sofa. The three of us made a cozy picture. I knew just how I would photograph it, if I were playing photographer right now instead of subject. It would make a lovely photograph; warm, dark tones, with man, woman, and dog—a happy trio—illuminated by the golden glow of the fire.

I had never felt so whole, so happy.

The past year had been the hardest of my life, but it had led me here, to this love, this connection, and this home that meant so much to me. I was exactly where I belonged, and I was with the man I wanted to spend my life with. It was more happiness than I'd ever expected to find, and my heart felt like it could burst from joy and gratitude.

I looked up at Emerson and stroked his beard with my fingers. "I love you," I whispered.

He turned his face toward mine, his deep-brown eyes crinkling up in a sweet smile. "I love you too, sweetheart."

"Isn't this just perfect?" I asked, snuggling in even deeper. "I wish we could stay like this forever."

"Oh, yeah?"

"Yeah."

He leaned in to kiss me, but a knock on the door interrupted us.

Emerson frowned. "Expecting anyone?"

"No, not tonight." I sighed and pulled away from his arms, pushing away the blanket so I could get up and answer the door.

A wave of anxiety hit me before I even reached the doorway.

I paused before opening it, feeling a fear I couldn't understand. Everything within me wanted to run back to Emerson, wrap back up in the blanket, and ignore whatever was waiting for me on the other side of that door.

Whoever it was knocked again, sending another wave of nerves through me. I closed my eyes and braced myself.

But when I opened the door and saw Janet, my stepmother, standing there with a worried look on her face, I was utterly confused. My fear vanished—or changed, rather—as I pulled her inside. No longer worried for myself, I was deeply concerned about her. It wasn't like her to travel without telling me, and I had never seen her look so pale.

"I'm sorry I didn't call you," she began, "but I didn't know what to say. I felt I just needed to come straight here. That you needed to see this in person."

"What is it, Mom?" My heart pounded in fear of the unknown.

"It's this." She pulled something from her purse and placed it in my hands.

I knew immediately.

It was Eileen's missing journal, the one I had searched for without success months ago, the missing piece of my mother that might finally tell me why she was murdered.

It was the clue that might help me finally take down her killer.

My hands shook as I took the journal from Mom. It felt as if the world was suddenly crashing down around me. All the normalcy of the past few months, settling into a comfortable routine with Emerson—it was over now. I knew that before I even read a single word. The weight of the journal in my hands was nothing compared to the weight on my heart. I knew, even then, that everything was about to change.

I walked numbly to my corner chair and fell into it, barely registering that it was a choice made to put distance between me and Emerson, from the life we had started building together.

My heart, my gut, my soul—they knew I was about to walk a new path. I only hoped that, at the end, I would finally find the answers I needed.

I hoped I would finally find my mother's killer—and that he would pay.

Mom let herself into the house, quietly closing the door behind her. She removed her gloves and scarf and hung them on the hangers by the door before taking the seat next to Emerson. My seat—at least until now.

They both just sat, waiting for me to say something, to do something. But I didn't know what to do.

I was afraid to open the journal in front of them, afraid of what would happen. Afraid of what I might see.

But I wasn't afraid for myself.

Emerson had been nothing but supportive of my visions and my search for Eileen's killer, and Mom was on board now, too. Her coming here with the journal proved that. She could have easily hidden it away and I never would have known about it. The investigation had basically faded away into nothing. Joe, the former sheriff and my investigative partner, kept telling me he was working it, but that it was a cold case. "These things take time," he always said, and I had been so happy building my life with Emerson that I had been more than willing to accept that.

I looked toward Emerson. Our eyes met in a long look, like we were both trying to communicate everything that had been left unsaid between us.

No, it wasn't for me that I was afraid to open the journal. It was for him.

Everything within me was firing off warning signals that once I opened this, things would never be the same. My mother had died because of whatever was in this journal. And over the past year, I had seen death up close and personal more than once. I was terrified, not for myself, but for the people I loved.

"I'm sorry," I said, faltering. "I think I need to be alone while I read this."

I couldn't block out the brief flash of hurt in Emerson's eyes. I didn't blame him. We had shared nearly everything for the past three months.

But he recovered quickly. "Of course," he said, standing up. "You and your mom need some time to catch up anyway. I'll head home." He walked over and kissed me softly, running his hand through my hair and cupping the back of my head. "Call me if you need me," he said quietly. "I'll check on you later. I love you."

"I love you, too," I said, looking deep into his eyes and trying to somehow convey everything I felt. Hoping somehow he would feel my love and know I was only putting distance between us to protect him from whatever darkness was coming. Because the one thing I was sure of at this moment was that the path I was about to walk was darker than any path I had ever walked before.

"Lock up behind me," he said, as if he somehow sensed the darkness too.

I nodded and kissed him again, quickly, before tears sprang up in my eyes.

All I had wanted when I moved here were answers about what had happened to the mother I had never known, but now there was so much more on the line. There was so much good in my life that I didn't want to lose. And now, I knew exactly how nasty things could get when a killer felt threatened. I had seen it firsthand, nearly lost my life more than once, and nearly lost two of the people I loved most in the world.

I put the journal down, gently, as if it were a bomb about to explode and destroy my home instead of just my life. I followed Emerson to the door with Thor on our heels. I gave Emerson one last hug before closing the door and locking it behind him. The room immediately felt colder, darker somehow without him here, and I was tempted to throw the door open and call for him to stay. I knew he would. He would curl up and sit with me while I read whatever my mother had written. While I learned the truth about why she had died.

But I also knew I couldn't have him here. Not yet. Not until I knew what I was dealing with.

Mom didn't say a word until I came back to the chair. "I'll just go to the guest room," she said with the slightest hesitation. "Unless you want me to stay with you?" Her tone seemed hopeful.

"No," I answered, shaking my head. "I need to do this alone. But thank you. And thank you for bringing it."

She nodded and gave me a small smile. "My suitcase is still in the car, but it can wait."

"No," I said, immediately relieved to have a few more minutes before opening Pandora's box. "Let's get it now and get you settled."

We headed out to the cold to get her bags. I was grateful for the reprieve and grateful for the crisp night air that seemed to jar me out of the heaviness that had fallen on me the minute I had seen the journal. Outside, underneath the moon and the stars, I felt better. I felt like I could breathe again.

But the feeling didn't last long. We had the suitcase inside and the doors locked again within minutes. Mom disappeared into the guest room to settle in, and I found myself alone with the book I had longed for—and now dreaded.

Chapter Two

Daphne

Instead of going straight to the journal, I went first to the kitchen to make myself a cup of tea. Maybe I was avoiding what needed to be done, or maybe Fiona had just rubbed off on me. Either way, it gave me another few minutes of reprieve.

It was strange, really. A few months ago, I had literally torn apart my house looking for that very journal. Back then, I would have given anything to find any clue as to what had happened twenty years ago. Now, I resented the journal's existence.

My sole purpose for moving here was to find my mother's killer. I should rejoice over the journal. It was the key I had been missing; it would reopen the door to the investigation for the first time in months.

And while part of me knew I dreaded reading it because of the danger it might cause the people I loved, I also knew part of me didn't want to rock the boat and ruin this life I was building for myself. The sheer selfishness of it all racked me with guilt.

My mother deserved justice, and I was the only one who could get it for her.

So I sipped my cup of tea, a blend Fiona had said was good for mental clarity. When I was ready, I finally sat down to open up my mother's journal.

A shudder went through me when I touched it again. I could almost feel the anxiety and darkness she had felt when she had written in it. I had first learned of the journal through a vision of her, a vision that had sent me to my knees. In it, she had been scribbling anxiously, obviously overwhelmed with worry, while I—the toddler version of myself—had played on the floor. I was helpless then. Now that I wasn't, I knew what I had to do. But oh how I hated stepping back into that darkness.

When I opened the cover, the first thing I saw was a letter tucked in the front. I pulled it out and saw it was addressed to me, in my dad's handwriting. My eyes immediately filled with tears as I began reading his words.

My dearest Daphne,

If you're reading this, then the cancer has likely won, and you've discovered, or are about to discover, the truth about your mother. I'm so sorry I never had the courage to tell you the truth myself. I hope, when you learn the truth, you will understand why and forgive an old man who was simply doing his best to keep you safe.

The truth is that you had a mother and a life I kept from you. Her name was Eileen, and she was the love of my life. We were soulmates, if there is such a thing. She was my every happiness. She loved you fiercely. You are so much like her.

She died when you were three, and I kept her from you, for reasons you will soon understand.

They ruled her death a suicide, and at first, I believed it. I was devastated and confused. We had been so happy together. But she had changed. She had become anxious, worried, paranoid, and depressed. I spoke with her doctor about it, and he tried to help. He prescribed medications. She was furious at me for going to him and refused to take them. She wouldn't talk to me about whatever was going on, but it was eating away at her soul. So when they told me she had killed herself, I believed it, until I found the journal which you now hold in your hands. After that, I knew she had been murdered.

You may remember having visions when you were a young child, and how

I would scold you for them and tell you to stop them. I don't know if you remember that or if you still have them now. Perhaps you blocked them out—I hope to God you did! But here is the truth. The visions you had were real, and so were hers. After finding this journal, I lied and told anyone who asked that hers were delusions, some form of hereditary mental illness. There had always been rumors about Eileen's sight, of course, but few people knew the truth. It was easy to dismiss it all. It killed me to say such things about Eileen, but it fit with the suicide story and helped give you and me both a level of safety while I made plans to get out of Rosemary Mountain.

I loved her deeply. You'll never know how much. But, as you'll see, I was trying to follow her wishes, which were to protect you at all costs. At all costs, dearest Daphne. Even if it meant hiding the truth about her from you.

Your mother, bless her, had a thing for justice. She simply couldn't stand by and let someone get away with evil. It was her greatest virtue and also her greatest selfishness. If she had only been willing to put her own family above her zeal! It's the one thing for which I've never been able to fully forgive her. If she would have walked away, then maybe she would still be with us. Maybe you could have grown up in her love. Because her love was a beautiful thing, Daphne. It was like sunshine itself.

So yes, I kept the truth from you because I wouldn't make the same mistake. I was so angry that Eileen had placed justice above her own family, and I promised myself I wouldn't let my hunger for vengeance ever get in the way of your safety. So, instead of fighting in Rosemary Mountain, I simply left. I left and took you with me and did my very best to keep my promise to Eileen to keep you safe. Whatever the cost.

As I said, I hope you'll forgive an old man if my choice was a mistake. If you haven't found it yet, there's a box in the attic with pictures of her and some of our old love letters. I look through them, even now. You look just like her, darling. I'm grateful that part of her lives on in you.

So now you will have the truth. But I caution you, dear girl. If any of your mother's zeal for justice lives within you, tamper it. Stay away from Rosemary Mountain, I beg of you. Let the past be in the past. Live your life knowing that you had two parents who loved you deeply, but don't go digging up old ghosts.

I love you, dear girl, and I shall always watch over you.
Dad

I was sobbing by the time I finished the letter, my shoulders shaking uncontrollably. Dad's explanation answered so many of my questions about why he had kept the truth from me. But it also raised new ones and increased the feelings that warred within me. I had come here for justice—but was that truly the right path? He had given up on justice in order to keep me safe. But in my heart, I couldn't believe that was right, either.

I couldn't imagine loving someone and just letting her killer get away with it. How could he have lived with that? How could he have allowed her killer to go free for all these years?

But hadn't I just been considering doing the same thing?

Everything within me was at war, and all I could do was sob.

I soon felt a hand on my shoulder, softly urging me to raise my head.

"I'm sorry. I'll leave you alone if you want. But I heard you crying and just wanted to check on you..." Janet trailed off, obviously unsure whether I would accept her support.

"It's okay," I said. I picked up the letter and handed it to her. "Read it."

"Are you sure?" She glanced at the letter and back at me with a hesitant expression.

I nodded and pushed the letter into her hands. I didn't want his words about Eileen to hurt her, but I needed a mom right now. I needed to talk this over with someone who could help me sort out my feelings.

She read it silently, a strange expression on her face, then handed it back. She sat down heavily, a pained look on her face. "Well. That explains a lot, doesn't it?"

"Yeah." I nodded. "I just... I just can't believe he walked away like that. I can't believe he lied about her, threw her under the bus. He did exactly what her killer wanted him to. He actually strengthened her killer's story, then ran away like a coward."

She winced. "Daphne, that's not entirely fair. You know I don't have any lingering feelings for your father, but you're not a parent yet. You don't understand what it's like to feel that kind of protective love for a child. He was just doing what he thought was best for you."

Some of the anger softened. "I know. And as angry as I am for it, I have to admit I was sort of considering doing the same thing."

"What do you mean?"

I just shook my head. "It's so selfish. But, Mom, I was finally happy, you know? Things were going so well. I felt like I had really found my place in this community. Emerson and I, well..." I blushed. "We love each other. We're happy."

"I know, honey." Her face twisted in sadness, some of which I knew was from the lack of love in her own life.

I stood up and paced, no longer able to stay still. "I've seen firsthand what can happen when we get involved in a murder investigation. Twice. And it seems like whoever killed Eileen is ruthless."

Mom nodded. "Yes, it seems that way. Lonnie was obviously terrified, which wasn't like him."

"But I can't just walk away. Can I?"

I looked at her, feeling the pleading in my very soul. I felt so torn. Torn between the part of me that was like Dad, that wanted to run away and forget it all in order to protect what was mine, and the part of me that was apparently like my mother. The part of me that wanted to finish what I'd started.

The part of me that wanted vengeance.

Mom sighed and rubbed her eyes. "Honey, you're the one who will have to live with whatever choice you make here. Can you walk away? Yes. Your father did, obviously. No one else knows about the journal. No one knows you have it. You don't seem to be on anyone's radar or in any danger at this point, and the novelty of Eileen Sullivan's daughter moving back seems to have dissipated. So if you want to bury the journal and forget it, then yes, you can. But I don't think that's really what you want."

"I don't know what I want right now," I said, giving the most honest answer I could.

"Then why don't you sleep on it?" she suggested. "There's no reason you have to read the journal tonight. Take some time to decide.

After all, as you said, there's a lot at stake. You've seen what happens during these things."

"What do you think I should do?" I asked.

She just shook her head. "I'm not giving any advice beyond what I've already given. Sleep on it. Then follow your heart."

I couldn't help but crack a small smile. "What happened to the version of you that always told me exactly what to do and how to do it?"

She returned my smile, but her eyes were filled with sadness and regret. "You're not the only one who changed this year." She stood up, came over to embrace me, and took my face into her hands. "Get some sleep. You'll know better what you need to do in the morning."

I nodded, then quickly hugged her again. "Thanks, Mom."

I picked up the journal and went upstairs, intending to follow her advice.

But hours later, with sleep still evading me, I picked it up again, knowing there was only one choice to make.

I was my mother's daughter.

And I chose to fight for justice.

CHAPTER THREE

EILEEN'S JOURNAL

Had tea with Fiona today. Daphne did the cutest thing! She got up from tea and toddled off, returning moments later with Fiona's midwifery bag. "Go," she said. Fiona laughed and asked if she was trying to get rid of her. But not five minutes later, the phone rang. Fiona was needed for a premature delivery. Fiona and I just looked at each other and smiled. It seems the sight was passed down to Daphne as well. Precious thing!

Daphne

WHEN MOM GOT up the next morning, she found me sitting in the kitchen, sipping my third cup of coffee, as I finished the last few pages of the journal. She rummaged through the cabinet in search of the Darjeeling tea I kept just for her, turned on the teakettle, then sat across from me, waiting until I closed the book.

Silence hung between us for what felt like an eternity until she finally broke it.

"So you decided to read it?" she asked. There was quiet acceptance in her voice, as if she had known all along what choice I would make.

"Yes. I couldn't sleep last night." I took a long sip of my tepid coffee. "I started it around one, then dozed for a few hours and finished it when I got up."

She nodded. "I don't want to pry," she said, after a pause.

"You're not prying," I said, reaching out to put a hand over hers. "I wouldn't even have this if it wasn't for you. Although, I completely understand if you don't want any part of it. It's not your battle to fight."

She placed her other hand on top of mine, sandwiching it between hers. "You're my daughter," she said simply. "Your battles are mine."

I smiled, again marveling at how our relationship had changed since Dad's death. I loved him dearly, but he had made some mistakes, and sabotaging my relationship with the woman he'd chosen to raise me was part of that. She had made mistakes too, certainly. But we had made peace with the past, and I understood her now. I was grateful to have her in my life, a feeling I couldn't have fathomed a couple of years ago.

"So do you have any answers?" she asked, eyeing the journal like it was a snake that might strike out and bite at any moment.

I let out a sigh. "Yes, and no. Mostly I just have more questions. But I learned a few things." I ran my hands over my face. "I think I need to talk to Fiona." Talking to Fiona had become an automatic response to everything in my life. Whenever anything happened, my first thought was to talk to her. "She lived here during that time," I said. "I think she can make more sense of it than I can. I just hate to bring her into it."

A smile played on Mom's lips. "I think Fiona's proven she can take care of herself."

I felt myself grin until the gravity of the situation hit me again. "I still hate getting her involved in something that might be dangerous, especially considering her heart." Fiona had landed in the hospital with a heart attack during the last murder investigation in which we had found ourselves.

"She was just napping, remember?"

I smiled again, despite myself. "I remember."

Fiona had slapped the doctor who called it a heart attack, insisting she had just been napping when Emerson found her unconscious. I knew Mom was trying to lighten the mood in an attempt to make me feel better. And it was working, a little. But the truth was, this was a dangerous situation. The one thing that was clear from Eileen's journal was her fear. She had been up against something so big she hadn't known how to handle it—or who to trust.

Joe had told me he thought Eileen had died because she was too trusting and always saw the best in people. But her journal made it clear that, as time went on, she didn't feel she could trust anyone at all.

I trusted Fiona though. And truth be told, I even still held some trust in Joe. I would be wary of him, and I wasn't ready to tell him about the journal. But I had come to think of him as something like a grandfather. In my heart, I believed he was protecting me.

But as I thought again about Fiona's heart and the danger I had already put her in, I felt a stab of guilt at dragging her into yet another investigation—especially when this one felt so much darker than the ones before. It weighed on my conscience, knowing that if anything happened to her, it would be because of me and this decision I had made to seek justice.

Not telling Fiona about the journal was unfathomable. She had been part of this from day one; I couldn't keep something like this from her. But the more I thought about it, the more I wondered if it was a good idea to keep everyone in the dark about the specifics I'd read. I would rehash what we already knew, hoping if we talked about it again, I might pick up on something I had missed when I hadn't known what I was looking for. But I wasn't sure I should tell them anything else, especially since I wasn't yet sure what information was responsible for Eileen's death.

Eileen had died for what she had seen. That much I knew for sure. I accepted that the same might happen to me. But I wasn't about to let it happen to Emerson, Mom, or Fiona.

In fact, the more I thought about it, the more sure I was about keeping the details from them. I would go ahead with the meeting, but I had every intention of keeping them on the wrong track until I had taken care of things myself.

• • •

I MADE plans with Mom to meet at Fiona's later, but there was someone else I needed to see first.

I felt overwhelmed with nerves as I stood on the front step of Emerson's log cabin, waiting for him to answer. I loved him, and I trusted him with my life. But things had never been easy for us. Our relationship had been complicated from the start, and I couldn't help but wonder if this was the event that would finally push him over the edge and make him walk away. Who would want to willingly get involved in yet another dangerous scenario like this one? He had moved to Rosemary Mountain for peace. I had given him the opposite, time and time again.

But when he opened the door and smiled at me, I felt myself relax. I let out a sigh and moved into his arms, breathing in his scent and letting it ground me. Sandalwood and cedar. It was a combination I had grown to love, ever since the day I had met him.

His fingers gently massaged my back as he held me. At some point, he maneuvered us into the house and closed the door to keep the heat from escaping. But I just stayed buried in his arms, not yet ready to come back to the real world.

Finally, I broke away.

"We need to talk," I said with another sigh.

His face immediately dropped. "Well, I can't say I like the sound of that."

I walked into his living room and plopped down on his couch, waiting for him to join me. "Thanks for giving me some time last night," I said when he settled across from me. "I was overwhelmed and needed to process everything."

"I understand," he said in a measured tone.

"I didn't want to read the journal," I admitted. "Everything has been so great. I resented its existence. Resented that I'm getting dragged into all of this again. It's hard for me to admit that."

He cocked his head. "Why is it hard for you to admit that? It makes perfect sense to me."

I ran my hands over my face in frustration. "Because it makes me a bad person. I finally have the key to finding out what happened to my mother, and I want to run away from it all to keep my own life comfortable."

He reached over and grabbed my wrist gently, bringing my hand into his. "You're not a bad person. Anyone would have mixed feelings about walking into something like this. Hell, you think I was excited to get orders to deploy to Afghanistan? I signed up for it, trained for it, and still felt sick when it was time to go."

"Really?" I smiled a small smile. "That makes me feel better."

"Really. And I bet Greg would say the same thing about getting called to go into dangerous situations in his job. We all have a survival instinct built into us, Daphne."

"I guess that's true." I turned my face toward his back window, watching his chickens pecking for food in the frosty grass. Their life was so simple I almost envied it. "I ended up reading the journal," I finally said. "I started it late last night and finished it this morning."

"And?"

"Eileen wasn't so helpful as to name her killer," I said with a wry smile. "But I have some things to go on. Mom and I are going to Fiona's in a bit to talk about the whole thing. I was hoping you might want to come too. But..." I trailed off, gathering courage for what I needed to say. "I understand if you don't want to be involved. There's no obligation here. I know you moved to Rosemary Mountain for peace, and, well, you found me instead. The last thing I want is—"

He cut me off with a kiss. "Daphne. Don't even start. I'm with you. I'll be by your side every step of the way."

My eyes filled with tears, of both gratitude and fear. And of guilt, for knowing I was going to keep him in the dark. "Emerson, it might be dangerous. And I could never forgive myself if something happened to you."

"Funny, because that's how I feel about you." He shrugged. "I know you have to do this. I've known it since I met you. I love you, Daphne. Do you really think I would make you face whatever this is alone?"

"I love you too. Emerson, I'm scared."

"What are you scared of?"

"That everything's about to change."

Chapter Four

Eileen's Journal

Daphne did the cutest thing today! A stray cat came into our yard, and Daphne got down on her hands and knees, mimicking her. She was meowing and trying so very hard to talk to this sweet kitten. The cat was scared to death, of course, and wanted nothing to do with her. I thought I should probably shoo the cat away, but eventually that scared kitty cozied right up to her! I ended up feeding the cat some cream, and it looks like we may have a new pet. Doc Rogers agreed to come over later to give it all the standard shots and such so that will be taken care of. It's a friendly little cat. Hopefully Lonnie won't mind the new addition.

Daphne

EMERSON and I drove together to Fiona's. I was more grateful than ever to have him with me, even though my fear was growing that telling anyone anything might be the wrong move. My mind kept flashing back to images of Emerson tied up and bleeding on my living room floor, suffering simply because he was with me and I had been the target of a killer. No matter how many times everyone told me it wasn't my fault, I couldn't shake the feeling that it was.

And here I was again, bringing everyone together for a fight that wasn't theirs, a fight that might endanger their lives.

I would have given anything to have been the one who found the journal so none of them would even have to know about it.

Fiona was waiting for us at the door, with a sober look on her face. I hadn't told her about the journal when I called and asked if we could meet, but she knew me well enough to hear in my voice that something was wrong.

She greeted me with a kiss on the cheek, then ushered us inside to get warm. "I'm making fresh coffee," she announced. "Figured we needed it. Can I pour you a cup?"

"Yes, please," I said, as I rubbed my hands together in front of the fire. It was chilly outside, but Fiona's house was always cozy, and I instantly felt better here.

Stepping into Fiona's cottage always felt like stepping into a storybook world. She had immigrated to America decades before, but her style was still heavily influenced by the Irish countryside where she had grown up. It was a soothing cottage, full of dark earth tones and cozy blankets, always deliciously fragrant from the dried herbs hanging in her kitchen. The fire was always lit, and the teakettle was always hot. It was a place where I felt instant peace.

"And one for you, Emerson?"

"Yeah, thanks," he said.

She started for the kitchen but stopped when she heard a knock at the door. "Now who in the world?"

"I forgot to tell you," I said. "Mom's coming, too."

Fiona gave me a strange look, then headed to the door to let Mom in. "Janet! So nice to see you again. Come on in. I was just making coffee for the young ones, but if I remember correctly, you're a tea drinker. Is that right?"

"Yes, that's right." Mom's voice was surprised. "Nice to see you too, Fiona."

"Come on in and warm up. I'll put on the kettle. I have a nice Darjeeling. How does that sound?"

"That sounds lovely. Darjeeling is my favorite. Thank you." Mom pulled off her scarf and coat. She started to walk in, then noticed our shoes sitting by the front door. We always took them off when we came inside, as Fiona never wore shoes in her house. Mom hesitated, then followed suit, slipping off her boots to reveal brown, woolen socks. I stifled a giggle. Despite the seriousness of the situation, I couldn't help but find the humor in what I was watching. I didn't think I had ever seen Janet Sullivan in her socks before. She was always a bit too proper to relax like that.

Fiona disappeared into the kitchen, and Mom sat on the couch. We fell into an awkward silence as if none of us knew exactly what to do.

Fiona finally came back with a tray in her hands and paused at the entry. "Well, I'll be! It feels like I just walked into a funeral. Daphne, stop this nonsense and tell us what's going on. Or am I the last to know?"

Emerson stepped forward and grabbed his mug and mine, then motioned for me to come sit by him on the couch. I did, taking comfort in the closeness.

"Well," I said awkwardly, unsure of how Fiona would react. "Mom found Eileen's journal."

Fiona paled. She handed a teacup to Mom, then took her own and sat down in her rocking chair. "Are you serious? The one we were looking for?"

I nodded confirmation.

"Mercy. Well, let's have it. Do you know who killed her?"

I shook my head no. "I'm afraid not. Listen, I want to talk to you about it. But I'm going to say the same thing to you as I did to Mom and Emerson. You're under no obligation to be part of this. I'm scared, Fiona. I'm terrified of what might happen if I dig into this. And I don't want you getting hurt again. I felt like I owed it to you to tell you I found it, but you don't have to get involved."

Fiona just rolled her eyes. "If you're done with your speeches, girly, get on with it. You know we're all in this together. So just stop all that nonsense and tell us what you found out."

Emerson turned toward me with a little grin, as if to say, "See?"

"Alright. Well," I sighed, "first there was a letter from Dad." I quickly recapped what it said.

Fiona listened, then sank back into her chair. "Well, that explains a lot, doesn't it? Can't say it makes me respect Lonnie much though. What kind of man just runs off and leaves his wife's murder unsolved?"

"He was protecting me." I felt as though I had to defend him, even if I agreed with her. "He did what he thought was right."

She raised an eyebrow but said nothing.

"Anyway," I said, wanting to continue without additional discussion of Dad. "The first part of the journal didn't seem like anything important at all. She wrote about little things I did or said, memories..." My voice cracked and my eyes filled with tears. I couldn't help it. Those things might not have been important for the investigation, but they meant everything to me. Seeing proof that the mother I couldn't remember had truly loved me, that she had loved being my mom, meant everything in the world.

Emerson put his arm around me until I could continue.

I cleared my throat when I could finally speak again. "About halfway through, the tone changed. She stopped writing her happy memories and started talking about a situation that was worrying her. It was vague at first, but she got more open as time went on. Part of it involved the vision I had here, a few months ago." I chose my words carefully, hoping to avoid the specifics of what had been bothering Eileen until I knew for sure what had gotten her killed.

Fiona nodded. "The vision you had where Don and Joe were talking together in the woods?"

"Right. She was following Don and saw his meeting with Joe. The journal says she confronted Joe, just like we did after the vision. He told her the same thing he told us, that he had taken a bribe from Don to look the other way over an embezzlement scheme at the church, and that it was his deepest regret."

Fiona just sighed. I knew hearing about Joe's sins bothered her as much as it bothered me. We both felt attached to him, and it was hard to know he had made such a terrible mistake.

Mom put down her teacup and turned toward me. "Well, we already knew about Joe and Don. Please tell me there was more, something that will give us a new lead to go on."

I nodded slowly. "There's more." How much more, I wasn't ready to say. "She talked about Don and how the money at the church didn't add up."

"That makes sense," Emerson added, "since Joe told us the same thing. But it's interesting she knew it too."

"Right." I nodded. "We know Joe continued investigating Don, even after the bribe. But then Eileen died, Don seemed to change his ways, and Joe basically dropped his investigation."

"None of that seems like a motive for murder," Mom pointed out. "Unless Joe was the one who killed her to keep her quiet about the bribe. Don had already been caught embezzling and had gotten away with it. He had Joe in his pocket, protecting him. And his church automatically believed everything he told them. They never would have believed Eileen over him. So why would he kill her for that?"

"Exactly," I agreed. "On the surface, the only one with motive there would be Joe." I felt like I was betraying him by stating the obvious. "But I don't think he's that kind of person," I insisted. "Bribery and murder are two very different things. Besides, there's at least one other person involved. Katie said, 'Don's not the one who runs this town.' And Christie told me about those texts between Don and someone labeled Mr. Boddy in Don's phone."

"Right," Emerson agreed, picking up where I left off. "And Mr. Boddy was the name of a character from the Clue movie. A character who was blackmailing everyone."

"Yes," I said. "So from those things, we have a couple of theories. I'm assuming Mr. Boddy is also the person Katie says runs the town. We don't know that for sure, but it feels like a safe assumption. So maybe Mr. Boddy was blackmailing Don about something else, something much bigger than the embezzlement, and Eileen found out about whatever that was. In that case, maybe Don killed her to keep himself safe. Maybe there was something in his past even he wouldn't have been able to get through without repercussions. Or maybe Eileen found out who Mr. Boddy was, and Mr. Boddy killed her to keep running his blackmailing scams."

"Or Joe killed her to protect himself," Mom added, refusing to let it go.

I nodded reluctantly. "I still don't think that's what happened."

"You're less willing to consider that an admitted dirty cop killed her than this crazy idea of a mysterious Mr. Boddy that no one else has ever even heard of?" She was incredulous.

Her words stung.

"I know it sounds crazy," I said, feeling defensive. "But my gut says Joe didn't do it."

Emerson took over, trying to soothe the tension. "Let's all agree that Joe is a suspect, but perhaps not a likely one. I agree with Daphne and Fiona. I don't think he would cross that line. Money is one thing, murder is another. But put Joe aside for right now. What ideas do we have for who Mr. Boddy could be? And who has enough power that Katie would have said he runs the town?"

Emerson gave me a pointed look. I knew exactly who he was thinking of, but Fiona said it before I could.

"Bill Brinksley," she spit out.

"Definitely a possibility," I agreed.

Bill Brinksley was the richest man in Rosemary Mountain—and Fiona's least favorite. He lived at the bottom of our lane and tried to exert authority over the whole thing. He had also given me a particularly hard time recently. He was powerful, he was rich, he held a surprising amount of influence over the town, and he had proven he was willing to lie and manipulate for his own benefit.

"But Katie's husband also had a lot of power," I pointed out. "As the town's only doctor for years, he had money and a lot of influence. And he tried to cover it up when Katie killed Don, so he's obviously not a totally upstanding citizen. As a doctor, he also would have had access to the sleeping pills that killed Eileen." And while I wasn't ready to share this with the group, Eileen's journal had given me other reasons to want to look more into Doc Rogers.

"I still think it's Bill," Fiona said. "Doc may have gone stupid and spent too much time thinking with his second brain when he met Katie, but again, I think there's lines he wouldn't cross."

"You *want* it to be Bill because he's the only person in town you don't like," I pointed out.

"Fair enough," she conceded. "Joe's been working the case for a few months. What does he think?"

I sighed. "I don't know."

"What do you mean you don't know?" Mom asked.

"He hasn't told me anything," I admitted. "He said he had a few ideas as to whom Mr. Boddy might be, but he's keeping me in the dark to keep me safe."

She just raised her eyebrows. I knew what she was thinking.

"I know how it looks," I said. "And despite my personal feelings, I will be cautious with him. I've already decided I'm not going to tell him about the journal yet. Let's keep everything said here today between us, okay? But right now, I think our focus needs to be on figuring out for sure who Mr. Boddy is."

"So what's our first step?" Emerson asked.

"Well," I said, "I think I need to talk to Katie. I've felt that way since the day she was arrested, but Joe kept telling me no. While I still don't believe he's the bad guy here, I've decided he doesn't get a vote anymore."

Emerson nodded. "Want me to call Greg and ask for a favor?"

"No," I said, shaking my head. "I'm going to call Jackson. He owes me one."

Emerson frowned. I knew he wasn't a big fan of Jackson's. He had felt some jealousy toward the man when he and I were broken up. But Jackson was just a friend, one who had already broken the rules to help me out before. He was also too young to have been involved in my mother's death, which was another mark in his favor.

"Do you want me to go with you when you talk to Katie?" he asked.

"No. I need to do this alone. Katie will be more likely to talk if it's just me. I'll make the arrangements, then tell you whatever I find out. In the meantime," I said, glancing around at everyone, "let's keep this all quiet, okay?"

Fiona frowned. "Got it."

We changed the subject and chatted about other things, for which I was grateful.

It meant nobody thought to ask me what was in the rest of the journal.

CHAPTER FIVE

EILEEN'S JOURNAL

Edwina had her baby today. I went to help Fiona with the delivery. New life! No matter how many times I see it, it's a miracle every time. I'm thinking of asking Fiona to train me in midwifery. Lonnie loves having me stay at home with Daphne. He takes such pride in being able to support us all. But I think I would enjoy a career of my own, and Daphne's such a doll when we help Fiona. She could train in it too. Wouldn't that be precious? Like three generations of midwives. Fiona's practically my second mom, so it would be like a family business!

I joked with Joe last week that maybe I would become a private investigator. After all, I've gotten some experience there, too. The idea seemed to irritate him though, like I would be working against him instead of with him if I went into business myself. He's such a grumpy old man sometimes.

I really would love something for myself though. As much as I enjoy helping Joe and Fiona, it's still just helping them with their own jobs. I think I'd really like something that was mine. Just mine. I hope Lonnie will agree it won't harm Daphne for me to do a bit more work. Sometimes I think I'll go crazy just sitting around the house when there's nothing to do!

Daphne

AFTER CHATTING ENOUGH to lighten the mood, the group dispersed. Mom announced she needed to head back to my place for a teleconference with her work. Emerson and I made moves to leave too, but Fiona held me back.

"Honey, can I talk to you privately for a bit?"

"Of course," I said with just a bit of hesitation. Emerson was my ride, and I wasn't looking forward to walking back to his place in this cold.

The mountain seemed to have dipped into temperatures so low I wouldn't have believed them possible before living here. I knew that was being a bit dramatic. Places farther north dealt with far lower temps than Eastern Tennessee every winter. But I sure wasn't used to the cold of the mountain in the depths of winter. Even breathing outside seemed to hurt, as the air was still cold when it hit my lungs.

Emerson seemed to anticipate my needs though. "I'll go warm the truck up," he said. "Take as long as you need. I'll wait for you."

I met his eyes and gave him a smile of gratitude. I felt so lucky to be with him. Rosemary Mountain had brought a lot of things to my life, both good and bad. But of the good things, he was definitely the best. Fiona was a close second.

When the door clicked shut behind him, Fiona took my hand and led me into her kitchen.

"Now, Daphne, I know you're not telling us the full story with that journal."

I started to protest, but she held up a hand to stop me.

"It's okay, honey. I'm not going to ask you to tell me anything you aren't ready to. I know you've got your reasons for keeping quiet. Now, if you're doing it just out of some misguided notion of needing to protect us, I hope you'll rethink that." She peered at me sharply. "We're all grownups here, and we all know what we're doing. I know you think this is your battle, and it is, but it's ours too, see? Eileen was like a daughter to me. You're not the only one who wants to see her killer pay for what he took from us."

"I know," I said with a lump in my throat.

"So I'm not going to pry because I trust you'll tell me what I need to know when I need to know it. But don't keep quiet just to keep me safe, okay? Let me help you."

I nodded, unable to speak for fear of what I might say.

"And speaking of helping you, I have some ideas for that," she said, getting up and going to her shelves of herbs. She looked through them, humming to herself, then chose a few jars to bring over to me. "Have you heard of mugwort, dear?"

"No," I answered.

"One of my favorite herbs," she said. "Although, who am I kidding? They're all my favorites. Anyway, you're familiar with this one, whether or not you know it. It's one of the herbs I put in your tea the day you had that vision of Joe and Don together in the woods." She peered at me sharply again.

"Oh, really?"

"Yes." She opened the first jar, filled with ground herbs, and began spooning some of it into a brown paper bag. "Mugwort's known for causing lucid dreaming. Drink a cup of tea, or even sprinkle it on your pillow at night, and you're more likely to dream. Some say it helps open up your third eye, see?"

"Okay." I nodded.

"And seeing as what happened to you that day, I'd say it does seem to help open up your own sight. And, well, if you're going to be digging into your mom's death, you're going to need all the sight you can get."

"I understand." I swallowed hard, hoping she was right and the sight would help me—not only with seeing the past, but also with the future. The more I could see, the better chance I had of getting us all through this without anyone getting hurt.

She grabbed a pen from her drawer and wrote out instructions on the bag. "This will tell you how to brew a cup of tea from it. It's not the most pleasant flavor on its own, so I'm going to add a few other ingredients. Any guesses as to why they call it mugwort?"

"I have no idea," I said with a laugh. I never knew where Fiona was going with her herbal talks.

"It was used to flavor beer, before they discovered hops."

"Interesting."

"Yes. I've experimented with that myself, but I think hops work a lot better. Anyway," she said, adding a few more herbs from different jars to the bag. "I'm adding some peppermint and chamomile. Makes a nice tea before bed. And one more thing."

Fiona rose again and went back to her herbal shelves, looking them over closely before finally finding what she was searching for. She came back holding an old pewter locket. She sat across from me, opened the locket, and spooned a small amount of mugwort inside.

"What are you doing now?" I asked, curious.

"Well, legend has it that St. John—John the Baptist, as you know him—wore a girdle of mugwort for protection in the wilderness. I don't have a girdle for you, but maybe this locket will help." She clicked the locket shut and held it out for me to take.

I looked at it and hesitated. "But, Fiona ... wasn't John the Baptist beheaded?"

She paused and cocked her head for a minute. "Well, yes," she admitted. "But he probably wasn't wearing it then."

I bit my lips to keep from laughing. I had gotten used to Fiona's superstitions and didn't want to hurt her feelings. I didn't have any faith that a locket of mugwort would provide me any protection, but I took it from her and placed it around my neck just the same. It would make her feel better, if nothing else. And I certainly understood the need to do something—anything—to protect those I loved.

I looked down at the pretty locket and made a vow that I would keep my family safe, even if it meant I had to do this alone.

Chapter Six

Eileen's Journal

Tonight was the most beautiful summer night. Lonnie and I dropped Daphne off at Fiona's and went for a ramble through the woods together. We took a picnic basket and spread out a quilt where we could see the best of the sunset, dipping down behind the trees. Lonnie surprised me with a bottle of wine and we ended up spending hours there, just the two of us, talking and kissing like we were silly teenagers again.

I told him about my desire to work, to have some sort of business of my own. But, as I expected, he wishes for me to continue staying home with Daphne, at least for now. I expected as much, but I admit to being a little disappointed. I adore Lonnie, but sometimes I think he is so focused on his own plans and desires that there isn't room for mine.

It's alright though. I adore my sweet daughter. Even now, as I write, I stop every few minutes to just smile at her as she plays. She's so darling, tending to her baby dolls with as much care as the best little mother. I don't mind savoring these precious moments with her. After all, there will be plenty of time to work later.

Emerson

I FIDGETED IN MY TRUCK, waiting on Daphne. I felt the same nervous anticipation I always felt when walking into danger. But this felt worse in some ways. I knew Daphne better than she realized. I could tell she had put up some kind of wall between us and that she hadn't fully let me back in.

I reached over to the glove compartment and pulled out the box I always reached for when thinking of her. I flipped it open and stared at it. An emerald, the exact color of her eyes, surrounded by diamonds. The moment I'd seen it, I'd known it had to be hers. I had carried it since the week she took me back, just waiting for the day I felt confident that if I asked her to marry me, she would say yes.

That day hadn't come yet, and now I was wondering if it ever would.

She was young. Eight years younger than me. Eight years that seemed more like a lifetime when you considered our life experience. Not that she hadn't lived a whole lot of life in her time here on the mountain. Nevertheless, it was a difference. And she was so damn independent. Refused to move any of her things into my cabin, even though she spent at least one night a week there. Never gave me so much as a drawer at her place, either.

She was so open, so loving, so warm. Yet she never talked about the future or even asked where things were going. All she would ever say was that she wanted everything to stay exactly the same.

The same.

It was driving me crazy. Worse, I felt like an idiot for *letting* it get to me. I was the man, after all. Most guys would think I had hit the jackpot. A great relationship with no strings, no commitment, no questions. Wasn't I supposed to be relieved she didn't want to talk about the future?

Nope.

I wanted to wake up with that woman every morning for the rest of my life, and I was ready to hear the same from her.

I had come so close to asking her last night. It had felt like the perfect moment. Then she said that whole thing about wishing everything could stay the same again. After that, Janet showed up and everything had changed ... just not in the way I wanted.

Daphne had to do this. I knew that. I just hoped she would let me be by her side through it. I wanted to protect her, obviously. But hell, it was more than that. I wanted her to finally let me in all the way.

I shut the box quickly and shoved it back into the glove compartment when I saw Daphne coming out of Fiona's front door. Fiona stood watching, looking older and more weary than I had ever seen her, as Daphne climbed into my truck. This was going to be tough on all of us who loved Daphne.

Daphne pulled the door closed and gave me a small smile.

"New necklace?" I asked, pointing at the locket hanging around her neck.

She reached up and wrapped her fingers around it. "Yeah. Fiona gave it to me for protection."

"Protection?" I raised my eyebrows. I had come a long way as far as Fiona was concerned and even made her medicinal teas a part of my everyday life. But there were some superstitions I could never take seriously.

"Mugwort," she said, a little grin playing on her face. She knew how I felt about things. "She says John the Baptist wore it for protection in the wilderness."

"Wasn't he—"

"Beheaded," she said, finishing my sentence with a nod. "Yes. But Fiona's quite sure he wasn't wearing the mugwort at the time." She giggled, then laughed until she had tears in her eyes.

I smiled and laughed with her, but inside, I was worried. Daphne seemed tired, different. Weary already from a battle we hadn't even fought.

"So, what now?" I asked.

"I need to talk to Jackson," she said, "to see if he can arrange a meeting with Katie. Do you mind if I have him come to your house? I'm not sure I want to talk to him about it over the phone."

I frowned. "That's fine, but why not the phone?"

"Just a gut feeling," she said.

I nodded. Daphne always went with her gut. "Alright. Yeah, call him and tell him to meet us at my place."

CHAPTER SEVEN

Eileen's Journal

I had a vision today, quite out of nowhere, and I don't know what to do about it. It was Don, the minister next door. He was with another woman—a girl, really. Now, I don't know what to do. I feel so terrible for his wife and want to let her know. On top of that, I'm worried about the girl he was with. She's much younger than him. Probably over eighteen, but it's still concerning. I just have a sick feeling about the whole thing. I need to find a way to tell Patricia. Maybe if I follow him for a while, I could get some proof to take her. Joe doesn't want me telling anyone else about the sight, so I can't exactly tell her I had a vision about the whole thing. She probably wouldn't believe me anyway.

Daphne

EMERSON MADE us another pot of coffee while we waited for Jackson to arrive. He had agreed to come over that morning, to my relief. I could tell he was curious about why I wanted to meet with him, but he didn't ask for details over the phone.

Jackson was a deputy who had recently been made detective in charge of a new investigative division in Rosemary Mountain. The running joke was that they hadn't needed one of those until I'd come along. It was a joke that never made me laugh. Instead, it rubbed me a little raw and reminded me of how my mere presence here had stirred up trouble for people who hadn't deserved it.

Emerson brought me a warm mug of coffee, made just the way I like it—my fourth of the day, something I would surely regret before the day was over—and pulled me toward him on the couch. I took the hot mug into my hands and drew a deep breath, trying to relax.

"You doing okay?" he asked quietly.

"Yeah." What else could I say? Truthfully, I wasn't sure how I was doing. My whole world had been turned upside down—again. But my decision was made. I was going to get justice for Eileen. Whether I was okay or not didn't really factor into anything. I just had to do whatever needed to be done, then pick up the pieces after.

We sat in silence for a few minutes before he prodded again.

"I notice you didn't volunteer a lot of information about what was in the journal." He said it as a fact, which somehow made me more uncomfortable than if he would have asked about it.

"I'm just not ready," I said. It was true on a thousand levels. I wasn't ready to tell them what the journal said. I wasn't ready to dive into this investigation.

I wasn't ready for everything to change.

But ready or not, change was here. All I could do was try to control the fallout by limiting who was in the cross fire when everything went down.

He took in a deep breath and sighed as if he understood my answer on more than one level, which, truth be told, he probably did. That was the thing with me and Emerson. Our very souls seemed connected, which was why it felt so wrong to keep any of this from him.

I began debating whether or not to just tell him everything. Of everyone involved, he was the one most able to protect himself against any potential danger. He carried a gun, he had military training, and he was best friends with the county sheriff. Getting him involved was completely different than involving someone like Fiona, a seventy-two-year-old woman with a heart condition.

I smiled wryly, despite myself. Fiona would strongly contest that assessment. She considered herself more than capable of handling every situation, and so far, she had proven that to be true. Still, it felt different to me.

And Janet was even worse. Janet didn't have any self-protection skills that I knew of, and absolutely none of this involved her.

Emerson was strong and capable though. Having him by my side through this... Could I risk that? It would make everything so much easier. But I knew I couldn't live with myself if something happened to him and it was my fault. His mother had already lost one son. I couldn't be the reason she lost another.

Jackson's sharp knock interrupted my thoughts, to my great relief. I didn't want to continue that internal debate because I knew I would give in and tell Emerson everything if I thought about it much longer. But risking Emerson's life would be selfish. I needed to stay strong.

I jumped up from the couch and opened the door to find Jackson standing there, wearing his customary grin.

"Hey, there, Daphne," he said, rocking back onto his heels.

"Hey Jackson," I said, smiling. We had dispensed with any formalities long ago, so I never referred to him as Detective Ford like most people did. "Come on in," I said, holding the door wider so he could come in out of the cold.

"Emerson," he said with a curt nod.

"Jackson, good to see you. Have a seat." Emerson's tone was friendlier than I'd expected, for which I was grateful.

"Will do," Jackson said, heading for the chair in the corner.

"Can I get you a cup of coffee?" I asked.

"Nah, I'm good. So what's all this about? You two having some sort of domestic squabble you need me to sort out?" he teased with his big grin.

I sat back down on the couch by Emerson and returned his smile. "Not quite. I was actually wondering if you would do me a favor."

"Well, I probably owe you one after your help on that last case. What can I do for you?"

"Well," I said, feeling a sudden wave of anxiety for even asking. "I was hoping you could get me in to talk to Katie."

He cocked his head, a questioning look on his face. "Are we talking about Katie Rogers?"

"That's right." I nodded. "I'd like to meet with her face-to-face. Privately."

"You know I've got to ask. Why are you wanting to talk to the woman who tried to kill you?"

I had already decided to tell him the truth rather than concoct some excuse. I could be honest without giving away anything about the journal.

"When she was trying to kill me, she insinuated she knew who killed my mother," I said flatly. "I asked Joe Hemsworth to question her about it, but to my knowledge, he hasn't followed through. Now I'd like a chance to talk to her myself."

Jackson's eyes got big, and he leaned forward, putting his elbows on his knees. "Well, I can't say I expected that."

"So can you arrange it? Please." I didn't want to beg, but I would if I had to.

He let out an exhale and shook his head slowly. "I'm sorry Daphne, but that's against policy. For one thing, Mrs. Rogers didn't add you to her approved visitors list. From there, it can take up to thirty days to apply and get approved. But that's kind of beside the point. It's our policy that crime victims can't visit the person accused of committing that crime."

I grimaced, momentarily deflated. "Is that the law or just a local policy?"

"Local policy," he stated, looking uncomfortable. "It's just a bad idea."

"Jackson, I wouldn't ask if this wasn't important," I said, realizing I was going to have to beg after all. "She may be the only person who knows the truth about what happened to my mother. Please. I know you've skirted the rules before. If there is even a chance you can make this happen, I'm begging you. I have to talk to her." I clasped my hands together, desperately hoping he would agree.

He fiddled with his collar, looking even more uncomfortable. "I need to think this over."

"That's all I'm asking," I said.

He stood up to leave, apparently no longer in the mood to chat with us.

"Jackson, one more thing," I said, jumping up before he could leave.

"Some other policy you're wanting me to ignore?" he asked, his eyebrows raised.

"No," I said with an awkward chuckle. "But can we keep this request between us? I don't want anyone to know I'm looking into my mother's death again."

A look of understanding flitted across his face before being replaced with his professional mask. He nodded slowly, then nodded once toward Emerson and walked out of the cabin.

Even though the matter was unsettled, I counted it as a win. He hadn't said no outright, and I felt certain he would try to make it happen if possible. I couldn't do anything else on that front, at least not yet.

But there was one thing I could still do. I needed to talk to Joe and try to get a read on him. Because while I had defended him to Mom, the fact was, Eileen hadn't fully trusted him. Not at the end. And while the thought of it killed me, I had to admit the truth. He had motive, he had means ... and he might have been fooling me all along.

Chapter Eight

Eileen's Journal

I went into town today to run some errands and saw Don. The vision I had of him and the girl immediately came flooding back, and I felt like I needed to do something. I ended up following him for a while, trying to gather more information. I don't think he noticed. He seems pretty distracted. I didn't see him doing anything suspicious though, and he never met up with the girl.

But something else came of all of it. He left his pen on the table after lunch and I picked it up. When I touched it, I had another vision of them together, and I feel even more uncomfortable. I can't put my finger on exactly why, other than the obvious fact that he's married and she seems awfully young. But I know there's a reason I'm seeing this. There has to be something I'm supposed to do about it. I just don't know what.

Daphne

I LEFT Emerson's and went to the one place I was dreading—Joe's. Just thinking about it put a pit in my stomach. I had never been to his house before, and I didn't know what he would think of me just showing up out of the blue. But I had to find out the truth. I had trusted him, primarily because Fiona did and partially because I just naturally liked the guy. But I had liked Katie too and that had obviously been a mistake. I was willing to admit I hadn't always been the best judge of character.

Eileen's journal made it clear she'd stopped trusting him, and I understood why, thanks to my own vision of him. Had I been in her shoes and had seen him talking with Don about something that obviously wasn't above board, I would have felt betrayed and heartbroken as well. It was clear she had adored him and thought of him as a partner. Knowing he was working with Don had to have felt like a knife in the back.

But I had known he wasn't perfect before getting emotionally attached. I understood why he had taken the bribe, and I believed him when he said it was the worst mistake he had ever made.

I just needed to know if that was true or if he was playing me.

If he was only guilty of taking a bribe and looking the other way on Don's embezzlement, that was one thing. But if Eileen was right about him not being trustworthy, and if he had anything to do with her death ... I couldn't even imagine the anger and betrayal I would feel.

The problem was, I would be relying almost totally on my intuition and, if it showed up for me, the second sight. If Joe had been lying to me this whole time, it wasn't likely he would tell me the truth now. And if he had been lying, then he was a very good liar.

I didn't want to go back to my house to make a cup of tea first, but I was tempted to try Fiona's mugwort anyway. I slipped out a pinch of the dried herbs and put them straight into my mouth, hoping the effect might be the same from just chewing and swallowing them. The taste was quite bitter, and I had to fight the urge to spit them out. I swallowed it all quickly, washing it down with my water bottle, shuddering over the taste. If it worked, it would be worth it. But I admit I had my doubts.

I braced myself and walked up to Joe's door, attempting to project confidence I didn't feel. I rang the doorbell and waited, glad he didn't seem to possess Fiona's gift of knowing I was coming.

That would come in handy if I needed to make a move later.

After a few minutes, he answered the door, smiling when he saw me. "Well, well, what do we have here? Find another dead body somewhere?"

I forced myself to smile. "Funny. No, I'm afraid not. Just thought I would stop by and see how the investigation into Eileen's death is going."

His smile faltered, but he swung the door open and invited me inside. "Come have a seat," he said. "Sorry it's just an old bachelor's pad in here."

Bachelor's pad didn't totally fit, but it wasn't off the mark, either. His house was nothing like Fiona's warm, cozy cottage. It felt sad and lonely inside, lacking more than just a woman's touch. The walls were empty, with no family photographs or signs of love. I immediately felt sad for him, knowing he had devoted his life to law enforcement and had lost his marriage in the process. It seemed he had been alone ever since.

But I couldn't allow my feelings to cloud my judgment. I hardened my heart and focused back on the reason I was here.

"So," I said, taking a seat on his grey sofa. "Give me an update on the investigation."

He didn't quite meet my eyes when he plopped down in his own recliner across from me. "It's like I told you before. This case is colder than cold, since it isn't even officially a case. I'm doing what I do. But it's going to take time."

"I hear you," I said, trying to not be confrontational. "And honestly," I said, as a lie began forming in my head, "I'm considering dropping the whole thing."

His ears perked up at that. "Really? Why?"

I shrugged. "Like you said. It's colder than cold. You've been working on it for, what, four months now? And you haven't gotten anywhere."

He looked at me with a look I couldn't quite place, like maybe he was trying to read me too. "You haven't accepted the suicide theory, have you?"

I shook my head slowly. "No. Not really. But I'm thinking more and more that Don was probably the one who killed her. It makes sense, right? And if he's the one who killed her, well, there's probably nothing we can do to prove it. He's already dead." I shrugged again.

He rubbed his chin and continued giving me that thoughtful stare. "Maybe," he finally said. "But I thought you were convinced this mysterious Mr. Boddy was behind the whole thing?"

I kept my own face thoughtful as well. "Yeah, but have you found anyone you think he could be? Rosemary Mountain isn't exactly full of mysterious bad guys." I cracked a grin, deliberately trying to put him at ease.

He leaned forward and put his elbows on his knees. "What's your game, kid?"

"What do you mean?" My skin went cold.

"Why are you acting like this?"

I shrugged again, attempting nonchalance. "I'm not acting like anything. I'm just stating the facts. Four months in and you don't have a single new lead for us to go on. Maybe it's just time to accept it's over."

"You're lying," he said, pointing a finger at me. "Don't think I can't tell. So I'll ask you again. What's your game?"

My eyes flashed with anger. "Maybe I should ask you the same thing."

He sat back, looking startled. "Excuse me?"

"You tell me the case is cold for months, but when I talk about dropping it, all of a sudden you have a problem with that? Which is it, Joe? Is the case dead or not? What are you not telling me?"

The question asked, I did my best to breathe and calm my emotions, trying to be as open as possible to anything the sight might give me. But it wasn't easy, considering the amount of anger coursing through my body. I hadn't realized until now just how frustrated I was with my supposed partner.

"Cold and dead are two different things," he said, as if talking to a child. "If you want to drop it and move on with your life, that's your business. I can still look into things on my end. That's my business."

"You've kept me completely out of the loop the whole time, so what difference does it make?" There was that anger flaring again. "What's the difference between me dropping it and moving on or me being with you when you won't tell me anything at all?"

"I'm trying—"

"I know, I know," I said, rolling my eyes. "You're trying to protect me."

He stared at me a long minute then sighed.

"Fine. You want to know what I've been up to? I'll show you."

He got up and walked out of the room, leaving me sitting there wondering what on earth was coming next.

CHAPTER NINE

Eileen's Journal

I did a little poking around and found out Don left his last church in a hurry after getting caught having an affair. I'm not sure if that makes me feel better or worse. Better, because at least Patricia already knows he's been unfaithful in the past. Worse, because it feels even more icky now.

I'm thinking I should tell Patricia. No wife deserves to be made a fool of like that.

Daphne

AFTER A FEW MINUTES, Joe returned, carrying a leather notebook and a handful of file folders. He motioned for me to follow him to the kitchen, where he spread everything out in front of me. My heart began racing. Here was proof, in front of me, that he really *was* investigating my mother's murder. I suddenly felt guilty for the way I had spoken to him, even if he deserved it for keeping me in the dark. Yet something inside me whispered that I shouldn't tell him about the interview with Katie. I knew what he would say. He would be against it, might even stop it. So, despite my guilt, I bit my tongue and focused on simply gathering as much information as possible from him.

"Most powerful man in town," he said, sliding into the seat across the table and tapping a photograph with two fingers. "Bill Brinksley. You met him yet?"

"No," I said, shaking my head. "Not in person. But I've heard plenty of stories, and of course, you know he gave me some trouble a few months back."

He grinned at that. "I'm betting you've heard a few stories from Fiona. She can't stand the man."

"This is true," I said, returning his grin.

"Anyway. When you told me someone with a lot of power may have been over Don or blackmailing him—whatever the case—I immediately thought of Bill. He's an obvious choice."

"Right," I said. "He's who Fiona thought, too."

"So," he said, pushing some notes toward me. "I've been doing some digging. Trying to find out how he made his money, see if it's on the up-and-up. Looking into his relationship with Don. Also, trying to verify his whereabouts the night Eileen was killed. But, you understand, we're talking about something from over twenty years ago. It's not quick work, especially since I'm retired and don't have the resources behind me to look into this officially."

"I get that," I said, nodding. "But what have you found out so far?"

He moved his head back and forth in an uncertain gesture. "As far as I can tell, he made most of his money in the eighties buying and selling real estate all over Arkansas and beyond. Putting in condominiums and apartment buildings for high profits. Buying land, getting it zoned for commercial use, reselling it for way more than he paid. Seems to have lots of friends in local government."

I stared at his picture. "Lots of friends, or lots of people he black-mailed in order to get them to do his bidding?"

He nodded, conceding the point. "Could be. But that's just speculation and no one I've talked to has said anything that would confirm such, although I will say this. Not all of his friends seem to actually like him very much."

"So where was he the night Eileen died?"

Joe shrugged. "Can't say for sure yet. It's not like I'm going to go up to him and ask him where he was that night. He was in town for her funeral, I know that much, because I remember him being there. And," he said as he slid a newspaper clipping toward me, "he was in town the day before she died." He tapped a face in the picture on the clipping. "There he is receiving a plaque for a donation to the hospital."

I studied the picture. There he was alright—a younger version of him, anyway. I disliked the man instantly, and not just because of how Fiona felt about him. Something about him, in both pictures, felt arrogant and entitled.

"So, odds are, he was in town," I murmured, still staring at the picture.

"Highly likely. He traveled a lot, so like I said, I can't say for sure yet. But yeah, odds are, I'd say he was in town. Don't know yet where he was the night it happened."

"So how are we going to move forward?" I asked, finally looking up.

"Cool your jets," he said, putting up a hand before whisking the picture and article away. "We're lacking more than that. We're lacking a motive for killing Eileen, which means we've got absolutely nothing whatsoever. Can't go accusing a man of murder with no evidence and no motive."

"Hmmmm." My mind went back to the journal. "I mean, Eileen had the sight. If he was involved in anything shady, she might have seen it. Maybe she confronted him and he felt threatened."

"That's a big maybe, and it involves something not many people knew about—or would believe to be true."

"Yeah," I said, momentarily deflated.

"Besides," Joe said, "he's not the only person I'm looking at."

I sat up straight again. "Who else?"

He slid another photograph toward me, a mug shot of a younger man. When I touched it, my senses immediately began buzzing. I felt overwhelmed with disgust, rage, and repulsion. In my mind, I saw images of him laughing, throwing a cigarette butt on the ground. Before I could stop myself, I pulled away from the picture and forced my eyes open, not wanting to experience any more of it—then instantly regretted it, in case it was important. I put my hand back on the picture, but got nothing this time.

"You getting something over there?" Joe asked, obvious curiosity in his voice.

"I don't know," I said. "Maybe. Nothing about Eileen. Just … feelings. I don't like him."

Joe raised his eyebrows. "Don't blame you. Not much to like there. His name is Russell Sharp. Here, we've got motive, seeing as I heard him threaten to kill your mama myself. But he's not likely to be any sort of power player like this possible Mr. Boddy. No connection to Don that I've seen, and not a particularly powerful person."

Russell. I had to force myself to not visibly react. I had read that name in Eileen's journal. My heart sped up again. "Why did he want to kill her?" I asked, staring at his picture.

Joe paused for a moment before answering. "She put him in prison," he finally said. "Manslaughter. Three years. There was absolutely no way we would have ever connected him to the case if it wasn't for your ma. She knew. Had a vision as clear as day. Told me where to go, and where the gun would be. Russell was furious, thinking he was going to get away clean. Had already done one year in prison and wasn't at all happy about going back." He paused again. "He threatened to kill her when we arrested him. Got out on parole just a few weeks before she died."

"And you didn't look at him for it back then?"

He shook his head slowly. "I'm afraid not. Thought it was all just hot air, to be honest. And like I told you before, there was no reason to say anything other than suicide."

"How did he know she was even involved?" I asked, confused. It had been my understanding that Eileen's work with Joe had been something of a secret, that they had tried to keep her gifts mostly under wraps.

He paused again. "They had a history," he said. "And she went with me when I went to arrest him. He knew."

I had so many questions, but only one seemed to matter now. "Then why haven't you gone to talk to him? He has a clear motive. He even threatened her."

Joe nodded slowly. "Again," he said, once more speaking to me as if I were a child, "her death, officially speaking, was a suicide, and I'm trying to keep it on the down-low that we're looking into this. He has a motive, yeah, but that's not enough to prove a case. I want more before I go talking to anyone. And based on what Katie told you about someone more powerful than Don killing your ma, he doesn't fit the profile."

"We've got to look into him more though," I said, "especially considering my reaction to his photograph."

"Agreed. But there's another option." He pushed a third photograph toward me, a face so familiar I knew I had seen it before, but I couldn't remember where.

"Who?" I asked, trying to remember.

"Doc Rogers."

I let out a deep breath. "Oh my goodness, yes. I only saw him once, and he's older now, but yeah." I looked up at Joe. "I'm glad to see you're considering him. I was wondering about him myself, but I know you two are friends, and I wasn't sure what you would think about that."

Joe looked grim. "Friends, yes. But he performed the autopsy. He's the one who signed off on suicide. It would explain why Katie knew something about the whole deal." He raised his hands in frustration. "I don't want to think it of him. But..."

"So what would the motive be there?" I asked, curious what he might say, although I had some ideas on that, based on Eileen's journal.

Joe grimaced. "Look, I hate to talk about my friend like this, right? But if this Mr. Boddy thing is real, Doc would be a candidate for it. He's not as rich and powerful as Bill Brinksley, but think about it. For decades, he was the only doctor in town. He knows everything about everyone." He gave me a pointed look.

"I gotcha. So if Mr. Boddy really was into blackmailing, like we suspect..."

"Right. Doc would be someone with the information to do that. And like Don, he's living in a pretty fine house for his position."

"I don't know about that," I objected. "It's a gorgeous house, absolutely. But doctors make good money."

"City doctors, sure," he said. "But small towns like this?" He shook his head. "There's not a lot of money in Rosemary Mountain, Daphne, unless you're Don Kistler, Bill Brinksley, or—"

"Or Doc Rogers," I finished, sighing.

"Exactly."

Someone knocked on the door, startling me and alarming Joe, who glanced at his watch and groaned.

"My poker game," he said with an apologetic glance my way. "We'll have to continue this another time." He quickly swept up all the notes and moved to put them back from wherever he had gotten them. "Listen, before you go," he said, pausing to turn back to me. "You know that game you tried to run on me earlier?"

"About dropping the case?"

"That's the one." He gave me a pointed look. "If I were you, I'd keep playing that game. You want to work with me on this, then fine, we'll work together. But for your own safety, and the safety of everyone around you, you need to keep them out of it."

I nodded, the weight of it hitting me in the gut again. Joe was the one person who cared as much about Fiona as I did. I knew he wouldn't take a risk that would put her in danger, and he would probably never forgive me if I did. Not that I would forgive myself. I sighed, hating this situation that was going to force me to be dishonest with the ones I loved most. But his words were the confirmation I needed that keeping them out of it was the right thing to do.

"Okay," I agreed, letting out a breath. "I won't let them in on it."

"Good." He nodded toward his back door. "Now do me a favor and go out that way, will ya? The last thing I need is any rumors about me having female company of your age." He winced.

I laughed. "Got it. And Joe?"

"Yeah?" he asked, turning back to me.

"Thanks."

He nodded again and hurried away, leaving me to slip out the back alone.

Chapter Ten

Eileen's Journal

I went to talk to Patricia today. She's a woman of faith and has always seemed sweet in the few interactions we've had. So I thought I would just tell her the truth about my visions and let her decide how to handle it. Boy was that a mistake! I thought she might not believe me, but that wasn't the issue. She was angry, which I expected. I just didn't expect to be the target of her anger! She accused me of trying to harm Don's ministry. I tried to point out that if he's having an affair, he's the one harming his ministry ... and if that girl isn't eighteen, he's breaking the law. She just got angrier and kicked me out. What on earth? I admit, I'm a little shaken about the whole thing. I've never seen someone literally shake with anger before. I only hope when she has time to process it she realizes her anger is because her husband betrayed her.

Daphne

AFTER TALKING TO JOE, I headed back home, where life resumed as normally as possible. Time seemed to stretch out more slowly than ever while I waited for Jackson to get back to me. Mom asked if she could stay with me for a week or two, acting as if she simply needed a vacation. All four of us—me, mom, Emerson, and Fiona—went to dinner at the Irish pub and managed to avoid any discussion of the situation. The evening still felt heavy though, with an elephant in the room that none of us could forget, even if we were all doing a wonderful job of not referencing it.

I knew Emerson wanted me to ask him to stay that night, but I didn't do it. I knew if I curled up in his arms, alone in the dark, I would end up telling him everything Joe had told me and what the journal said. So I said goodnight to him and sent him home.

I wondered if he could sense the distance I was putting between us.

The next morning, I had a text from Jackson. Just three words. *Come at noon.*

My heart beat a little faster when I saw it. It felt like everything was happening so quickly now. I felt certain Katie held at least some of the answers. I regretted the time wasted waiting for Joe to arrange a meeting that had never happened. But I knew, as much as I hated to admit it, that the reason I hadn't pushed harder was because I had grown content with my life as it was. I had wanted to pretend I had tried my hardest so I could enjoy my new life in Rosemary Mountain.

But pretending was over. I was going to do this for real now.

Emerson was at work, so I sent him a quick message letting him know it was happening that day. He immediately texted back, telling me to be careful and to let him know what I found out. *I will,* I wrote back, even though I knew I was only agreeing to the first one.

"Do you want me to go with you?" Mom offered as she watched me nervously apply some lipstick.

I wasn't sure why it felt so important to look my best for this appointment. Maybe I was still intimidated by Katie. Maybe I needed her to know she hadn't broken me, that I was healthy and confident and, unlike her, free.

Or maybe I just wanted to hide how scared I really felt.

"No," I answered after a pause. "I need to do this alone."

Mom bit her lip. "Daphne, you're going to be face-to-face with the woman who tried to kill you. It would be normal to be shaken up after something like that. I could at least drive you so you're not driving home upset and emotional."

I turned toward her and pasted on a smile. "I'll be fine, Mom. Really. I need to do this alone."

"Why?"

"Why what?"

"Why do you need to do this alone?" She stared at me as if knowing, somehow, that my words were about more than meeting with Katie. "Why won't you let me support you?"

"It's just a meeting," I said lightly, wanting to avoid any real discussion. "I promise, if I need to break into any offices, you're the one I'll take with me." I grinned, trying to lighten the mood.

She didn't smile. "I'm worried about you. About all this. It's a lot, you know. Something about you changed after you read that journal."

"Nothing changed. I'm fine," I insisted. But I saw the worry on her face and sighed. "Look," I said, my tone softening. "Yes, it's a lot. And honestly, I was really enjoying my life before you brought the journal here. I had sort of moved on and put this whole thing behind me. So it feels heavy to pick it back up again. But I promise. I'm fine."

"I should have just buried it somewhere," she said, shaking her head. "I thought bringing it was the right thing to do, but now I feel like I made a terrible mistake."

"It wasn't a mistake." I reached out and put my hands on her shoulders, trying to convey how much I meant it. "You said it before. This is why I'm here."

"You have a choice in the matter, you know," she pointed out.

"I know. But I've made my choice."

And I was determined that absolutely nothing would stop me this time.

I felt like a bundle of nerves as I drove to the county jail, but by the time I pulled into their parking lot, I was oddly numb. It was like I had simply shut off part of myself in order to do what had to be done ... and in order to protect myself from any of Katie's mind games.

Still, as I walked down the hallway to meet Jackson, my heart pounded in my chest. He was standing outside his office, waiting on me.

"Hey, Daphne," he said, his usual grin missing. He seemed more worried than I was.

"Hey. Thanks for doing this," I said. I hadn't realized I would be asking him to go against policy, and I truly hoped he didn't get into trouble.

He nodded, still unsmiling. "Just so you know, it's on the up-and-up. I ran it past Greg. I know you asked me to keep it between us, but that's just not possible in this situation. In good news though, I guess you've built up quite a bit of trust with him, because he said if Katie was willing to meet, we could make it happen. I didn't tell Katie what you wanted to talk about, just that you wanted to visit her. She seemed excited and immediately agreed to add you to the list. Didn't even bother checking with her lawyer, even though I advised her to."

"Thanks, Jackson. I really appreciate it."

He gave me a serious look. "I need you to understand we pulled a lot of strings to make this happen so quickly. This is a big favor. One I'm still not too comfortable with."

"I understand," I said.

"And look, Katie's attitude about meeting with you creeps me out, honestly. Be careful in there, okay? She—"

"She likes to play mind games," I said, finishing the sentence for him.

"Exactly. I'll be honest, I really don't think it's a good idea for you to talk to her, and I would be highly suspicious of any information she gives you. I don't think you can trust her to tell you the truth." His tone was flat.

"Got it," I said.

"And I would avoid talking about anything involving the case against her. Everything will be videotaped, of course. But we don't need anything messing up the case. Got it?"

"Yes, I understand," I agreed.

"Alright. Follow me."

. . .

I sat at a cold steel table in the visitor's room, trying not to shiver. I always felt cold and shaky when I was scared, and today was no different. But at least I still felt somewhat detached from what was about to happen. I wasn't thinking at all of what Katie had done to me. I simply wanted answers.

I was just afraid of what those answers might be.

Katie flounced into the room with an excited look on her face. Somehow she still managed to look gorgeous, even in a jumpsuit, without the benefit of makeup or her hair styling tools. It was frankly annoying.

"Well, hello, bestie," she said with a wink. "I appreciate you coming to see me. That's got to look good for my trial, right?"

"Sure," I said flatly.

"So, girl, how have you been?" she asked as if we were just two women meeting up for a coffee date. It was surreal.

"I've been great," I said in a measured tone. *No thanks to you.*

"Well, that's great to hear," she said in a tone that would have come across as warm and genuine had I not been looking at her eyes.

I could see the sharp glint in them now. I was angry at myself for missing it for so long, for getting taken in by her to begin with.

"So tell me," she said in her teasing way. "Did you ever get to have any *fun* with good old Emerson, or are you still pining after him and hoping he'll be *relationship* material?"

Yes, there was that sharp glint there, with words chosen intentionally to hurt me.

But her words no longer had any power over me, at least where Emerson was concerned.

"We're together, if that's what you mean," I said, keeping my face blank and my tone even.

There was a look of surprise in her eyes before she shut it down. "Well, good for you!" Once again, if I hadn't known her better, I would have thought she was being genuine. But her eyes revealed the truth of her sarcasm.

"I'm not here to talk about me though," I said.

She just laughed. "Well, if you're hoping for some juicy news from me, I'm afraid I'll have to disappoint you. Unfortunately, my life has been a bit, well, boring lately." She rolled her eyes and tossed her hair back.

"I'm not here to talk about you, either," I said. "I'm here because the last time we spoke, you started a conversation we didn't get to finish."

"Oh?" she asked, one eyebrow arched.

"I'm here because I want to know who killed my mother."

Her face instantly changed. "I can't talk to you about that," she hissed, leaning forward across the table. "Are you trying to get me killed?"

I kept my face placid. "In all fairness, you literally tried to murder me."

She rolled her eyes.

"But come on. What do you mean?" I leaned in closer. "Why would you be in danger?"

"Sweetie, I told you. You don't know anything about how this town works. Look, I'm sorry about your mom. I really am. But I can't help you." She started to get up and walk away.

"Wait," I called, desperate now. "Please."

She hesitated for a moment. As afraid as she was, I knew she couldn't resist the emotion in my voice. She enjoyed it too much—enjoyed the power she held over me. She fed off of that power.

She came back to the table, wary. "I'm not telling you anything. We can talk about something else, but not that."

"Just let me talk. You don't have to say anything." I took a deep breath, praying my sight would help me read between the lines. Then I spoke again, not waiting for her to agree. "Don didn't kill my mom." I said it flatly and watched for her reaction.

There it was—a little flash. Fear and knowledge, written as clear as day on her face before she could wipe it away.

"Someone more powerful than Don killed my mom."

Again, a flash of confirmation in her eyes. She drew herself back and eyed the video cameras. "I won't answer any of your questions," she said loudly, as if for the benefit of anyone who might be listening. "I won't help you in this ridiculous quest. Your mother committed suicide. Everyone knows it. You need to get a life."

"Did Don know who killed my mother?"

Again, the smallest flash. I was on the right track.

"Was Dave involved?"

"Of course not," she spat out, her arms crossed. This time, I couldn't tell. I didn't quite believe her, but I wasn't sure.

"Did she get killed because of something she knew?"

Oh yes. That confirmation was as plain as day. But the fear was growing. I could tell I was about to lose her. I took a chance and broke a rule, reaching out to grab her by the hand, hoping I might get something more—anything. And it worked. The second I touched her, I saw a dark room. Men were talking, gathered around a table in some sort of meeting, but I couldn't tell who it was. The room was filled with thick cigarette smoke, and Katie was observing quietly from the corner, hoping to not be seen.

She yanked her hand away and leaned back, eying me like an animal in a trap.

"Take my advice," she said, pointing a finger at me. Her hand shook slightly, and she shoved it behind her, still embarrassed to show weakness. "Drop this. Your mom committed suicide. You survived yours. Don't throw that away."

With that, she pushed away from the table, turned her back to me, and announced to the guard she was done.

Chapter Eleven

Eileen's Journal

Last night, I told Lonnie about my vision and subsequent conversation with Patricia. He was frustrated with me too, telling me I should have stayed out of the whole thing. He's proud of me when I help Joe solve cases. I know that. But he wasn't proud of me for this. He said their marriage wasn't any of my business and I was just drawing attention to myself—attention that could be dangerous.

Maybe he's right. Maybe it isn't any of my business. But I feel like I'm supposed to do something about it, and I don't know how to explain that to him.

He loves me so much; I know that. But he's always been wary of the sight. I think he would be happy if it just went away. He worries so, especially since the threats last year.

Part of me wishes I would not have gone to Patricia, and part of me wishes I simply wouldn't have told Lonnie about it!

Jackson

When Katie ended the visit, I walked back to my desk and plopped into my chair to brood. I had pulled strings to make the visit happen because I wanted whatever information Daphne learned from it. But unfortunately, I hadn't learned a thing.

Except that Katie was scared. That much was obvious, and that was interesting.

But until I knew for sure who she was scared of, I wouldn't know what I needed to know.

I drummed my fingers on the table, mulling the whole thing over. What were the odds that Katie really knew something? And if she did, which part of it did she know?

This whole thing could blow up in my face and destroy everything I had spent my life building.

I jumped when Greg stuck his head out of his office and called for me. He was the last person I wanted to see right now, but I didn't have a choice in the matter. When he called, I answered. So I pushed away from my desk and headed toward his office.

"Have a seat," Greg said, his tone friendly but authoritative.

I obeyed silently.

He stared at me for a long minute, like he could read my thoughts, then nodded. "So, what did we find out?" He put his hands together, his pointer fingers pointed straight toward the ceiling like a prayer. Ironic, since I was the one doing the praying.

I cleared my throat. "Not much. Katie's scared. Terrified, I'd say. Put on a show for the cameras about how she wouldn't tell Daphne anything. She insisted it was suicide and basically told Daphne to get a life."

Greg took it in and nodded slowly. "That's interesting, that she put on a show for the cameras."

"It is, isn't it?" I had thought the same thing and didn't like it at all.

"Hmmmm." Greg put his hands behind his head and stretched back in his chair. This was his favorite way to think.

I knew to just sit quietly until he spoke again.

After a few minutes, he sat back up. "Jackson, do you still have the report on Eileen Sullivan's suicide?"

"Yes, sir." My heart pounded in my chest, but I kept my face calm. At least, I hoped I did.

"Good." He nodded again. "Bring it to my house tonight. Bring a pizza too. And let's keep this between us."

"Understood." I stood, knowing he was dismissing me.

"I like pepperoni," he called as I walked out of the room.

"Got it," I called back.

But I wasn't thinking about pizza. No, I was thinking about the ghosts from my past, and wondering how close Daphne was to digging them up.

I was trying to figure out how far to let her go before I stopped her myself.

Chapter Twelve

Eileen's Journal

Lonnie wanted to talk again today. He made me reread the threatening letters from last year, making me feel quite guilty, which was likely exactly what he wanted. I know he wants me to stop investigating altogether, even wants me to stop helping Joe. I understand. Those letters were awful, full of horrible words. But what he doesn't seem to get is that this is who I am. The sight is a gift. A responsibility. If I'm shown something about a crime, I have a responsibility to pursue it! It would be wrong not to, like the parable of the talents. And besides, as awful as those letters were, they have nothing to do with this situation at all. Don may be a lousy husband, but he's no murderer. And the man who wrote those letters is in jail, where he can't harm me.

Daphne

I drove home slowly after meeting with Katie. I hadn't really gotten any new information, but her reaction confirmed my own thoughts. Eileen's murderer was still at large.

The journal would not be enough to prove anything. In fact, I was painfully aware that some entries in the journal would only seem to back up the story everyone had been so happy to accept—that she was losing her mind, becoming paranoid, and killed herself because of it.

I would need something bigger, something undeniable.

I just had absolutely no idea yet where to find it.

And if I couldn't find it, I would have to figure out a way to lay a trap for the killer.

In the meantime, I knew Mom and Emerson would both be waiting for answers. I could honestly tell them I had learned nothing new, but I wasn't sure how long I could keep that up. I suddenly regretted our team meeting. It would have been a much better idea to simply pretend the journal said nothing at all and that the case was dead from the start. If I had been thinking on my feet, that's what I would have done. But the sheer emotion and anxiety of it all had clouded my judgment. Now I had to figure out how to handle things.

Maybe it wasn't too late. Maybe I could at least convince Mom the case was dead and get her to go home.

If I was going to lay a trap for a killer, I would feel a lot better about having her out of the way.

Emerson and Fiona would be harder sells. For one thing, they both seemed able to read me like a book. It was impossible for me to get anything past Fiona, and Emerson always seemed to see to my very core. Fooling them would be much harder than fooling Mom. But if I could at least get Mom safe and out of the way, I would feel better.

I took some deep breaths and practiced my story before I got home, grateful that Emerson was at work. It would be easier to convince Mom to leave if it was just me and her.

"Good! You're back," Fiona said the moment I opened the door.

I hoped the shock on my face came across as surprise at seeing her and not the way it felt—like she had caught me red-handed in the cookie jar, trying to get away with something.

"Fiona," I said, attempting to mask my instant guilt. "I didn't know you were coming over today."

"And I didn't know you were meeting with Katie today," she

replied, peering at me with those sharp eyes, with just a hint of accusation in her voice.

"It was sort of a last-minute thing," I said, shrugging off my winter coat. "I guess Mom filled you in?"

"Emerson texted and asked me to come check on you after, see how it went and all."

"Oh, that's sweet of him." *And more than a little frustrating, considering. Could he read my thoughts from a distance?*

"Fiona made tea," Mom said, gesturing at the tray sitting on the coffee table. "We've been waiting for you. Come, tell us what you found out."

I unwrapped my scarf slowly and hung it and my coat in the closet, using the opportunity to hide my face as I spoke.

"Unfortunately, there's not much to tell," I called from behind the closet door. "She was excited to see me, but she refused to talk about Eileen. I don't know. Jackson and I were talking beforehand about how she seems to enjoy playing mind games with people. Maybe that's all it was when she acted like she knew something. Just another way to torture me."

My speech over, I emerged from the closet, hoping my face wore a mask.

"Hmmmm…" Fiona said, her sharp eyes still peering at me.

"Well, that's a disappointment," Mom said, sighing. "I was sort of hoping she would just, I don't know, tell you and all this could be over."

"She probably would if she actually knew anything," I said. "I get the feeling it was just all a big game to her. I'm thinking Joe was right. Maybe this case is colder than cold."

"It sounds like you're giving up! You can't give up now! You just got the journal. Isn't that what we've been waiting for?" Mom protested.

"Aren't you the one who said Dad hid all this from me for a reason?" I pointed out. "Even in his letter, he said to stay away from Rosemary Mountain."

"So that's it, then?" Fiona asked. "You've decided it's a dead end?"

"It's not a decision. I think it just is what it is," I said, unable to meet her eyes. "I know we got all excited about the journal, but we're exactly where we were before it, aren't we? We haven't actually learned anything new at all. The case is dead."

"Hmmmm," Fiona said. I wasn't looking at her, but I could just imagine the look on her face, the one she always had when she wasn't buying what I was selling. "So, Janet, does that mean you'll be heading back to Little Rock soon?" Fiona asked, turning her attention to Mom.

My heart beat a little faster, grateful she had asked the question I was afraid to.

"Well, I don't know," Mom said, faltering. "I mean, there's no reason for me to rush back. But if Daphne doesn't need me to help..." she trailed off and looked at me helplessly.

My guilt immediately intensified. I could see she was hoping I would ask her to stay, but I couldn't.

"Oh, I hate for you to take off more time from work just for me," I said. "I really feel we're at a dead end here. I don't have any other ideas at this point. All we're doing is rehashing what we already knew. If anything changes, I'll call you, of course."

I felt terrible as I watched Mom's face fall. Her ideas of courtesy and social customs were too ingrained for her to continue staying with me without an invitation, but I could see she really wanted to.

I just couldn't let her.

"Well," she said, lifting her hands helplessly. "I guess that's that. I'll head home first thing in the morning."

"Why don't we go to dinner again tonight? All three of us," I suggested, wanting to make some sort of offer to assuage my guilt. "We can have a girls' night. Maybe even catch a movie after."

Mom smiled faintly. "Well, that would be fun."

Fiona clapped her hands. "A girl's night is just what we need. Janet, have you been to Marco's yet? Daphne, we should take her to Marco's!"

I giggled despite myself. Fiona loved pizza so much it was almost an obsession. She typically cooked either Irish or traditional Southern fare at home—a menu that perfectly reflected her own Irish/Southern fusion charm. But she suggested Marco's nearly every time we ate out. Not that I blamed her. Real Italian food was hard to beat, and Marco's was incredible.

"No, I don't think I've been there yet," Mom answered.

"Oh, you'll love it!" Fiona clapped her hands again. "I'm just going to run home and finish up my chores so we can go have us a good time. Daphne, why don't you swing by and pick me up in a couple of hours and we can all ride together. Oh, this will be fun!"

Mom and Fiona got to chatting eagerly about movie options (not that there were many at our tiny theater), which made it feel like it took forever to get Fiona out the door. Thankfully, Mom had perked up at the idea of our night out, and she excused herself to shower and get ready right after Fiona left.

Her absence finally gave me the one thing I had been thinking about ever since I'd left the county jail—another look at Eileen's journal.

Chapter Thirteen

Eileen's Journal

I told Joe about the vision, to see if he can find out who the girl is and make sure she's okay. He was angry I told Patricia. I told him he was right, I shouldn't have. I should have gone to him first. But initially, I thought it was a marital issue. Patricia's reaction, and the fact that I keep having visions even after telling her, tell me it's more than that. I'm really worried about that girl, even though I don't know why.

Daphne

I reread several entries from Eileen's journal and added some notes to my own notebook. I still wasn't sure how I was going to set a trap, especially since I didn't know who I was trapping. But I at least had some ideas for where to investigate next. I just needed to make sure I could do so without drawing any attention—from anyone.

My thoughts in order, I turned my focus toward getting ready for our girls' night. I was glad we were doing it, mostly for mom's sake, but for my own as well. The last couple of days had been tense. I was looking forward to putting everything out of my mind for a few hours.

It was a morbid thought, but part of me felt like I needed to make the most of this time with Mom. After all, I was getting ready to take down someone who had successfully gotten away with murder for decades. This could end badly for me. If something happened, I wanted Mom's last memories of me to be happy.

After I dressed, I knocked on the door to the guest room.

"You ready?" I called.

"Just a minute!" she answered.

I stood waiting until she opened the door looking flushed and happy.

"You look pretty, Mom," I said. She had swept her dark hair back into a graceful French twist and had put on a deep-red sweater that really set off her hazel eyes.

"Thank you," she said, smiling. "You do, too."

I had dressed up just a bit too, even though a girls' night with Mom and Fiona at a pizza place wasn't exactly cocktail-dress worthy. Even so, I had wanted to look—and feel—good, so I had slipped into a brown suede miniskirt and a forest-green sweater. I knew the sweater brought out the green in my eyes and played nicely with my strawberry-blonde hair. Besides that, forest green always made me think of Emerson, as it seemed to be his favorite color to wear. I had bought this sweater because it made me think of him, and wearing it made me feel like part of him was with me.

I was missing him terribly and regretting the distance I was putting between us, despite knowing it was the right thing to do.

"So, are you ready?" I asked.

"Yes! This will be fun. Does Marco's have good cocktails?"

I laughed. "Honestly, I've never ordered one from there. I'm not even sure I've looked at the drink menu. I guess we'll find out."

WE PICKED up Fiona and headed into town together, all seemingly in great moods, ready to have fun. I stayed quiet in the car while Mom and Fiona chatted away, my heart swelling with gratitude and love for both women. Tonight, I would block out the guilt of keeping secrets from them and make the most of this time, savoring every moment. I smiled, listening to them discuss the hotness level of popular Hollywood actors. Yes, this night was already turning out to be exactly what I needed.

Marco's was filling up when we arrived, but that didn't matter for us —all Fiona had to do was wave to Marco when we walked in and he immediately came over to escort us to her favorite table.

"Ahhh, Fiona!" he said, kissing her on both cheeks. "It's been too long! And Ms. Daphne! But who is this lovely woman?"

Mom beamed, a little flush in her cheeks.

"This is my mom, Janet Sullivan," I answered, making the introduction.

"So nice to meet you!" he said. "Welcome to our humble little family restaurant. Follow me." He led us to Fiona's preferred spot in the back and handed us menus. "But you may not need them," he said with a wink. "Fiona, you'll be happy to know I was in the mood to make *sfincione* today!"

Fiona and I immediately handed our menus back.

"Sign me up," I said.

"I knew this was going to be a good night," Fiona sang out.

"What's *sfincione*?" Mom asked, uncertain.

"It's a Sicilian specialty pizza," I explained. "It's incredible. You'll love it."

Fiona leaned forward, whispering, "It's a recipe from the old country. It's not on the menu, and Marco only makes it when he's in the mood. But he knows I love it, so he always saves some for me."

"I got to try it my first night here," I added. "It's really something special."

Mom shrugged and handed her menu to Marco. "I guess make that three."

"Wonderful!" he said, beaming.

"Ah, do you have a cocktail menu?" Mom asked as he started to leave.

He just waved her off. "Yes, but forget the menu. If you want cocktails, we will make you something special."

Mom blinked a few times before turning back to us. "He seems nice," she said, fidgeting with her napkin. "But I really would have preferred to choose my own cocktail."

I stifled a grin, knowing just how much she was struggling internally. Janet Sullivan was not someone who liked to have decisions made for her.

"I'm sure it will be great," I reassured her. "And if not, we'll go somewhere else after this where you can pick whatever cocktail you want."

"That's right!" Fiona chimed in. "The night is young, and so are we!" She cackled, and I grinned again.

"Well, hello, ladies." A familiar voice cut into our laughter.

I looked up to see Greg, our county sheriff, and Jackson both standing over our table.

"Oh, hi," I said, my laughter immediately dying. No matter how much I liked the two of them, I couldn't quite relax around Greg.

"Enjoying a night out?" Jackson asked with a grin.

"Girls' night," I said. "I guess it's boys' night for you? Emerson will be sorry he missed it."

"Boys' night, yeah," Greg said. "This guy was supposed to bring a pizza, but he forgot it." He clamped his hand on Jackson's shoulder. Jackson immediately winced. "So we had to come over here to pick one up."

Greg was talking to me, but his eyes kept turning to Mom. I stole a glance at her and noticed she was even more flushed than earlier as she smiled up at him. It hit me like a ton of bricks. There was a mutual attraction there, and I wasn't at all sure what to think of that.

I spoke before I could stop myself. "Um, since you're here for pizza too, would you like to join us?" I asked.

Jackson immediately spoke up. "No, we have some—" but Greg squeezed down on his shoulder again and Jackson immediately shut up.

"We'd love to join you for a quick slice," Greg said, smiling again at Mom.

She blushed and my eyes grew wider.

No, I wasn't at all sure what to think of this.

Greg slid in beside Mom on her side of the booth, and Jackson pulled up a chair to the end. I couldn't help myself. I pulled my cell phone out of my purse and immediately texted Emerson.

• • •

Me: You will never believe what is happening right now.

Emerson: What? I hope it's good, because this is the most boring shift in history. Entertain me, please.

Me: I'm at Marco's with Mom and Fiona, and Greg and Jackson came in. There are definite ... sparks.

Emerson: Between Greg and Jackson?? What the hell?

Me: No, silly. Between Mom and Greg.

Emerson: Oh. Yeah, I could see that.

Me: What?? How can you see that? I don't know what to think of it. I invited them to join us and he and Mom are sitting together in a booth now. Mom's blushing. BLUSHING, Emerson. I've never seen her blush. I don't even know what to think.

"Daphne," Mom spoke, interrupting my exchange. "Stop being rude and put away your phone right now. You have an entire table of people here to visit with. What on earth could be more important than that?"

"Sorry, Mom," I said, feeling my face go red. "I was texting Emerson."

"Oh." She smiled. "Well, maybe that is more important."

I had to stop my jaw from dropping to the floor. Was Mom getting ... soft? About love?

"So?" Greg asked expectantly.

"So what?" I asked, my face blank. I had no idea what he was talking about.

"I guess you missed that whole conversation," he said, grinning. "Whatever you and Emerson were talking about must have been pretty interesting."

I blushed furiously.

"Oh my," Mom said, covering her face. "Please tell me you weren't *sexting*," she said, mouthing the word. "Daphne, that's really inappropriate, no matter the circumstances."

"Mom! No." I wanted to crawl into a hole and die.

Greg cleared his throat awkwardly. "Well, anyway. I guess you missed it, but Janet here said she's heading home in the morning because you've decided to drop this investigation into your mother's murder. Is that a fact?"

I swallowed hard. I found it incredibly difficult to lie to Greg. He had a way of looking at me that just intimidated me to my very bones.

"Well, I didn't really find out anything," I said, evading the question. "Like Jackson and I were talking about beforehand, Katie likes to play mind games. That's probably all this was. She may have just been teasing me about knowing something because she enjoyed having that power over me."

"Gotcha." Greg nodded. "Well, you'll understand I'm relieved to hear you're going to stay out of things, considering my position. But I do hope talking to her somehow gave you the closure you need."

I swallowed hard again, this time with a lump in my throat. "I don't know that I'll ever really have closure," I admitted.

The table grew quiet and awkward, as if my admission had made everyone uncomfortable. Thankfully, Marco chose that moment to bring over a tray of cocktails, giving us a chance to change the subject.

Mom drank hers quickly and ordered a second, declaring it the best surprise cocktail she had ever tasted.

But I just twirled my straw, taking tiny sips now and then to make it look like I was playing along. That quick exchange with Greg had brought all the darkness back, and all I could think about was getting through the night so I could dive into my investigation the next morning.

CHAPTER FOURTEEN

Eileen's Journal

I saw the girl today—not in a vision this time, but in real life. I had left Daphne with Fiona so I could run some errands in town, and there she was, straight from my visions, walking across Main Street. For the first time since this started, I felt this moment of hope, like maybe this was what it was all for. Maybe I wasn't supposed to tell Patricia. Maybe I was supposed to help the girl herself. So I went after her and asked if we could talk...

Daphne

WHILE EVERYONE WAS EATING pizza and chatting happily, my mind was a million miles away. All I wanted to do was figure out who had killed my mother. Was it the mysterious Mr. Boddy, like I had long believed? Or was it Russell, seeking revenge for his prison sentence? Or was it someone else, someone even closer to home? Was there something I had been missing this whole time?

I tried to smile and play along with our happy party, but faking it was more difficult than I had expected. I felt so much guilt for having put the investigation on the back burner, and additional guilt for bringing it back now, potentially endangering everyone I loved. Damned if I do, damned if I don't. Either way brought guilt, and I couldn't really enjoy myself or our impromptu party with all of it hanging over my head.

I spied Christie waiting tables across the room and decided to go talk to her. She was the one who'd told me about Mr. Boddy to begin with. Maybe she had remembered something in the months that had passed since then. Any lead would help at this point.

I slid out of the booth and told everyone I would be back in a few minutes. Fiona, always quick to the point, asked where I was going.

"I haven't chatted with Christie in a while," I said, attempting nonchalance. "Just wanted to catch up with her and see how the baby is." I gave her a faint smile.

"Oh, that's nice," Mom said, having heard all about Christie after the first investigation. "I hope things are improving for her."

"Yeah, me too."

Fiona just shot me a keen look, like she could read right through me. But all she said was, "Tell her I said hello, would you? I'll pop in on her and the baby soon and bring her some more tea."

I nodded and left them, relieved Fiona hadn't said more.

Christie had returned to the kitchen by the time I got away, but I peeked in and motioned to her. Her face lit up when she saw me. She put down her tray, wiped her hands, and walked over to me, her face flushed. It struck me once again just how naturally pretty she was, with rosy cheeks and curly blonde hair piled high on her head. She was genuinely sweet too, and I hoped she would find someone soon—someone who would love her and treat her the way she deserved. Other than her baby, she was practically alone in the world, having been kicked out of her family for getting pregnant out of wedlock. She had lived in her car until Marco and Sophia had taken her in and given her a place to live.

"Daphne! I haven't seen you in a while," she said, smiling up at me. "Do you want to see some pictures of the baby?"

"I'd love to," I said, smiling back at her. "Do you have a few minutes to take a break?"

"We aren't too busy. It should be fine." She called back to Marco, "Hey, is it okay if I take five to show Daphne some baby pictures?"

He grinned and waved a hand toward her, letting her know it was fine.

"Come on," she said, pulling me toward the back offices. "I'm dying to get off my feet for a few minutes."

We stepped into the back office, where she immediately plopped down on the couch and stretched, yawning as she did. "He's not sleeping through the night right now," she admitted, "and boy am I tired." She pulled her cell phone out of her pocket and showed me a picture of him.

"He's darling," I said, meaning it. He had her same rosy cheeks and blonde hair. Thankfully, I didn't see a bit of Don in him. I hoped it stayed that way.

"Thanks," she said, gazing down at the picture with obvious adoration before swiping to the next photo for me.

"Such a cutie," I cooed. "Who watches him while you work?"

"My parents, believe it or not," she said with a little smile. "They started coming around after he was born. I think Marco said something to them."

"Oh wow," I said. "That's progress. Have you moved back in with them?"

She shook her head. "No, not yet. Things are still tense. But it's getting a little easier all the time. It helps that they adore him."

"Do they know he's Don's?" I asked. Christie had initially refused to tell anyone who the father was, not wanting to get Don in trouble. After all, he had been three times her age, married, and the pastor of the local church. The whole thing had barely been legal, and certainly would have ruined him.

She shook her head slowly. "No. I still haven't told them. I haven't told anyone else, actually. I know he's dead and all, but..."

"But you still don't want to hurt his reputation."

She nodded, tears pricking her eyes. Christie was way too sweet and kind for her own good. Don had done her wrong in pretty much every way possible, yet she still defended him. I always wanted to shake her, talk some sense into her. But she was so fragile that I could only be gentle with her, even if it meant biting my tongue. Constantly.

"Speaking of Don," I said, changing the subject. "Christie, I need to ask you something."

"What?"

"Have you thought of anything else that might be a clue to who Mr. Boddy is?"

Her face reddened. "Not really, why? It doesn't matter anymore, right? After all, it was that Katie girl who killed Don, not Mr. Boddy."

Her words said no, but her eyes said yes.

I forced myself to stay calm. "Right, Katie killed Don. But there's a chance Mr. Boddy killed someone else once." I looked at her and bit my lip, wondering if I should tell her the truth. I finally decided to trust her, knowing her sweet nature would make her want to help if she realized it was personal to me. "Christie, Mr. Boddy may have been the one to kill my mother. That's why I'm trying to find out who he is."

Her eyes went wide. "Oh no! Really? You think so?"

"I don't know for sure. There is another possibility. But this Mr. Boddy person is definitely someone I need to talk to, and since you're the one who found out about his existence, I thought I would check with you."

She looked down at the ground. "I don't want to get into trouble."

My heart picked up speed when I realized she really did have something. I put my hand on hers and tried to be as reassuring as possible. "You won't. I promise."

She chewed her nails nervously, pulling her shoulders in as if protecting herself. "You know how the police never found Don's phone after he died?"

My heart nearly stopped as I realized what she was saying. "Christie. Do you have Don's phone? The one he used to contact Mr. Boddy?"

She bit her lip and nodded.

I wanted to jump up, cheer for joy, and dance around. This was by far the biggest break we'd had in finding out who this guy was. Surely Joe could trace the calls. If not, maybe Jackson would do it. I wasn't sure how all of that worked, but it was an actual connection to Mr. Boddy himself. It was pure gold.

"Christie, is there any way you would consider letting me borrow that phone for a little while? It could be a game changer."

"But won't I get in trouble for taking it?" She asked the question in a tiny voice, like a child afraid of punishment.

I paused before answering. I had kept Christie's name out of things completely. As far as I knew, neither Greg nor Jackson knew Don was the father of Christie's baby or that she had talked to me the first time around. I had told Greg about Mr. Boddy, but he hadn't taken it seriously, primarily because he'd thought I was delusional at the time.

But they had looked for the missing cell phone, and I really didn't know how big of a deal it would be if they found out Christie had taken it. She had taken something that was potential evidence in an upcoming murder trial. That might be a huge deal. It dawned on me that my taking it from her might also be illegal.

I let out a breath and ran my hands over my face. "Honestly? I don't know. Why did you take the phone to begin with?"

She blushed again. "I didn't mean to. Not exactly. We were together right before ... well, before he was killed. He left it behind on accident. Once he was gone, it was like the only piece of him I had left, you know? Except the baby, of course. I mean, I was supposed to just play the part of a random church member, with no one ever knowing about our relationship. Sitting at the funeral, in the back, while everyone made over Patricia." Her eyes filled with tears again. "I don't know. It just felt right to have something of his. And"—she blushed again—"I was afraid there might be pictures of me on it."

"I see." I let out another deep breath and gritted my teeth.

Everything within me said it was a terrible idea to take the phone, but it was the only shot I had, and I wasn't willing to get Christie in trouble. I would take my chances and get Joe to help me use it to find Mr. Boddy.

"Look," I said, "if you let me borrow the phone, I won't tell anyone about your involvement. And you shouldn't, either," I warned. "It might get us both in big trouble."

She nodded, grateful. "I won't tell anyone. I don't have it here. But

I'll get it to you. I want you to figure out who killed your mother, and I'll help if I can." She squeezed my hand and gave me a smile of solidarity.

"Thanks, Christie. I really appreciate it."

She smiled again. "I better get back to work now. I'll bring the phone next time in my purse. Whenever you can stop in and get it, I'll have it for you, okay?"

"Okay."

I followed her out, trying to ignore the nagging feeling that I was making a terrible mistake.

CHAPTER FIFTEEN

EILEEN'S JOURNAL

The girl's name is Becky. I told her I knew she was having an affair with Don Kistler and that I worried she was in trouble. She just laughed at me and said I was being stupid, that she wasn't in trouble at all—she was protected. Strange word to use. I tried to talk some sense into her, reminding her he's married and unlikely to leave his wife for her, but she just rolled her eyes and said I didn't have a clue what I was talking about. Said I wasn't living in the real world and she was fine, thank you very much. I told her I had a bad feeling something was going to happen to her. She just laughed and walked away.

I left feeling even more troubled, although I don't know why. I've done everything I can do, as far as she goes.

Daphne

I HUGGED Mom goodbye the next morning, feeling equal parts guilt and relief mixed with sadness over the whole thing. I was relieved to know she would be out of danger while I did whatever I needed to do. But I felt guilty lying to her. And above all, I felt a sense of grief, knowing it was entirely possible this whole thing was going to blow up in my face in one way or another. I couldn't shake the feeling that everything was going to change, that this goodbye was more than just a "see you later." If nothing else, this chapter of my life was ending, and I didn't know what was on the other side. That scared me more than I could say.

After I was sure she had made it a ways down the road and wouldn't be coming back, I put away my work for the day and got ready to go out. I had decided to visit Don's church. I wouldn't break in this time— I was going to do things the honest way. But I hoped to gather some information there, either through conversation or the sight, that might help me get a little more clarity on who exactly was behind Eileen's death.

As I was making a travel mug of coffee to go, I heard a knock on my door. My immediate reaction was hope that it was Emerson, but another part of me hoped it wasn't. I missed him like crazy, but I needed more time. Seeing Katie had brought back the old nightmares of him tied up, helpless, being tortured because of me. I couldn't bear to put him in danger again or risk putting his mother through another scare. No matter how much I wanted him—needed him—I had to keep my distance until this was done.

I opened the door feeling a bit of trepidation, warning myself to keep my guard up. But instead of Emerson, I found Fiona on my steps, smiling brightly.

"Oh, good morning," I said, opening the door for her. The last thing I wanted was company, but I couldn't send her away. She would know something was up if I wasn't open and friendly.

"I came prepared!" she said, patting the bag she wore across her body.

"Oh, a new purse?" I asked as I closed the door behind her. I looked at the bag she was patting and realized the fringed leather crossbody was twice the size of the one she normally wore.

"Not new, just not usually needed. But I figured I better be prepared this time around. Packed the nine millimeter. I don't plan on letting anyone get the jump on us this time! So, where do we start?"

"What do you mean?" I really hoped she wasn't going where I suspected she was going.

"With the investigation of course," she said. "Great move, by the way, sending Janet home. She's not used to this stuff like we are. Doesn't quite seem to have the spirit for it. Would probably just get in our way. Not that I don't like her, mind you," she said, wagging her finger at me. "I do. She's a real sweet lady. But I agree with you on this one. I think we better keep this to us and Emerson." She nodded enthusiastically, as if we had been on the same page the whole time.

I bit my lip and tried to figure out the best way to respond.

"So, go on now," she continued. "Fill me in. What really happened with Katie? And what did Christie have to say last night?" She perched on my fireplace hearth and leaned forward eagerly.

I took a seat on the couch across from her and kept my tone measured. "I was telling the truth, Fiona. Katie didn't say anything. I really think she was just playing mind games with me. And Christie showed me some baby pictures. That's all."

Fiona clucked her tongue, disappointment clouding her face. "Daphne Sullivan, I didn't think you had it in you to lie to old Fiona. I have to say I'm hurt."

"I'm not lying," I protested. "You can ask Jackson. I'm sure they recorded the whole thing. She was excited to see me but completely clammed up when I asked about my mother. I asked her several questions and she didn't say a word to any of them. She said my mother committed suicide and ended the interview. That's the truth."

Fiona raised an eyebrow and gave me a pointed look. "And maybe that is technically true. But you and I both know you have ways of getting other information."

Guilt shot through me again. "What do you want me to say, Fiona?" I raised my hands helplessly.

She shook her head. "Girly, you and I both know you're hiding something. You didn't tell us the whole truth about that journal." She pointed a finger at me. "And you're not telling me the whole truth now."

I started to protest, but she cut me off.

"Don't. Now I told you I trusted you to tell me what I needed to know when I needed to know it. I know that journal had to have been hard for you to read and you just might not have been ready to talk about it. But this is different. You have it in your mind you're going to cut all the rest of us out and do this alone, don't you?"

I let out a frustrated sigh. "Wouldn't you do the same?"

She moved her head back and forth, contemplating. "It's hard to answer that. Maybe you're right. Maybe I would. But I'm telling you, this is a bad idea."

"Getting any of you involved in this in the first place was a bad idea," I said. "Look at everything that's happened!" I got up and started pacing, feeling too much anxiety to sit still. "Fiona, a man *died* the first time I was investigating this. Emerson got hurt. He and I both almost got killed. And not too long ago, you had a heart attack, all because you were protecting *me*. Then, thanks to me, we both got practically kidnapped by a murderer. He held a gun up to you, Fiona."

I was pleading with her now, begging her to realize the seriousness of all this. "I cannot be responsible for anyone else getting hurt."

Now Fiona was the frustrated one. "If you think any of that was your fault, you're crazier than I thought you were. You aren't responsible for what any of those people did."

"And if you get killed investigating this with me?" I stopped pacing and looked her in the eye. "Do you really think there's any world where I wouldn't feel completely and utterly responsible for that? Do you think there's any possible scenario where I wouldn't live the rest of my life in misery, believing it was my fault? You know about survivor's guilt," I pointed out. "You're the one who educated me on it. Do you seriously think that if something happened to you, or Mom, or Emerson, that I could ever live with it and be okay? I cannot—I will not—put any of you in danger again. Not even for this."

Fiona stood up and walked toward me. "The three of us are stronger together. You know that. How do you think *I* would feel if you walk into this alone and get hurt? How would Emerson feel? You know what he went through when he lost his brother. What do you think he'll go through if he loses you too and didn't even have a chance to stop it?" She poked a finger into my chest, emphasizing the point.

I let out a breath, letting the ramifications of that wash over me.

I collapsed onto the couch and held my head in my hands.

"Fiona, I don't know what to do. I feel like I'm in this impossible situation where people are going to get hurt no matter what choices I make."

"Well, if that's the case, then don't you think the smartest thing would be to let us all in so we can face this together? Emerson and I are grownups. Let us make our own decisions. And I don't want to speak for him, but I suspect he feels exactly as I do. We're stronger together, and there's a better chance of us all coming out of this alright if we go into it together."

Her words made sense. I couldn't deny that. But I also couldn't deny this feeling in my gut, a feeling that something terrible was going to happen.

And, selfish though it may be, I couldn't live with that ... even if it meant forcing them to live with it instead.

"I need to think about it," I said. I looked up at her and saw obvious disappointment on her face.

"Well, you know where I am if you need me," she said stiffly. Then she walked out and left me behind to wonder if I was doing the right thing or making the biggest mistake of my life.

Chapter Sixteen

Eileen's Journal

While I was working in the garden this morning, an owl flew over and perched in the tree near the house. It gave me chills. Fiona says there's nothing really to the idea of the owl being an omen of doom. She says the owl is a symbol of wisdom, intuition, and good medicine. But today, I couldn't help but feel this one was a warning, a warning that something terrible is going to happen...

Fiona

I heard the owl before I saw it. A Great Horned Owl. I could hear it hooting from the direction of my house as I walked the trail that led from Daphne's place to mine.

I came out from the cover of trees and spotted it.

"What are you doing here?" I muttered, staring at it as it perched on the branch of the oak tree that grew beside my garden.

I liked to think of the owl as a totem for my medicine. I had always sort of thought of it as a sign of blessing.

But I knew well that it was also considered an omen of death.

And things just weren't sitting right in my soul today. I didn't have the sight, no. But I could feel things. And I had felt things going wrong the night before Daphne showed up on my doorstep telling me she had found Eileen's old journal.

Daphne was making a mistake, that was for sure, keeping me and Emerson out of things. Oh, I knew she thought she was doing what was right, protecting us. But that girl had a blind spot. Took everything that had happened before to heart, thinking it was her fault. And I couldn't shake the feeling that it was going to get her hurt.

Trouble was coming, that much was for sure.

I walked to my chicken coop, calling for my hens. Owls rarely hunted during the day, but you just never knew. I scattered some grains in the pen, getting the chickens under cover. They had a pen attached to the coop where they could still forage a bit, with a wire netting over top to protect them from predators.

Not that wire netting would stop a predator intent on his next meal.

I finished feeding my chickens, keeping a wary eye on the owl.

"You leave my chickens alone, you hear?" I called out when I was done, pointing my finger at the owl. It just stared at me, unblinking.

I went back into my house and put on the teakettle. Times like this called for a good cup of tea, something comforting. A little of this, a little of that. I pulled some of my favorite herbs and put them in my strainer, then poured the hot water over them, taking a deep inhale of the herbal aromatics. Nothing like a good cup of tea to put you to rights.

The owl hooted again outside my window, letting me know things weren't put to rights yet after all.

I carried my cup of tea to the living room and pulled out the box I kept hidden in the closet there. I brought it over to the couch and opened the top, taking out the picture I hadn't looked at since the day Daphne had shown up next door.

Eileen, in her favorite sundress, holding Daphne on my front porch. Me beside her, the beaming stand-in grandma. Lonnie on the other side, the proud daddy. Joe behind the camera, taking the picture. I remembered it all like it was yesterday.

"Oh, Eileen," I whispered, looking at the picture sadly. "What did you get yourself into, girl?"

Chapter Seventeen

Eileen's Journal

I had another vision, this time about Don and money. I can't explain it, but the money doesn't add up. This vision was different from what I normally see. It didn't seem real, is what I mean. More like . . . a weird dream, where you know it means something, but it's not actually what happened. Normally I see what happened, as if I'm replaying a movie. Or what's going to happen. But this was completely different. Symbols, maybe? It's so hard to explain. All I know is that the money doesn't add up.

Daphne

WHEN FIONA LEFT, all I wanted to do was curl up on the couch and have a good cry. Once again, I resented the journal's existence. Although, that wasn't entirely true. I wanted to finally solve the mystery of Eileen's death. I wanted answers. I wanted justice.

I just wished I would have found the journal before settling in here, before I had developed the relationships I now had with Mom, Fiona, and Emerson. Before I had anyone to lose.

Now, it felt like I was going to lose them either way. Fiona was angry, that much was clear. Emerson had been great so far, but I knew he wouldn't tolerate being avoided much longer.

It felt like either I went into this with them and risked losing them that way, or I kept them out of it and lost them anyway.

It wasn't fair.

But it also wouldn't be fair to risk their very lives for a battle that wasn't theirs, so it would just have to be this way.

I put aside my feelings and bundled up to move forward with my original plan of investigating at the church. The money was the key to this, that much I knew. Eileen had mentioned it multiple times in her journal, and Joe had told me as much back when he and I were making our agreement to investigate together. There was too much money for a church that size, and I needed to find out why.

I sent Joe a quick text before I left, letting him know about the cell phone. He texted back quickly, telling me good work and to let him know when I had it in hand. He could pull some strings and try to trace the number. One victory secured, I felt a little boost of confidence heading to Don's church.

As I pulled into the church parking lot, I felt a shimmer of doubt. I wanted to do things the right way this time, but why on earth had I expected that anyone here would want to talk to me? Everyone who went here hated me. They had to. I was the reason their beloved pastor was dead, at least as far as they knew.

His wife certainly blamed me, that much was for sure.

The only hope I could hold on to was that Luke, Don's son, had told me that his older brother Matthew would be inheriting the church. And based on the way he described Matthew, I was hopeful I might get somewhere. According to him, Matthew was "good," whatever that meant. I could only hope it meant he might be willing to help if there was something funny going on with the church finances.

Of course, Luke wasn't exactly known for being stable, so who knew if he was a good judge of character? His idea of a "good" man might differ greatly from my own.

I took a breath and steeled myself, then forced myself to walk through the front doors of the church.

The receptionist's face turned to ice when she looked up and realized who I was.

"Can I help you?" she asked, her lips set in a thin line. I was grateful she was at least pretending to be polite, rather than immediately calling for security to throw me out.

"Hi." I offered her a timid smile and stuck my hands in my pockets so she wouldn't see them trembling. "I was wondering if there was any way I could speak with Matthew? I believe he's the new pastor here?"

She sniffed. "Well, you heard wrong. Matthew is *not* the new pastor here. At least not any longer. He resigned several weeks ago. However, if you want to speak with Reverend Pierce, I can ask if he has a minute or two to spare for you. He's a very busy man though, and you did not make an appointment."

My brain was running at full speed. This felt like incredible news. Surely a new pastor, whoever he might be, would be more willing to talk to me than Don's son.

"I would really appreciate it," I said, trying to convey genuine gratitude. "I really need to speak to someone."

"I'm sure that you do," she said, turning her nose up slightly as she turned away from me to make the call.

I gritted my teeth and planted a submissive smile on my face, refusing to let her disdain ruin my day. I was so grateful for at least a chance—and even more grateful that it was with someone new, possibly even an outsider. I didn't know how Don's church operated, but at our home church back in Arkansas, ministers could be sent to the parish from just about anywhere. It was entirely possible this Reverend Pierce wouldn't have any sort of grudge against me at all. Maybe he wouldn't even know who I was! I couldn't have asked for more.

After a few moments, the receptionist turned back to me, her tone still frosty. "Reverend Pierce says he has just a few moments he can spare you. I believe you know where the office is." She shot me a pointed look.

I immediately felt a stab of guilt, knowing she was the one who had seen me breaking into that very office on a security camera. "Yes, I remember," I said with an awkward smile. "Thank you."

She turned away, and I walked down the hallway, sighing with relief to have that bit over with.

. . .

REVEREND PIERCE'S door was closed when I got there. I knocked loudly, feeling braver than I had when I'd approached the receptionist. I didn't recognize his name, which made me hope I was right about him being an outsider. It would be such a relief.

"Come in," his voice boomed.

I opened the door, immediately confronted by the overwhelming dislike I felt for Don's old office. The whole place seemed to have been designed to make guests feel uncomfortable. It screamed money, prestige, and coldness.

Exactly like the man sitting behind the desk.

I only had to see him to realize I had miscalculated. His whole energy felt exactly like Don's, only worse somehow. Colder. Cruel. I felt sick to my stomach.

But he was still an outsider. Maybe he was the typical charismatic, overly groomed, domineering pastoral type. But that didn't necessarily mean he was shady like Don. I still needed to talk to him to see what I could find out.

I approached his desk warily. "Thank you for seeing me," I began. I walked to one of the stiff-backed chairs in front of his desk and sat down.

He immediately raised an eyebrow as if letting me know I had broken some unspoken rule about sitting before being asked. I felt even more uncomfortable and squirmed a bit in my seat.

"I'm Daphne Sullivan," I said. "I appreciate your time."

"Reverend Pierce," he replied. "What can I do for you, Ms. Sullivan?" Brusque and to the point, but not rude. And if he had any recognition of my name, he didn't show it.

"This is going to sound very strange," I said. "And you may not have been here long enough to even know. But I have some concerns about how the money is being handled at the church. There have been some rumors, you see. I was wondering, does the church ever put out public financial statements? Or have you had a chance to take a look at things?"

Even as I spoke the words, I could feel that this whole thing was a huge mistake. The look on his face grew colder with every word I said, and I felt myself shrinking beneath his gaze.

"I'm not sure what rumors you may have heard, but I can assure you that everything here is handled with the utmost accountability. However, as I'm sure you will understand, *you* are not on our board of elders. You're not even a member here. So I fail to see how any of this is your concern." He raised his eyebrows.

I bit my lip and took another breath. "I know it sounds strange," I said, giving him an apologetic smile. "And what I'm referring to is from over twenty years ago, certainly not anything from during your tenure here."

"You used the present tense when you asked," he pointed out.

"Did I? I misspoke. I'm specifically looking at the nineteen nineties. I understand I'm not a member here or, as you pointed out, on the board of elders. But perhaps there are some financial statements from back then I could look at..." I trailed off. I could see from his face that this wasn't going anywhere.

"I'm afraid I can't help you," he said with an expression that contradicted his words. "I'm not aware of us having kept any such records for so long."

Shouldn't financial records be kept indefinitely? I kept my thoughts to myself and offered him a tight smile of my own.

"I understand," I said. "Thanks anyway."

He nodded. "I'm sure with your *concerns* you're not interested in pursuing membership here." He stated it as a fact, with another raised eyebrow.

"Um, not at this time, no," I said awkwardly.

"Then I'm sure you'll understand I have a number of members who need my time today." He gave a pointed look toward the door, dismissing me.

"Of course. Sorry to bother you."

I left his office and thought to myself that I might have actually just met a minister I disliked even more than Don Kistler himself.

Chapter Eighteen

Eileen's Journal

I followed Don again. I was out in my garden and I saw him leave his house, look around to make sure no one was looking, then duck into the woods. Daphne was playing at Fiona's, so I decided to go after him. I know the woods well, and Fiona has taught me how to walk through them silently.

I feel sick. This time, he met with Joe. Joe! I can't believe it. They're working together? I wanted to throw up, watching them in the woods. Joe told him things had gone too far, but Don said HE would decide that. He said Joe was on his payroll and not the other way around. I can't believe it. How could I never have seen it? I've been working with Joe for years at this point. How did I never see he was dirty? My heart grieves the loss of trust, the loss of what I thought was a true friend. If Joe is involved in whatever this mess is, then what hope is there of making things right?

Don said "what has to be done." What does he mean? Is the girl in trouble? Something else?

Emerson

I woke up feeling listless and alone. I was missing Daphne. The few texts we had sent back and forth weren't cutting it. I missed her in my arms, in my bed, in my life.

I was trying to be patient and give her time with her mom, but it was more than that. I could practically feel the distance she was putting between us and it worried me. And only partially because I wanted to spend the rest of my life with her.

I knew Daphne and the lengths she would go to in order to find out what had happened to her mother. I couldn't help but feel that part of why she was pushing me away was so I wouldn't be there to stop her.

That feeling made me sick and helpless.

I spent the morning at home, taking care of my animals and catching up on a few projects. But when I hadn't heard from Daphne by lunchtime, I was over it. Distance be damned. I was going to check on her.

But I stopped short of my truck when I got a call from Greg.

"Hey, man, what's up?" I asked, retracing my steps back to the front porch of my cabin.

"Just following up on a conversation I had with Daphne last night," he said.

"Oh, yeah?"

"She said she was dropping her investigation. Does that sound right to you?"

I sat back in the chair on my front porch. "Dropping her investigation? That's the first I've heard of it. Although, I've barely talked to her in two days."

Greg chuckled. "Everything okay on the home front?"

"Just giving her some space to spend time with her mom." *Or trying to.*

Greg's tone changed. "Oh yeah, her mom was there last night too. Janet's a real interesting lady. Sophisticated type. Real different than the women from around here."

Now it was my turn to chuckle.

Greg immediately cleared his throat and turned serious again. "Anyway," he said, "it doesn't sound like Daphne to drop things, does it?"

I shook my head no even though he couldn't see it. "Not at all. She probably just doesn't want you monitoring her."

"That's what I was afraid of. Find out what you can for me, okay?"

"Why are you asking?" I cut straight to the point.

Greg cleared his throat again. "Look, man, I've got a bad feeling about this. I'll tell you, I'm doing a little digging into Eileen Sullivan's death. Katie's reaction to that interview with Daphne didn't sit right with me. It may be nothing. In fact, I'd say there's a real strong chance it's nothing at all. But I've got that little tingle, a little feeling something's off. So I'm going to make sure. The last thing I need is Daphne getting in the way or getting caught up in something dangerous again. So can you help me out? Keep an eye on her. Make sure she really is dropping it. Keep her busy." He chuckled again. "I'm sure you have ways of keeping her busy, don't you?"

I rolled my eyes. "Greg, you know I can't tell that woman what to do."

"Oh, I'm well aware of that." He laughed out loud this time. "You tell her she has to stay out of it, and she's just stubborn enough to dive in because of it. No, don't tell her what to do. Just manage things, see? Like I said. Keep her busy."

I rolled my eyes again. "I'll do my best."

"Don't tell her I'm looking into things, okay? That's also the kind of thing that will make her go crazy, thinking she needs to help."

"Got it. But let me ask you something, Greg. What's that tingle telling you? How dangerous are you thinking this might be?"

Greg was entirely too quiet, for entirely too long. "Like I said. It's probably nothing. But I won't lie to you. I've got a bad feeling about this one."

I let out a deep breath. "Keep me in the loop."

"Will do."

The line went dead, and I stared mindlessly at my truck, trying to figure out my next move.

Chapter Nineteen

Eileen's Journal

I broke into Don's church last night. It makes me nervous even thinking about it—I can't believe I broke the law! What else am I supposed to do, though, when the man who is the law here seems to be as dirty as the man I'm investigating?

I'm just grateful Lonnie showed me those lock-picking skills. I wasn't very good at it and it took forever. I was sure someone was going to catch me! But I got in and the place was empty, thank goodness.

I went to Don's office and looked through all of his files, but couldn't find any financial information. I guess either he keeps that offsite or maybe they have a treasurer or something in charge of all of that. I'll need to do a little digging to find out.

As I was leaving, I got the feeling someone was watching me. I could feel it, chills up my spine, like someone was lurking in the shadows of the parking lot as I left. I admit I'm a little scared...

Daphne

I left the church and sat in my car, trying to figure out what to do next. In the end, I decided I still wanted to talk to Matthew. Maybe he'd resigned, or maybe he had been forced out. If he was an honest man and something shady was going on with the church finances, maybe he was forced to leave because he wouldn't take part in it. I wouldn't know unless I talked to him, and even though the idea of going to him still made me feel a little ill, I had to try.

Unfortunately, I didn't know where he lived, and I didn't really have anyone I could ask. Fiona would know, but asking her would clue her in to what I was doing. Emerson might know, but that posed the same problem. Greg, Jackson, and Joe would all tell me to stay out of it, and those five people were basically the extent of my resources in Rosemary Mountain.

Except the library. I realized I could do something slightly unethical and find Matthew's address from his library card records. I had been working part time as a temp at the library for a while, and it would be easy enough to do, assuming he had a library card.

I drove straight to the library and walked in casually, announcing to the new librarian that I had left something in the back. She just smiled and waved me on through to the back offices. I headed straight for the computer and logged in, then did a patron search. *Bingo.* Matthew Kistler lived just a few blocks away, in the older part of town.

I wrote the address on a Post-it, then left, waving goodbye to the librarian as I did. She smiled and waved, but barely looked up and didn't even ask if I had found what I was looking for.

Matthew's house was a small, brick ranch. It was very modest and a bit rundown, but you could tell he and his wife took pride in it and tried to make it as nice as they could. The yard was trimmed nicely, and there was a pretty welcome mat out front. I walked up to the front door and knocked nervously, bracing myself for rejection.

A pretty young lady with a baby on her hip answered the door with a questioning look on her face. "Can I help you?" she asked.

She didn't seem to know who I was, or at least wasn't reacting to it. I was happy either way.

"Is this Matthew Kistler's home?" I asked.

"It is," she said, still uncertain.

"I was wondering if I could—" but I got cut off by Matthew himself before I could finish my sentence. I could hear him before I could see him, asking who was at the door.

"It's a lady needing to talk to you," the woman answered to the man I still couldn't see.

He popped his head around the door and my eyes instantly went wide. Matthew was the spitting image of his father—at least, how I would imagine his father had looked thirty years ago. But despite their resemblance, they seemed as different as night and day. Matthew's face was kind, and he looked down at his little wife with love. I instantly felt more comfortable.

"Of course," he said, opening the door a little wider. "Come on in."

It was obvious at first glance they didn't have much money. The home appeared to have been furnished with well-worn secondhand furniture and cheap art prints in poster frames. But I took an instant liking to the house anyway. It felt warm and loving, welcoming to anyone who visited. It was the complete opposite of Don's old office in every way.

I spied two young girls peeking out from the corner, both blonde-haired and blue-eyed like their mother. They waved shyly when I smiled at them. I half expected Matthew to shoo them off, but he invited them into the living room with us. When he took a seat, they both crawled onto the arms of the chair he sat in, wrapping their little arms around his neck as they continued staring at me with obvious curiosity. It spoke volumes that they were that comfortable with him, knowing what I knew about Don as a father. Luke had been right. This man was not his father's son.

Matthew gestured for me to sit as well. "What can I do for you, Ms. Sullivan?"

"You know who I am?" I asked, surprised.

He gave me an amused smile. "It's quite a small town."

"I guess I'm surprised you invited me in if you know me," I admitted.

His face took on a look of deep contemplation. "Not everyone blames you for what happened to Dad," he said, his voice kind. "I know you've gotten some flak around town, but that's unfair. It was his own mistakes that led to his murder, not yours."

Tears pricked my eyes unexpectedly, as a wave of emotion passed over me. I hadn't realized how much part of me longed for forgiveness for Don's death even though I wasn't directly the one who had caused it.

"Thank you for saying that," I said, my voice strained. "But for what it's worth, I'm truly sorry it happened. And truly sorry that my moving here seems to have instigated it."

He smiled a sad smile. "I think we both know it would have happened eventually, even without you moving here."

"Maybe," I said, although I didn't really agree. I still felt responsible for his death, and part of me always would, no matter how many people tried to tell me it wasn't my fault. I had given Katie the exact doorway she needed, and I would always regret it.

"Now, you obviously came here for a reason, and I hope it wasn't just to talk about Dad," he said, his tone friendly. "What can I do for you?"

I eyed his young daughters. "Perhaps we could talk alone?" I asked.

He raised an eyebrow, then told the girls to run help their mother in the kitchen, where she had disappeared as soon as I had come in.

"Thanks," I said when they left. "I wasn't sure if this would be sensitive or not. There's no easy way to say this, and I'm sorry to bring up such a negative topic, but, well, I'm still looking into my mother's death, and..." I swallowed hard, bracing myself for his reaction, but his face remained neutral.

"Before she died," I finally continued, "She was concerned about your church finances. She said that the money didn't add up, that there was too much of it. I also know, from other sources, that your father had been suspected of embezzlement, and, well, bribing a public official." I swallowed again, realizing just how awful and awkward this conversation really was.

But Matthew just nodded gravely, listening. When I didn't go on, he took the lead.

"Ms. Sullivan, I've heard the rumors about you investigating your mother's death. Do you really believe she was murdered?"

"I do," I said, nodding.

He nodded too. "Her death stands out as a minor epoch in my own life. I was a kid myself, but I remember it being a fairly dramatic event for the town, and a source of gossip at the church for quite a long time." His gaze drifted off, like he was remembering.

"After hearing the rumors that you came here believing my dad had killed her, I did a lot of reflecting on that time period, trying to remember anything that might help you, one way or another. It wasn't easy. To be honest with you, for most of my childhood, I tried to stay out of Dad's way as much as possible. Spent most of my time in the woods, alone with my books." He smiled that sad, tired smile again, reminding me once more that Don had left an entire list of victims in his wake. "I will say, I do not believe my father was capable of murder, no matter what his other sins were. I don't think he was responsible for your mother's death. But," he said, glancing toward the kitchen. "Why don't we step outside into the backyard and talk about the other?"

"

I felt a little wave of nerves for the first time since I had met him. But I wanted answers, so I agreed, reminding myself that he was a completely different person than his father.

I followed him into the backyard, where he gestured to two rickety patio chairs.

"Thanks for coming out here," he said. "I know it's chilly. I'll try to keep this brief. But I don't want Laura to hear our conversation and worry. She's already worried enough, frankly."

I nodded and gave him a reassuring smile, but stayed silent. It was a skill I had learned from both Joe and Fiona. People talk more if you just stay silent and let them.

"As you probably know, I was the associate pastor of the church while my father lived."

I nodded again.

"Upon his death, they installed me as head pastor. It was always the plan for me to take over for him when he retired. Or so I thought." He frowned. "As associate pastor, I had a long list of duties but no authority. I was kept in the dark about virtually everything. I simply showed up for work and did anything Dad didn't want to do. Hospital visits, funerals, midweek services, that sort of thing."

I continued nodding and giving him all the reassuring vibes I could. Not that it seemed to matter. He seemed eager to tell his story.

"As head pastor, I assumed that would change and I would finally have some authority over how things were run. But I soon found out differently. I, too, became concerned about finances specifically. See, I know our congregation quite well. After all, I've been the one actually ministering to them for the last few years. And the salary increase I got as head pastor, well... To use your own words, it just didn't add up. If you assume every member gives a ten percent tithe—doubtful, but let's assume it—it just doesn't add up."

He held up his hands helplessly. "This is Rosemary Mountain. It's a small town, a rural community. People here don't live on much. Call me stupid, but I never realized how much money Dad was making. We didn't talk about money growing up, and to be honest, it's just something I never thought about. Working at the church, I really only focused on my role. I never worried about the money. But I started thinking about it after receiving such a dramatic increase in pay. So I asked to see our financial records..."

My heart sped up just a little, and I leaned forward, eager to hear what he would say next.

He lifted his hands again. "An innocent request, don't you think? For a pastor to see the financial records of the church he's leading? But apparently that was off-limits. I received what felt like a warning, to put it bluntly. A warning to stay out of things. Stay in my lane. When I pushed the issue, the elders immediately asked for my resignation."

"Wow," I said, finally speaking. "So that's why they have someone new."

He nodded slowly. "Yes. Someone handpicked by that same board."

"Why didn't you say no?" I asked. "I mean, can they really make you resign?"

He sighed. "They have ways, trust me. But," he continued, lifting a hand to indicate he didn't want to talk about that, "I shared your concerns, obviously, about the money. Unfortunately, I'm out completely and have absolutely no way of helping you look into that."

I grimaced. "That is unfortunate. I went to the new minister today and asked him about it. It didn't go well, as I'm sure you can imagine."

A worried look crossed his face. "You went to Reverend Pierce and asked him about all this?"

"I did."

He hesitated a moment, then spoke again. "Ms. Sullivan, I feel the need to tell you to be careful. I'm not at all certain what's going on. But there's definitely *something* going on there. And if you're right that your mother was killed, and if she was killed because she was looking into this..."

"I know," I said quietly. "I'm very aware."

He sat silent for another minute. "I wish I could help you," he said finally. "But I have a family. And frankly, keeping them safe is my top priority at this point."

"Trust me. I understand that too."

After all, keeping my family safe was my own top priority.

CHAPTER TWENTY

Eileen's Journal

Don came over to confront me today. Wanted to know why I was stirring up trouble between him and Patricia, and why I was accusing some innocent girl of something that wasn't even true. I told him he was the one making trouble, stepping out on his wife with someone half his age. I also asked him how the church paid for his expensive house. He was enraged. I immediately regretted it. I admit, I'm more scared of him than I thought...

Greg

I took another look at the file spread out in front of me. It seemed completely in order, a simple case of suicide. Eileen Sullivan's body was found with a note and an empty bottle of pills, pills which the autopsy confirmed as the cause of death. Multiple people reported the victim to have been spiraling with anxiety and depression for weeks. Simple. Clean.

"So, what am I missing?" I mused. Because my gut told me I was, indeed, missing something.

Truth be told, when Daphne moved to Rosemary Mountain claiming her mother was murdered, I thought the girl was more than half crazy. And, well, after getting to know her a bit, I still thought she was a bit crazy, to be honest. But she also had her head on her shoulders, and she'd been right more than once.

I tapped my pencil on the file folder, thinking again about Katie's conversation with Daphne. I'd watched the video a few times, and when Katie looked up at the video cameras, there was genuine fear on her face.

Why?

Why would she be afraid unless she had something to hide?

And since she hadn't been around these parts when Eileen Sullivan died, it only made sense that she wasn't hiding her own involvement in the situation. But judging by the look on her face, that girl was as convinced as Daphne was that Eileen had been murdered. And what's more, she seemed to be scared to say anything about it.

I wanted to talk to her myself, that was for sure. But not yet. Not until I knew what I was dealing with here. If possible, I preferred going into a situation already knowing more than the person I was questioning. Here, I was completely blind.

Doc Rogers, Katie's husband—ex-husband? Did the marriage still count if he was testifying against her for murder? Either way, Doc was the one who had performed Eileen's autopsy and ruled it a suicide. Joe Hemsworth, the former long-standing sheriff of Rosemary Mountain, had signed off on it. Both of them were highly respected citizens. Best of the best. Loved by all.

And there was the rub.

I scratched my chin and mulled it over.

Even now, after that whole mess with Katie, people still adored Doc. They were quick to forgive him, putting all the blame on her for manipulating a lonely widow. And he had been completely cooperative since the day he'd realized we had her for murder. He might have initially tried to protect her, but he seemed remorseful for that. Like he had a conscience. So the whole town had forgiven him, no problem. It was Doc after all. The man they quite literally entrusted with their lives.

As for Joe, people around here seemed to think he walked on water. They had entrusted their lives to him too, and by all reports, he had done a fine job as sheriff. Loved by all. Which, admittedly, had made it hard since I had taken over. No other sheriff had lasted long after Joe retired. Joe had always won his elections by a landslide, if he had to win them at all—half the time, from what I had heard, he had run uncontested. His face was the face of law enforcement in these parts. When he'd decided to hang up the badge, people were initially eager to run for the job, excited for their first chance to even try for the position. But nobody had made it past one term yet. The two sheriffs in between me and Joe hadn't even tried running again. By the time I moved to Rosemary Mountain and ran for the job, it seemed nobody else wanted it. I also ran uncontested, but it wasn't because Rosemary Mountain residents were eager to vote for me.

Nobody seemed to like that I did things differently than Joe. I was an outsider and could never fill his shoes. Some flat out said it, even yelled it from their cells if I made them spend a night in jail for acting out the kind of country nonsense that passed for a good time out here. Others just let me know by their general attitude in our interactions.

I had always told myself it was just following his act that made me feel a bit, well, uncomfortable with him. But now, my mind was starting to go places I didn't feel good about.

If—and it was a big *if*—Eileen Sullivan had been murdered, Joe wasn't necessarily involved. Depending upon the manner of homicide, all it would have taken was Doc covering it up. Maybe not even him. If someone had forced Eileen to take those pills, the way Katie had tried to force Daphne, Doc and Joe both could have been totally in the dark about what really happened. Show up at the scene, see the note and the pills, autopsy confirms—why question it? I had to admit, I probably wouldn't have.

Katie's nerves though. That cast a dark light on Doc because of the connection to Katie.

But if Doc was the only one involved, then why would Katie have been so scared looking at the camera?

Doc didn't have access to those recordings.

But Joe... Well, Joe still had a lot of people who were more loyal to him than they were to me, that was for sure.

And while I was still relatively new to Rosemary Mountain, I had been noticing some other things that just didn't sit right. Things that raised a few red flags for me. I had been quiet about these things so far, not wanting to ruffle any feathers. Watching, waiting. Gathering information quietly, making sure I wasn't jumping to conclusions. That's the way I handled things.

But maybe it was time to do a bit more than watching and waiting.

I dialed Jackson's number. If I was going to figure things out, I was going to need a few more files to look at. Along with a giant-ass pot of coffee.

Chapter Twenty-One

Eileen's Journal

I feel so sick. Lonnie is starting to worry. I want to tell him about all of this, but fear how angry he'll be at me for investigating. This all feels too serious, too real ... especially knowing Joe is involved. Everything within me is screaming danger, and part of me thinks I should just bury my head in the sand and walk away.

But the visions won't stop. Visions of Don and that girl, visions of money, and others I can't even understand. I don't know why they keep coming or what I'm supposed to do, but I can't walk away while they haunt me.

Daphne

I left Matthew and sat alone in my car for a few minutes, trying to figure out what to do next. It was clear I would get nowhere trying to find out about the church and the money on my own. But I still wasn't sure how much I should tell Joe about my own investigations.

And I sure wasn't going to bring in anyone else.

I refused to accept a dead end though. I still had the cell phone, which might identify Mr. Boddy. That was even better than financial info, and it was actually within my reach.

Before going to see Christie, I stopped at a new children's store in town and bought diapers, wipes, and a sweet little outfit for her baby. I wanted to give her something as a thank-you for her help. It was also a way to sneak in a few necessities without it looking like charity. I never wanted to make Christie feel that way; I simply wanted to be a friend to her. The store wrapped everything for me in a gift bag with pastel dinosaurs on it. I smiled, knowing Christie would love it.

I swung by Marco's on my way home, hoping Christie would be there with the phone. Marco greeted me with a smile.

"Ms. Daphne! Back so soon! Let me take you to a table."

The regret on my face was real. One whiff of the garlic and freshly baked bread in his restaurant and I was practically salivating. "I'm not here to eat, sadly. I brought a baby gift for Christie," I said, holding up the bag to show him.

His face lit up. "What a lovely gesture! Unfortunately, it's her night off. Do you want to leave it here for her or come back when she's here?"

"I'll come back. I'd like to see her reaction when she opens it."

He nodded. "Understood. She's off tomorrow too, but try back the next night."

"I'll be here." I waved goodbye and left, disappointed, but I reminded myself it was just two more days. Two more days and I would have the phone that would lead to Mr. Boddy himself. In the meantime, I had at least one more trick up my sleeve. If it worked, it might open up some more leads. It's all I had, but at least it was something.

I PULLED up at home and saw Emerson sitting on my porch. My stomach immediately went to knots. He knew where my hideaway key was; he easily could have let himself in. Why was he sitting on the porch, waiting for me? Had something happened to Mom or Fiona?

"What happened?" I called out, practically tripping out of the car. I was so worried I could barely think straight, much less walk correctly.

"Nothing happened," he said, lifting a hand in a "just pause for a sec" gesture. "I just missed you, that's all."

"But you're on the porch," I said, still fearful that something was about to drop.

"It's a nice day," he said, shrugging. He reached for me as I made it up the steps and pulled me to him on the porch swing he had hung for me just two weeks ago.

Two weeks that already felt a lifetime away.

He pulled me onto his lap and nuzzled my neck. "Can't a man just miss his girlfriend?"

"You promise nothing's wrong?" I asked.

"I promise. Well, except that I've barely seen you this week."

"I know." I sighed and snuggled in closer, finally relaxing as I felt his strong arms around me. For the first time in days, I felt home. At peace. Safe. "This week has been crazy, hasn't it?"

"Yes, it has." He was quiet for a moment. "So, Greg tells me you're dropping the investigation." His voice was quiet, level, without a hint of accusation in it.

I opened my mouth to confirm, but I couldn't. In that moment, I realized I couldn't lie to him, even to keep him safe. I wanted to. Oh, how I wanted to keep him so far away from all of this. But I couldn't bring myself to lie. Not again.

I pulled back so I could look him in the eye. "I can't," I whispered, shaking my head.

"Can't what?" His eyes bored into mine, expecting—demanding— the truth.

"I can't drop it," I whispered, begging him to understand. "But I also can't endanger any of you. Not again."

He let out a breath. "I figured that was about the gist of it. You're still investigating. You're just keeping it a secret from everyone."

I nodded slowly.

"So why did you tell me?" he asked.

"Because I couldn't bring myself to lie to you," I said.

"Well, that's good, I guess." His face said otherwise. He looked up at the ceiling of the porch and let out another long sigh. "Look, I'm not supposed to tell you this," he said, "but since you were honest with me, I'm going to be honest with you. Greg called me."

"About what?"

"About all of this. He has a funny feeling too. I have explicit instructions to not tell you this, but he's looking into your mother's death, and he wants you to stay out of it."

"Emerson, I can't—"

"I know," he said, holding up a hand. "I know you can't stay out of it. I'm not asking you to. All I'm asking is that you not push me out."

I took a deep breath and tried to figure out what to say. The truth was I couldn't agree to that at all. I didn't want to lie to him, but I still didn't want him anywhere near this. My mind immediately flashed back to his muffled sounds as Katie had sliced his arm with her knife, hurting him to make me do what she wanted me to do. I shuddered and closed my eyes, trying to force the images out of my head. He was here. He was safe. And I would do whatever it took to keep it that way.

"So what's our next move?" he asked, interrupting my thoughts.

"Well," I said, feeling a bit awkward now. "I feel like I've gotten as far as I can with talking to people."

"Agreed, at least for now. So what next?"

"Well ... I thought I would try Fiona's mugwort."

"Fiona's what?" His face was blank.

"Her mugwort. An herb she gave me. It's for opening up the sight."

He raised his eyebrows. "Ah. I see."

"I know that probably sounds weird to you."

He opened his mouth, then closed it again before twisting his lips and shaking his head. Then he let out a loud laugh, lasting so long I started giggling as well.

"You know, that would have sounded totally cuckoo to me a year ago. But you and Fiona have both gotten me to change my thoughts a bit when it comes to that. If you think it will help you see something that gives us a stronger lead to go on, then hell, I think you should try it."

I tucked my arm underneath his and rested my head on his shoulder. "You're amazing, you know that?"

"Yep," he said, making me laugh out loud again, darkness forgotten —for a little while at least.

. . .

EMERSON CAME in and we played house like everything was normal. We managed to find dinner ingredients in my pantry and fridge even though they were still never quite as well stocked as his or Fiona's. He caught me up on his shift at work, and I told him all about how weird it was to see such an obvious mutual attraction between Mom and Greg.

I still wasn't sure what I thought about that. After all, as much as I liked Greg, he *was* the man who once slapped handcuffs on me and carted me off to jail.

Emerson was all for the idea though.

"Wouldn't it be great if they ended up together?" he asked. "Greg's a good guy, you know that. He could use someone like your Mom in his life, and I've always gotten the feeling that she's lonely. She could use someone like him, too."

"Why is he single?" I asked, curious. "I'm assuming divorced?"

"Then you would assume wrong," he said, tossing me a carrot to chop. "He's actually widowed."

"Widowed?" I was surprised. After all, Greg was still relatively young. "Wow. That's so sad."

Emerson nodded in agreement. "It really is. They married young, but she died just a few years after. Car accident, I think. He doesn't talk about it much. Never to me. I've only heard the rumors."

"Wow." Suddenly I saw Greg in another light. I still wasn't sure I wanted him and Mom to, well, *do* anything. But I felt a newfound sense of empathy for him, and my respect for him had grown.

Losing someone you loved so young, then staying single all those years... My heart went out to him. Emerson and I weren't even married and I knew losing him like that would shatter me. Knowing Greg had lost his wife so young was absolutely heartbreaking.

We turned the conversation to lighter subjects and ate our dinner, much like old times. I cherished every single moment of it. I still had this feeling that everything was going to change, that I was going to lose everything—and everyone—no matter how hard I tried to keep them. But I would savor every single moment of normalcy with Emerson in the meantime. Or at least I would try. I couldn't help but get emotional if I even thought about my feelings of doom.

"Hey, what's wrong?" he asked, reaching to wipe the tear that had fallen despite my best efforts at keeping it at bay.

"Nothing," I said, shaking my head to change the subject.

"It's not nothing if it's making you all teary-eyed over there."

I shrugged and shook my head again. "Like you said earlier, it's all just heavy. To be honest with you, I just have this feeling that everything is going to change."

He frowned. "You keep saying that. You really hate change, don't you?"

"I do," I said earnestly. "I wish everything could just keep going on exactly as it was. Things were perfect until Mom arrived with that journal. And while I know what I'm supposed to do—what I *have* to do—I can't help but resent the fact that everything changed ... and that I feel like it's going to change again."

"What if it's a good change? A change for the better. Change isn't always bad, you know." He poked me playfully, but his face was dead serious.

"It is to me," I said with a painful laugh.

He looked deep in my eyes, as if trying to read beneath the surface. "You really think everything was perfect until the journal arrived? There's nothing you would change about your life before that?"

"Nothing," I said.

"Not one thing?" He pushed. "You would really want everything to continue going on the same way it had, never moving forward in life? Never progressing to the next phase?"

I blinked, trying to read him. This was obviously important to him, but I couldn't be certain why. I had always felt in my heart he would want to move back home to his family in Wisconsin after healing from his brother's death. He only came to Rosemary Mountain because he blamed himself for it, and being around his family was too painful. I knew he missed them terribly. Now that he was done punishing himself, there was no reason to stay away. I wondered if that was what this was about—if he was ready to move on to the next phase of his own life.

The thought made my stomach drop. I didn't want to hold him back from the family I knew he missed, but selfishly, I desperately wanted him to stay. I was getting to the point where I couldn't imagine my life without him in it—a dangerous point because I knew how much it would devastate me when he finally walked away.

"I was very happy with the way things were," I said, choosing my words carefully. "If it were up to me, yeah, I would have kept everything the same. But I understand if that's not enough for you."

He seemed disappointed in my answer, hurt even, but he didn't say why. I knew I had missed the mark somehow, but I was afraid to open that can of worms. Not tonight. I needed just a little more time, a little more strength before I could handle him telling me he was moving back to Wisconsin. So I didn't push, and he just stood up and began quietly clearing the dishes from the table.

Even that little change brought me back to reality, reminding me that, as nice as our normal dinner had been, it was time to get to work.

My eye caught the mugwort sitting on the counter. *Please, oh please work*. I was desperate. All I could hope was that somehow this would open up my sight and I would have a vision that included a face or a name, anything to prove what really happened.

With Emerson still slowly washing dishes, apparently deep in his own thoughts, I got up and put on the kettle to brew the mugwort tea. He glanced over and saw what I was doing.

"It's time, huh?" he asked.

"Yeah," I said, letting out a sigh. "It's now or never, I guess."

He nodded again, drying his hands on a towel, then leaned up with his back against the sink and gave me another deep look. "Do you want me to stay or go? Will having me here, I don't know, interfere somehow with the process?"

I wanted him to stay. Oh, how I wanted him to stay! But the truth was I did wonder if having him there would interfere. When he was around, all I could think of was him. I wanted his hands on me, wanted to be close to him. Wanted everything to just be normal. If he stayed, I would end up so focused on him that I couldn't really open up to whatever I needed to see.

"I want you to stay, but I think you should probably go," I said softly, knowing it would hurt him. Again. It seemed all I did these days was hurt everyone around me.

His face flashed with disappointment, but he didn't say anything.

He just nodded and put the towel down on the sink before coming over to kiss me goodbye.

"Be careful," he said, stroking my cheek and looking at me like he was memorizing me. Like he was saying goodbye.

Maybe I wasn't the only one who sensed the coming darkness.

"I won't lie," he said. "It makes me nervous for you to experiment with an herb when we don't know exactly what it's going to do to you. I understand you need this to work and you need me to leave, but I wish I could stay to take care of you."

"I trust Fiona. Don't you?"

"I do," he agreed. "But that doesn't mean I won't still worry about you."

I gave him the most reassuring smile possible, considering my own doubts and fears. I trusted Fiona completely. I had no concerns about my safety using any herb she gave me. But I was terrified about what I might see. "I'll be fine," I said.

"Alright," he said. "I'll get out of here. Call me if you need me."

"I will," I said and kissed him again. I wrapped my arms around his waist and held on tight, burying my head on his shoulder. *If only things could stay like this, just a little longer.*

He held me too, until the teakettle began to whistle. My mind went to Cinderella. The clock struck midnight and she was separated from her prince, doomed to leave his arms and go back to the darkness of her real life.

He reached behind me to turn off the burner, kissed me again, then left, leaving my house feeling more empty than it had ever felt before.

I FELT an unexpected sense of reverence while brewing the tea. I desperately wanted it to work, and not just because I thought it was the key to figuring out what had happened to my mother.

I wanted another vision of her because it was a piece of her. I had so few of them.

Every piece mattered.

So when the tea was finished, I carried it upstairs and out onto my deck, in the cold night air. I held the cup in both hands and sipped the tea slowly, my eyes closed. I sensed, somehow, that I needed to focus on my intention. So I did. I breathed in deeply and focused on "opening up," as Fiona had once described it.

I felt a deep sense of calm come over my body. The tea was surprisingly relaxing.

But no visions.

I finished the tea and sat there for a while, still trying to remain open, hoping that something would happen. But other than the relaxation in my body, nothing did.

I was disappointed, but I reminded myself that Fiona had told me to drink it then pay attention to my dreams. Even though nothing had happened right away, maybe the tea would still work as I slept. Just to be safe, I tucked a sprinkling of the herbs under my pillow.

I fell asleep quickly. Hours later, I awoke abruptly, my heart pounding.

I had dreamed of her. Not about Becky, or Don, or Joe, or whoever had killed her. Just her. It had been so vivid, so real, that I half expected to see her in the room.

In my dream, she had embraced me. Gazed at me, with eyes so tender and full of love it made my heart physically ache.

It was a love I had hungered for my whole life.

I had seen her face so clearly, had seen the way her green eyes sparkled. So like mine, yet different somehow.

"Oh, my Daphne," she had said, reaching out to touch my cheek. "You have made me so proud."

Her voice. How could I ever have forgotten it? Hearing it felt like an awakening of memories that had been hidden just below the surface, but always still there—this piece of her that was always with me, would always be part of me, even if I had somehow forgotten.

"Don't go," I whispered. "Please."

But she just smiled sadly, then faded away as I woke.

It was just a dream.

But I knew I would carry it with me for the rest of my life.

Chapter Twenty-Two

Lonnie told me to stop obsessing about the girl. But how am I supposed to stop? I've been racking my brain trying to figure out how all of this fits together: Don, Joe, the church money, and the girl. I admit, I don't like the places my mind keeps going. I hope, with all my heart, there's some innocent explanation for all of it. But if there were, I wouldn't be having these visions.

Emerson

I LEFT Daphne alone to drink her mugwort tea, even though I really wanted to stay. Mostly I wanted to just make sure she was okay, to see for myself that she didn't have any reactions to it or fall apart after any vision it brought forth. But for my own sake, I was glad to get away for just a bit.

I pulled my truck up to my cabin and turned it off, sitting there in the silence instead of going in. Once again, I pulled the engagement ring from my glove compartment and looked at it.

Daphne had confirmed my fears when she'd said she didn't want anything to change. I had dropped what felt like a thousand hints over the past couple of months, but the answer was always the same. She was happy exactly as we were. She didn't want anything to change. She was just enjoying the moment. Any time I even tried to bring up the future, she changed the subject.

I had been determined to convince her to marry me, but I was starting to wonder if I needed to face the facts. She had made it abundantly clear, over and over again, she wanted nothing to change. She seemed determined to not take even one step forward from where we had been since the night we got back together. What was it going to take for me to get the picture? Hell, when she said, "I understand if that's not enough for you," in that mournful tone, I felt like she was about to break up with me then and there, just for wanting more.

I stared at the ring again. I had imagined the proposal ten different ways, but one thing had always been the same. Her *yes*.

What if the answer was no?

I closed the box, put it back into its hiding spot yet again, and braced myself for the cold of the outdoors—and the cold of a house without Daphne in it.

Thor was waiting for me at the door. Old Faithful. I cracked a smile as I scratched his ears. "You didn't mind committing to me, did you, old boy?"

His tail thumped the floor as he rewarded me with kisses.

I let him out the front door to do his business. He came back quickly, as eager as I was to get warm and settle in. But he kept going to the door and whining, making me think he hadn't taken care of things after all. I opened the door to let him back out, but he just stood there, looking at me with one of those expressions only the smartest dogs can wear. He was trying to communicate something, and I, the dumb human, wasn't getting it.

"What is it, boy?" I asked, scratching behind his ears again. When it was clear he wasn't going to head back out, I closed the door—then I got it. He missed Daphne, too. He was hoping she was going to come in after me.

I sighed. "Well, aren't we just a pair of pathetic men?"

He whined a little, agreeing.

I just shook my head and headed to the kitchen to brew up some tea of my own. Hawthorn tea for me. Another one of Fiona's recipes, meant to cure heartache. She had given it to me to help heal the wounds left by my brother's death. But I was hoping it would ease the heartache that was developing over Daphne. Not that it was over. Not by a long shot.

I wasn't going anywhere. If she wanted things to stay exactly the same, well, I would just settle into being Mr. Long-Term Boyfriend. That was a future too, if not the one I wanted. I wanted her though, more than anything else. So I would just have to be content with the way things were.

Could I though? Could I be content playing long-term boyfriend, always held at arm's length?

It bruised the heart, that much was for sure.

Chapter Twenty-Three

Eileen's Journal

I went to Bill's today. It was awkward. But he's the most financially savvy person I know, and I need answers. I tried not to give him too much information, but I asked him what he would think if he knew a business was bringing in large amounts of money, larger than would make sense for their operation. He gave me one of those long stares of his, where you don't know if he's just thinking things through or if he didn't hear you at all. He finally said it sounded like money laundering. Money laundering! Exactly what I was afraid of. I asked him if he could tell me more about how that worked, but he said he was busy and had no more time for me. Then Billy walked in and things were even more awkward, so I left.

Daphne

I woke up the next morning and knew I needed to make things right with Fiona. I still had every intention of protecting her, but I couldn't bear for our relationship to be broken.

Reuniting with Emerson last night had made me realize Fiona was right. We were all stronger together. Spending just a few hours with him had given me strength I didn't know I needed. Beyond that, I was tired of hurting the people I loved. I was tired of keeping them at arm's length.

Unfortunately, that didn't change the responsibility I felt to keep Fiona safe or the promise I had made to Joe to keep her out of the investigation. Her physical heart was weak—a scientific fact I still struggled to wrap my mind around, considering how strong her spiritual heart was. I had no idea how I was going to be honest with her and also keep her safe, but I would figure out a way. She would just have to accept that I didn't want her investigating with me.

As if anyone could ever tell Fiona Flanagan what to do.

Before I went to Fiona's, I wanted to go to Bill Brinksley's to see if I could get any information or pick up anything from him. First, I brewed myself a cup of mugwort tea. The flavor was actually growing on me. It had done something for me last night, that was for sure. I even had that little experience, a flash of something, at Joe's after simply chewing some leaves beforehand. I felt like Fiona was right. As crazy and unbelievable as it seemed, something about the herb helped open me up more, and I needed to be open more than ever.

I drank my tea and tried to focus on my intention, but I struggled to focus on it when all I could do was try to think up ways to actually get into Bill Brinksley's house. He wasn't a fan of mine, even though we had never met. What excuse could I use to get in there?

In the end, all I could come up with was copying Fiona's neighborly way of popping over with baked goods to say hello. Technically, I was pretty sure in Southern culture it was supposed to be the original neighbors bringing over items to introduce themselves. But since he never had, I would switch it around.

Unfortunately, I lacked Fiona's baking skills. There would be no fresh apple pie from me, proudly presented to Bill, hot and fresh out of the oven. What I did have was some take-and-bake cookie dough in the freezer. That was simple enough and could pass as a homemade treat.

Cookies in the oven, I put together a small basket with some pretty tissue paper in the bottom. When the cookies were done and mostly cooled, I stacked a few in the basket and put a pink-checkered ribbon on top. There. It was cute, it was undeniably Southern, and it was my ticket into Bill Brinksley's home.

Hopefully.

I drove to his house, not wanting to waste the time it would take to walk there. Plus, I wanted to have an easy getaway, just in case. Between Joe, Fiona, and what I knew of Bill's reputation, there was a solid chance he was the mysterious Mr. Boddy I had been looking for. And that meant there was a chance he was dangerous.

I pulled up to his driveway, shuddering at how foreboding his house felt, then shook myself. I was being silly. If I saw this house anywhere else, I would think it was beautiful. A bit ostentatious, sure. But beautiful. It only felt foreboding because of my thoughts about it. I needed to shake those off, put a smile on my face, and act neighborly, no matter how I felt inside.

I rang his doorbell and waited nervously, reminding myself that he might not even be there. I wasn't sure which would be worse—facing him or not having the chance to.

But I didn't have to wait long. The door swung open quickly, and a grumpy-looking older man with white hair and bushy white eyebrows stood behind it practically glaring at me. He was dressed casually, in a sweater and jeans, but his clothes had that understated expensive look. They paired nicely with the Rolex on his wrist and the leather loafers on his feet.

"Well?" he said, obviously irritated I hadn't introduced myself yet.

"Hi," I said, putting on a fake smile. "I'm Daphne. I moved in down the road a few months ago and am still trying to meet all my neighbors." I held out the basket to him. "I baked you some cookies. Peanut butter."

"I'm allergic," he said flatly, still with a scowl on his face. "What are you trying to do, kill me?"

"Oh," I stammered, caught off guard. "Oh, no, I'm so sorry. I know how serious peanut butter allergies are. I didn't know." I could feel my face go bright red.

He stared at me again. "Daphne. Would that be Daphne Sullivan? Lonnie and Eileen's kid?"

"Yes," I said, still beet red.

He stared at me a long second, then held the door open wider. "Well, come on in then."

"Um, okay. I'll just leave these outside. Again, I'm so sorry. I didn't know about your allergy." I bent down and put the basket of cookies on the step to pick up again when I left.

"Bring them," he said, scowling again. "I lied about the allergy."

"Oh. Um. Okay." I picked the basket back up and followed him into the house, feeling more off balance than ever.

The inside of Bill's house matched the way he dressed. It was understated but elegant and obviously expensive. The outside of his house might have looked too ostentatious for the area, but inside, it felt like old money that didn't need to brag too much, with gorgeous wood paneling, old world oil paintings, and high-end furniture. Yet it somehow felt comfortable, lived in, and not like a museum on display. I was trying to reconcile it with the grumpy man in front of me and couldn't quite do it. I had never heard anyone mention him having a wife, but I felt certain this house had been decorated by a woman.

"I love your house," I offered. "It's beautifully decorated."

He glanced around, as if noticing it for the first time. "Oh. Yeah. Thanks."

"You are Bill Brinksley, right?" I asked, wanting to verify. I still felt unsure of myself, as the man standing in front of me wasn't anything like I expected.

"That's right," he confirmed, plopping into a chair.

I stood awkwardly until he rolled his eyes and gestured for me to sit. After placing the basket of cookies on the coffee table, I chose a high-backed leather chair near his and sat down gingerly, folding my hands in my lap, trying to think of something intelligent to say.

He looked at me with frank curiosity. "So you're Lonnie's kid." It was a statement, not a question.

"That's right," I replied, grateful he'd started a conversation first.

He nodded absently. "Lonnie was a good kid. Good friends with my son."

"Oh," I said with a prick of surprise. "I didn't know you had a son."

He pointed a finger at the family photos sitting on his baby grand. I got up and walked over to them, curious about the family of this hated yet powerful man. Sure enough, there were photos of him with a wife and a son, ranging from the 1970s through the 90s, I guessed, based on the outfits in the photos. Nothing recent, except a portrait of a middle-aged man who I assumed was the son.

"Is this him?" I asked, pointing to the picture.

He nodded.

"I'd like to meet him sometime. It would be fun to meet someone who knew my dad back then."

"How is Lonnie?" Bill asked absently.

I looked up, surprised. "Haven't you heard yet? He passed away several months ago, before I moved here."

He looked at me sharply. "Oh, yes. That's right. Now I'm the one who's sorry. It was thoughtless of me to forget."

"It's fine," I said, waving him off.

"Lonnie and Billy—my son—ran around together back in the day. Small town, same high school. They were the same year," Bill explained. "They grew apart after high school. Different life paths and all, some misunderstandings. But your father spent more than one night here when they were kids and then in high school."

Bill actually grinned, recollecting something. "I'm afraid I wasn't the most responsible parent. I think your father had his first cigar and his first whiskey here, both on the same night. Turned green and threw up all over the lawn."

I eyed him curiously. "You speak of him fondly," I commented, returning to my seat.

"Lonnie was a good kid. A good friend to Billy, until they weren't." His absentminded tone returned.

"So, I'm curious. If you were so fond of Lonnie, why did you accuse him of stealing from you a couple of months ago?" I asked the question coolly, curious about his answer.

He turned his attention toward me, the absent expression replaced by the shrewd eyes of a businessman. "Money, my dear," he said simply. "A little white lie that positioned me to potentially claim a small fortune, with extraordinarily little effort on my part. It wasn't personal. Simply business."

My temper flared slightly, but I reined it in and kept my tone calm.

"Your little white lie caused quite a bit of trouble for me. And you look like you already have a small fortune. So forgive me if I'm surprised you would find it so easy to lie about a dead man, hurting his reputation *and* his daughter, just to increase your bottom line a bit."

He shrugged. "You shook it off quickly. No harm. As I said, it wasn't personal."

I fought back a retort and took a deep breath, reminding myself of why I was here. "Is your wife home?" I asked, keeping my tone casual. "I'd love to meet her, too."

"Dead," he said, staring at me.

"Oh." I blushed, once again thrown off balance by his abruptness. "I'm so sorry. I should have realized."

He simply stared at me, silent. It was quite unnerving.

"At least you and your son have each other," I said, trying again to break the awkward silence. I had never met anyone I'd had so much difficulty talking to.

"Not really," he said, that odd, absent expression returning.

I relaxed slightly, relieved that his eyes drifted away from me.

"Billy and I are on different paths, too," he said finally. "A little falling out of our own."

I was dying to know more, and was trying to come up with a tactful way to ask about it, when he abruptly stood.

"Well, thank you for your visit, Daphne. But I have business to attend to."

"Oh, of course," I said, standing. I couldn't help one last effort though. "Do you mind if I use your restroom before I go?"

He looked at me sharply, as if seeing through me, then gave a quick nod. "Down the hallway, to the left," he said. "Make it quick. I have a call in ten minutes."

"Absolutely." I gave him my warmest fake smile and walked down the hallway straight to the bathroom, hoping beyond hope the mugwort would work exactly as I needed it to.

Chapter Twenty-Four

Eileen's Journal

Another letter arrived today. It caught me off guard, as I thought all that was over. But no, it looks as if I have one more thing to worry about. He says I should watch my step and hinted that he's out of prison. I thought he had another year left. Nobody warned me he was going to be released early. Normally I would take it straight to Joe, but I'm still not ready to face him about what I saw. And I can't tell Lonnie, not when he's already so worried.

Daphne

I walked down the hallway and slipped into the guest bathroom, closing the door behind me. I locked it and leaned against it, my nerves overtaking me as I looked around the small room for something physical I could hold that might give me something—anything. I needed information, a knowing, a vision. And I was running out of time.

But as I closed my eyes and leaned against the door, opening myself up to the surrounding energy, I realized I was in the wrong place to do this. The guest bathroom was too impersonal, too far removed from the family who lived here.

It wasn't devoid of memory though. Almost immediately, I was hit with a montage of images, all featuring the last person I would expect—my father.

Lonnie as a kid, getting cleaned up after what had apparently been a fun—and messy—time outside with his friend. Lonnie as a young teen, rinsing off a scraped knee and covering the wound with a Band-Aid. Lonnie as an older teen, sneaking in here with ... oh no, with my *mother*, closing the door and kissing her quietly, like they were afraid to be seen. Eileen pushing him away, acting shocked, then kissing him back before pulling away again, this time surprised by her own response. Eileen running out, closing the door behind her. Lonnie leaning against the sink, looking both sad and overjoyed at the same time. And later, Eileen alone in the bathroom, staring at herself in the mirror with a strange expression on her face, touching her fingers to her lips ... then sliding a diamond ring off her finger and putting it on the granite countertop as if she didn't know what to do with it.

My eyes opened, my heart pounding, as it hit me what I might have been seeing. That ring looked like an engagement ring, but it was *not* the ring Lonnie had saved in their box of memories. Had she been engaged before Dad? Had she been engaged to Billy? Was their breakup the reason Lonnie and Billy "went different directions," as Bill had said?

I didn't have the answer, but I knew I needed more. Thankfully, I was heading next to the one person who would know.

The sun was shining as I stood on Fiona's front porch steps, bringing welcome warmth to the mountain. Both good omens, I thought, although I felt distinctly uncomfortable standing outside, waiting for her to answer the door. Normally, she always seemed to sense when I was coming and was waiting with the door wide open before I even made it out of the car. The closed door felt like a clear message that things had changed between us.

Her face confirmed it when she finally opened the door.

"Good morning, Daphne," she said stiffly.

"Good morning, Fiona," I said, keeping my expression meek.

She stood and looked at me for a minute, then rolled her eyes. "Well, come on in then." She opened the door wide in invitation.

I slipped off my shoes and stepped into her living room, taking a deep breath as I did. The air was scented with rosemary and lavender, two of my favorite scents on earth. I spotted the oil diffuser in the corner and realized Fiona was diffusing my favorite blend. I couldn't help but smile. Maybe she had sensed I was coming after all.

"So you've come to your senses, have you?" she asked, locking the door behind me, then heading to stoke the fire.

I nodded. "Sort of."

She turned to me and raised an eyebrow. "Now what does 'sort of' mean, missy?"

"I'm sorry for not being honest with you," I said. "You're right. We're stronger together, and I don't want to do anything to hurt our relationship. I'm done lying and sneaking around. But I still don't want you getting involved with this. Fiona, it's dangerous."

"Oh, pish posh," she said, waving a hand. "Coffee?"

I nodded yes and followed her into the kitchen.

"I'm seventy-two years old," she began. "So what if it is dangerous? I've lived a long life. If it's my time to go, it's my time to go. Lord knows I'd rather go out having some fun than sitting here alone in this house."

"I'm not sure hunting down a killer is something I would consider fun," I said. I helped myself to a mug and poured a steaming cup of coffee from her French press, then joined her at the rough wood kitchen table.

She shrugged. "Good point. Fun may have been the wrong word. The point is the same though. You'd think I was a child or something," she muttered.

"Not a child." I reached out and put my hand over hers. "Just one of the very few family members I have left. I want to talk to you because I know you might be able to help me put together some of the pieces to this puzzle. But I need you to promise you'll stay out of the investigation, because I can't bear losing you, too."

At that, her eyes filled with tears. "Alright, alright. Fine. I'll stay out of it. You got your promise out of me. Now sit yourself down and ask me what you need to ask me."

"Was Eileen engaged to Bill Brinksley's son?" I asked, before taking a long sip of my coffee. Fiona's coffee always tasted better than what I made at home, even though I bought the same beans as her and had watched her preparation carefully in order to copy it. Mine still fell short. The woman was pure magic in the kitchen.

A look of disgust flitted across Fiona's face. "Oh my. I had forgotten all about that. Yes, as a matter of fact she was. For a brief period, anyway. Why do you ask?"

I explained about the vision in Bill's bathroom.

"Well, isn't that interesting?" She tapped her chin with her long finger, contemplating. "Goodness, that was a long time ago. Let me see what I can remember. Like Bill told you, Billy and Lonnie ran together. School buddies, you know. Oh, Billy had it bad for your mama. Took her to his senior prom." She smiled at the memory. "I never got the impression your mama felt quite the same way about him. I think it was always Lonnie for her, but Billy asked first, and Lonnie was too good a friend to make a move on Billy's girl ... for a while, at least."

"So what happened?"

"Truth be told, I don't know all the details, honey. I know Billy asked your mama to marry him in a grand display, which was an odd thing to my way of seeing, because anyone who knew Eileen would know that's not how she would want it. Plus, it's not like they were going steady or anything. A few dates here or there, but nothing serious. When he asked, I think Eileen felt she had to say yes. Her parents were all for it, of course, with Billy's dad being the richest man in town and living in that fine house. With the proposal being in front of everyone and her parents encouraging her and smiling so big, I think she didn't know what to do but say yes."

Fiona leaned back in her chair, her eyes raised to the ceiling, lost in memory. "You know, everyone was rejoicing and happy and celebrating, except one person. That's the part I'll never forget."

"Who?" I asked.

She looked at me in surprise. "Lonnie, of course. He looked stricken, like his dog had just died. I walked over to him and asked if he was okay. He said something about having waited too long. I knew then what he was about. I told him they weren't married yet." Fiona shrugged. "Only a couple of weeks went by before that ring was off her finger, and soon after, she and Lonnie were an item and all was well with the world."

"Except Billy's world," I said, an eyebrow raised.

"Except that," she agreed.

"Do you think Billy is the type who would have gotten revenge?"

Fiona screwed up her eyes, thinking it over. "If you're asking if I think he would have killed Eileen, all those years later, over the whole thing, I think the answer is no. He gave Lonnie a black eye," she admitted. "Their friendship never recovered. It was over for all of them after that, and a bit of a rivalry existed between the households from then on. But I'd be awfully surprised if he had anything to do with your mother's death."

I mulled it over. "But if his father really is Mr. Boddy, that old hurt could have been a factor in what happened."

Fiona nodded, ceding the point. "Bill was mad, that's for sure. Said some awful things about Lonnie, like how Lonnie wasn't from the right side of the tracks. When that didn't work, he said some ugly things about Eileen. Was embarrassed for his son, you see."

I did see. And it was just one more thing to keep in mind as far as Bill Brinksley was concerned.

"Where is Billy now?" I asked.

"Oh, he lives in town," she said, "in one of those fancy houses downtown. Historic district. I don't see him often, to tell you the truth. He travels a lot, like his dad, and he doesn't visit the lane much. He and his dad had a falling out too—don't ask me about what, because that seems to be a town secret that got locked down tight. No one knows but the two of them, and neither of them seems apt to talk about it."

"Interesting," I said. To me, that was yet another checkmark on the tally. If Billy had truly loved Eileen and had found out his father killed her, that would definitely be a reason for falling out—and a reason for staying silent about it. It was a lot to think about.

"I also wanted to ask you about something else," I said, changing the subject.

"What's that?"

I rehashed my dream from the night before, then asked the question that had lingered, unspoken, in my thoughts all day. "Do you think it was real?"

"What do you mean by real?" she asked with a curious expression on her face.

"I mean, do you think my mother really visited me last night? Or are dreams just our own mind processing things? Was it just me seeing what I wanted to see, and hearing what I wanted to hear?" A lump developed in my throat, making it hard for me to say the words. "Do you think she's really proud of me?"

Fiona reached for my hand and squeezed it. "Honey, I *know* she's proud of you. If you're asking me, I do believe our loved ones sometimes visit us in dreams. You know, I was real close to my grandmother. She's the one who taught me about plants and what to use for medicine, back in Ireland. Another life," she said, her eyes going dreamy as she remembered a part of her story I still knew little about.

"Anyway," she continued, "the night she died, I dreamed of her. She came to me and said she had to go, but she wanted to check on me and make sure I was okay. I woke up and knew immediately she had passed. Found out for sure the next morning. For the first few years she was gone, now and then she would show back up while I was dreaming. It was always the same. Just checking to see if I was okay."

Fiona shrugged and took a sip of her coffee. "Can I prove, by science, it was anything more than my mind? Of course not. But I'll tell ya, there's a whole lot on this earth that's true that science just hasn't caught up to yet."

Her words gave me comfort. I squeezed her hand, grateful to have found the kindred spirit I never knew I needed.

And I promised myself that, no matter what it took, I wouldn't let her put herself in danger this time.

CHAPTER TWENTY-FIVE

Eileen's Journal

Another threat in the mail today. That's two this week. Like the ones from before, it said horrible things. I hid it, along with the first, from Lonnie. I hate hiding things. But I don't know what else to do right now.

Jackson

MY STOMACH TWISTED in knots as I drove down the gravel driveway. It had been years since I had been down this road—a road I promised myself I would never return to. But thanks to Daphne, here I was, back in the one place I didn't want to be.

Home.

The word made me sick. Who would want to come from this? From *him?*

I killed the car and trudged to the door, with every step feeling like I was wading through mud. I hated this place. Hated him. Hated myself for lying to Greg about where I was and why I needed a day off.

Hated every bit of it.

But what had to be done had to be done.

I pounded on the door, feeling the weight of my fist hit heavy. It felt good.

"Yeah, yeah, I'm coming," came the voice from inside. A voice that threatened to turn my insides to liquid. The voice that haunted my nightmares.

The lock jiggled. I took a breath and braced myself, planting my feet and widening my shoulders. I wasn't a boy this time. I was a man. And I refused to let him see he still intimidated me.

The door swung open. Not even a hint of recognition in the man's eyes. Oh, but I recognized him. He was older, yes. Thinner, with more lines on his face than he should carry at his age. But that was the mark of a life lived poorly.

"Hi, Russell," I said with a grimace.

Recognition finally dawned. "Well, well, well. If it isn't young Jackson. Bold of you to show your face around these parts." He made a face of disgust and spit on the grass beside my feet. "We don't take too kindly to members of your profession, in case you don't remember."

"I remember," I said evenly. "Aren't you going to invite me in?"

He rolled his eyes and walked back inside, leaving the door open. I took that as an invitation and walked in behind him, closing the door behind me.

"What do you want?" he asked. "Here to put me back behind bars?"

"That depends. Should I?"

He plopped down on the hard wooden chair beside his kitchen table. The entire place felt dark, dirty, and rough. Just like when I'd lived here. I tried to block out the memories threatening to overwhelm me. I wasn't here for memories. I was here for information.

"Oh, I walk the straight and narrow these days," Russell said, with a sly grin that told me otherwise.

Lucky for him, I wasn't here about that though.

"Aren't you going to sit down?" he asked, with false hospitality, gesturing at the couch behind me.

I almost vomited when I turned to look at the same filthy, roach-infested couch that had been here when I had the misfortune of living here too, the same one he made me bend over every time he felt like taking a belt to me.

No, I wouldn't be sitting on that couch.

"I'll stand," I said, keeping my voice even.

The sharp glint in his eye suggested he knew exactly why I'd refused to sit on the couch. He grinned triumphantly, and I immediately changed my mind.

No way would he ever hold that kind of power over me again.

"Well, maybe I'll have a seat after all," I said. "Who knows? This conversation might take longer than I expect." I cracked my knuckles, a subtle threat of my own, and planted myself on the couch with a nonchalant look.

There was surprise and a twinge of disappointment in his eyes, a recognition of that loss of power he loved so much. I took it as the win it was and used the opportunity to ask what I'd come here for.

"Tell me about Eileen Sullivan's death."

He let out a barking laugh. "Is that what you're here for, boy? Don't you have better things to do with that high and mighty job of yours?"

I stayed silent, waiting for him to get around to it, keeping him locked in a stare down until he finally broke.

"I don't know anything about that woman's death," he finally said. "Other than that she deserved it, and I hope she suffered like she made me suffer."

"You suffered because of your own choices," I pointed out.

"Choices?" He scoffed. "What choices? Grow up here, like this, you don't have choices. My only choice was to survive, till that bitch took it upon herself to get involved."

The anger flared inside me, anger at his complete lack of empathy for any human being other than himself.

"*She* took it upon herself to *get involved*? Seriously? That's the way you see it?" I didn't even try to contain my anger.

"It's the truth," he said, that sick smile on his face. He pulled a cigarette from his pocket and lit it, taking a puff as if he didn't have a care in the world.

"You screwed up," I said, using everything within me to keep the emotion out of my voice. "Let's get that straight. But that's not what I'm here to talk about. I'm here because I want to know what happened the night Eileen died."

He let out another laugh. "Do I have to say it again, boy? I didn't kill her. Wasn't anywhere near her place that night. Don't even think you can go pinning that on me. But"—he leaned closer, lowering his voice—"we both know she had it coming, don't we?" He winked at me, and it took everything within me not to haul over and slap that smirk right off his face.

Instead, I clenched my fists until the rage passed, reminding myself it wasn't worth the assault charge he would almost certainly get thrown at me. It also wasn't worth anyone finding out about his connection to me.

"Do you have an alibi?" I asked, gritting my teeth.

He shrugged. "I was with you, wasn't I? You'll vouch for me, I'm sure. After all, what kind of irresponsible father would I be if I left my son home alone at that age?" He winked again.

I began debating whether the assault charge might be worth it after all.

"I hear Eileen's girl is living back in Rosemary Mountain," he commented, staring at me with his beady eyes.

"Where'd you hear that?" I asked.

He spit on the ground. "News gets around. Is she anything like her mama?"

"I don't know what you mean," I said. But I did. Oh, I knew exactly what he meant.

He grinned, recognizing my bluff. "Them Sullivan women are dangerous," he said, taking a long drag of his cigarette. "They're nosy. Seem to get off on telling other people's secrets. There's a secret or two you wouldn't want the world finding out, now isn't there? Yep, you gotta watch out for them Sullivan women. World would be better off with none of them in it, if you ask me." His eyes glinted as he grinned.

My blood ran cold. I couldn't be having this conversation. I stood up to walk out without saying a word.

"You leaving so soon, boy?" he called out. "Ain't gonna sit around and ask how your old man's been all this time? Ain't gonna help me out with some of those honest dollars you're so busy earning?"

I put my hand on the doorframe and paused. Slowly, I turned around to face him, one last time. "Yeah, I'm leaving. And you better hope you never see me again. Because if you do, it will only be because

I'm hauling your ass into jail. Call me 'boy' all you want. Try to make me feel small. Here's the damn truth of things. I'm not a boy anymore. I'm a detective now. And I'm damn good at what I do. So mark my words. If I'm taking you in? You won't be getting out again. I'll make sure of it."

"Is that a threat, boy?"

"Nah." I shook my head. "It's a promise."

He laughed, but I could see the fear in his eyes, and I rejoiced over it. I turned on my heels and walked out, hoping I never set eyes on this place ever again.

But in the privacy of my car, my confident swagger disappeared and my hands shook uncontrollably as I tried to grip the steering wheel. The honest truth was I was still as terrified of him as ever.

I was even more terrified about my world imploding if anyone found out my connection to him. Which meant if he really was the one who killed Eileen, I had a choice to make—take him in or cover it up.

I hated myself for it, but I wasn't at all sure what choice I would end up making. Because he was right. I knew exactly how dangerous those Sullivan women were. And I absolutely did not want my own secrets getting out.

CHAPTER TWENTY-SIX

I talked to Joe. I couldn't take it anymore. I told him I saw him and Don in the woods. He was so ashamed. I thought he would break down right then and there. He explained how he had taken a bribe to look the other way when he discovered Don was embezzling money, which may explain everything I was seeing with Don and the church. Embezzlement is bad, but better than money laundering! At least the crime would be contained to one person.

Joe asked me not to turn him in. Said it was the biggest mistake he's ever made and he's back on the straight and narrow. I told him I would think about it, but really, how could I turn him in anyway? I have no proof whatsoever. It's their word against mine. At least for now.

It's brought up quite the internal struggle. I love Joe like a father, and I believe him when he says he made a mistake. Everyone deserves second chances. Yet what he did was wrong. So very wrong.

And it still doesn't explain the visions of the girl.

Daphne

After visiting Fiona, I headed home, hoping to soak away the stress in a long, hot bath. I needed time to think, to process everything I had learned, and to take stock of where I was and what was coming. My whole nervous system felt exhausted already, and the fight hadn't even started.

I had just settled into my bath, a glass of wine in hand, when my phone rang. I groaned, annoyed at the intrusion, but knew I had no choice but to at least look at it. With everything that was going on, I couldn't afford to miss a phone call.

So I stepped out of the bath, ignored the soapy water dripping on the floor, and padded over to my phone sitting on the bathroom counter. *Joe.* My heart immediately beat a little faster.

"Hey, Joe," I answered, hoping I sounded calm.

"Daphne. I may have something. You busy? We need to talk."

I glanced over at my hot bath and the glass of Merlot sitting on the edge and sighed. "I can make time. Why don't you come over? Just give me fifteen minutes."

"I'll be there in ten," he said before hanging up.

I allowed myself one moment of regret before heading back to drain the water. So much for relaxation.

The phone rang again before I even had a chance to get dressed. It was Emerson this time.

"Hey, babe," he said, his voice warm.

I closed my eyes and wished he was with me. Just hearing his voice made me miss him even more. "Hey sweetie."

"Want to come over for dinner tonight? I'm making beef stew, your favorite. I thought we could open a bottle of wine, have a nice dinner, and relax. Catch up after everything." His voice was low with that little bit of gravel that always made me go weak at the knees. Suddenly I missed him so much it made me ache.

"That sounds amazing," I said, my voice full of regret. "But I can't." I bit my lip, wondering how he would take this. "I sort of have plans tonight."

"Plans?" He chuckled. "Let me guess, Fiona wants you to come over to help her charge her crystals under the full moon or something?"

I could hear the warmth in his voice. No matter how much he teased Fiona, he adored her.

"I wish," I said, laughing. I didn't know what to say next though. I didn't want to tell him Joe was coming over, because he would want to come over and get the update too. But I knew Joe wouldn't like that. He might not even tell me everything if Emerson was here.

"Listen," I said, glancing at the clock on the wall. "I'm so sorry, but I've got to go. Can we take a rain check on dinner? Maybe tomorrow night?"

"Sure," he answered, his tone changing. "We can take a rain check. I have to work tomorrow though, so that's out." He paused, then spoke again. "I really miss you, Daphne."

"I miss you too." It was true. I missed him so much I almost couldn't take it. "Listen, I have to go. I'll call you later," I said, before hanging up. I hated cutting it short, but I was down to five minutes before Joe arrived, and I couldn't exactly open the door naked.

JOE ARRIVED PROMPTLY, as promised. I had just slipped into jeans and a sweater and poured out my wine, putting on a strong pot of coffee instead. If he had something, I needed to be sharp. We sat down at my kitchen table, with one of his manila folders between us.

"What did you find?" I asked, too tired for small talk.

"Maybe nothing. Maybe something," he said, always annoyingly calm, as he flipped over the top of the envelope, revealing Russell's photograph underneath.

"Russell Sharp," I said, exhaling loudly.

"You remember his name," he said, looking mildly impressed.

"Of course I do." How could I forget the name of the man who had made me feel like that when I touched his photograph?

"Did I tell you what he did that got him sent to prison?" Joe asked.

I shook my head no.

"Game of Russian roulette," Joe said, pulling another photograph out of the envelope. This one was of a crime scene, a victim with a gunshot wound to the head.

I recoiled in disgust.

"At least that's what he claimed after he was arrested," Joe said. "And his friends backed him up. It was his gun and his idea to play. He bullied and goaded them into it, 'cause that's the kind of person he was. His buddy here," he said, tapping the photograph of the victim, "lost. Obviously. Russell was smart. Knew it looked exactly like a suicide, which, technically, it was. And that's what we called it, until Eileen told us the truth of what happened. He would have gotten off free and clear if not for her. Thanks to her knowledge, we nailed him. All I was hoping for was a negligent homicide conviction, but he went away for manslaughter. It was a huge win."

I stared at his picture again. "So he went away for a death that was initially ruled a suicide?"

Joe nodded.

I swallowed hard, suddenly feeling sick. This new information made me even more concerned. If he wanted revenge on Eileen for his arrest, how better than to pull off another murder that looked like suicide? From a killer's point of view, it was practically poetic—words Katie had used when talking about my own death.

"So that's old news," I said, swallowing hard again. "What did you find out?"

"Well, I told you I had heard him threaten Eileen myself," Joe said. "She was there when I arrested him, and, well, like I said, they had history. He wasn't a fan of her or her abilities. As I was putting the cuffs on him, he yelled out he would kill her someday. While he was in prison, he had somebody on the outside send her some threatening letters. Awful things. But of course, he was locked up and couldn't do anything. After a few months, he seemed to get bored and move on. I figured it was over."

"But?" I asked, knowing it wasn't over at all.

Joe nodded. "I talked to an old buddy of his this morning. A guy he looked up right when he got out. This was just a few weeks before Eileen died, remember? Anyway, according to this buddy, he was still spitting mad at her. Put all the blame on her for his prison stay. In his mind, they played a harmless game. It was just bad luck his buddy lost, certainly not his fault."

"Harmless," I said, almost shaking with anger. "Wow."

Joe nodded again. "Right. Obviously, the courts disagreed with him. His buddies testifying against him also went a long way."

"But he still blamed her..." I mused.

"And that's not all," Joe said. "Not only was he still mad at her, he was pissed as hell at his buddies for testifying against him."

"I'm not surprised," I said.

Joe pulled out two more photographs. The first was of a car, crumpled almost beyond recognition, at the bottom of a cliff. The other was of a man slumped over in his recliner with a gunshot wound to the head.

"Who are they?" I asked, even though I felt certain I knew.

"The two buddies," Joe said. "Both dead within six months of Russell's release. Both ruled suicide."

I put my elbows on the table and held my face in my hands, suddenly feeling even more exhausted than before. "So you're thinking he killed them?" I asked, despite again knowing the answer.

"I didn't say that," Joe said carefully. "But it sure seems like a big coincidence, doesn't it?"

I nodded, wrapping my arms around my body as if I could somehow comfort myself. It was all so heartbreaking, thinking that Eileen and these other men might have died at the hands of Russell, all payback over having been caught. It made me sick.

"Why did nobody put this together before?" I asked, distraught. "Three deaths of three people he hated, all within six months of getting out of prison? Seems like someone should have noticed this a lot sooner."

Joe sighed. "I wish I could tell you law enforcement worked like the movies, kid. But it doesn't. Look, this one here," he said, pointing to the guy in the recliner, "moved out of Tennessee. This happened in Georgia. Gunshot wound to the head. The gun is in his hand. There's a suicide note on the table. It's clear cut, right? This guy is a nobody as far as law enforcement is concerned. They don't have time to go digging up everything from his entire life just to make sure he did, in fact, off himself when all the evidence points to that."

I nodded, biting my lip. It all seemed so unfair, but I knew he was right.

"This one," he said, pointing at the car. "He had been an anxious mess ever since his buddy died. Talked about suicide more than once to his friends. Felt overwhelming guilt about how the whole thing had played out, seemed to have some sort of PTSD from the whole thing. His blood alcohol level was through the roof, he was the only one in the car, and he had told his mom not an hour beforehand that he wanted to die for what he had done. Again, clear cut. No reason to go looking into involvement from anyone else."

I stared at the pictures again. Three deaths was a big coincidence, but Joe was right. These really looked like suicide. I didn't know what to think. "Do you really think Russell may have been able to pull off three murders, all staged to look like suicide?"

Joe sighed and leaned back, his hands behind his head. "You had to know Russell. He's conniving. Cutthroat. Way smarter than he looks." Joe shrugged and put his hands back down. "I'd say it's possible. And with us now having a witness that even after his prison stint he was still obsessing about Eileen, well..."

"Yeah," I said, still focused on the pictures in front of me. "Plus, with the letters she was getting..."

"What letters?" he asked.

I looked up and immediately realized my mistake. "Didn't you say he had sent her letters?" I asked, trying to cover for myself.

"Yeah. I told you he sent her letters while he was in prison. But that had been over and done for a long time," Joe said, his sharp eyes peering into me. "Had the letters started up again?"

I bit my lip, not wanting to tell him about the journal. But if Russell really was behind this, I might have to produce the journal as evidence.

"Yeah, I think they had," I said slowly, still arguing with myself about how much to tell him.

"Is that the sight telling you that, or do you have some of them?" he asked, his tone mild.

I didn't answer.

"Could be important evidence," he said.

"Neither," I said, finally deciding to be honest even though I wasn't at all sure it was the right move. "I have an old journal of Eileen's from shortly before she died," I explained. "In it, she mentioned getting some threatening letters."

"Interesting," he said, rubbing his beard in thought. "Might have been nice for you to mention that to me when you found it. Any chance I could read that journal?"

"It's in Little Rock," I lied, still unable to bring myself to share the journal with him. "At my Dad's old house. I read it when I was going through his things. Unfortunately, I don't remember it having much information in it that would be relevant to this. That's probably why I forgot about it until now." I offered him a faint smile. "Unless you're interested in cute stories of me as a toddler, playing with my new kitten and getting into all sorts of trouble."

He grinned lazily, leaning back in his chair again. "I had forgotten about that cat. Cute little thing. You carried it everywhere, and crazily enough, it didn't seem to mind. Did Lonnie let you take it to Little Rock when you moved there?"

"I don't remember," I said. "I don't have any memories of it." It made me sad, even now, to have zero memories of my mother and our life together before her death.

He nodded. "I know that's hard for you. Well, listen, if you have any plans to go back to Little Rock soon, you might pick up that journal and let me have a read. You never know, it could have something in it you might not have picked up on."

"Great idea," I said, pretending to agree. "I don't know when I'm heading back next, but I'll keep that in mind. In the meantime, what are we going to do about Russell?"

"I've got some ideas," he said. "I've got a few more people on my list to talk to before I go talk to him myself."

"Keep me in the loop?" I asked.

"Of course, partner." He grinned again. "You do remind me of your mama, you know?"

I smiled but didn't mean it.

Because all I could think about was the look on his face when I'd told him I had her journal.

CHAPTER TWENTY-SEVEN

Went to the grocery store today. Ran into Patricia. She looked at me with pure hatred. Maybe it's my imagination, but I feel like everyone is looking at me weird, watching me. Am I just being paranoid? Am I losing my mind?

Emerson

I PUT my phone down and stared at it for a minute. Daphne was being cagey and weird, and I didn't like it at all. I knew it probably had to do with the case. What I didn't know was why she wasn't letting me in on it. Once again, her actions were letting me know exactly where I stood, and it wasn't where I wanted to be.

I picked up my phone again and called Greg.

"Hey man," I said. "You free tonight?"

"I'm free," he answered. "What do you have in mind?"

"Wanna shoot some pool at the pub?"

"Sure. What time?"

I glanced at the beef stew I had made just for Daphne. It was good stew, but I didn't feel like eating it anymore.

"Thirty minutes?" I suggested.

"Alright," he agreed before hanging up.

I pulled the pot off the stove and set it aside to cool. Then I grabbed my jacket and walked out the door, leaving the stew behind.

I made it to the pub first and was already munching on fish and chips when Greg arrived. He slid into the booth across from me and frowned.

"You couldn't wait on me?"

I grinned at him. "Not my fault you're late. I'm starving."

"Sorry about that. Crazy day at work."

"Oh yeah? Are the lovely citizens of Rosemary Mountain giving you trouble, Greg? Some dog peeing on someone else's bush?" I grinned again, my mood having improved already—and only partly because I was on my second ale of the night.

He rolled his eyes at me. "Not exactly. Had a tip come in on the case Jackson is working, but he wasn't there to handle it and it wasn't the kind of thing I could delegate. So I had to cover for him." He groaned. "He owes me big time."

"Where is Jackson?" I asked, curious.

Greg shrugged. "Beats me. Said he needed a couple of days off. Real mysterious about the whole thing. Whatever it is, he's serious about being out of pocket. I tried calling him five times today and he didn't answer." Greg grinned suddenly. "Want to know what I think?"

"What?"

He leaned forward, faking a whisper. "I think young Jackson's found himself a lady friend."

"Oh, yeah?" I grinned.

Greg nodded. "Yep. I'm guessing for whatever reason he isn't ready to tell me about her. But I think he snuck away to spend some extra time with her."

"Well, good for Jackson," I said, taking another swallow of ale. Truth be told, I was a little bothered by Greg's confession. I had always suspected Jackson had a thing for Daphne. He was always overly interested in her, to put it mildly. His sudden disappearance, combined with the way Daphne had blown me off without explanation, had me suddenly feeling more than a little uncomfortable.

"Let's play pool," I said, shoving the food away and downing the rest of my ale in a single swallow.

"You okay, man?" Greg asked, cocking his head.

"Yeah." I shook it off. "I'm fine. Let's just play." I needed a distraction, something to get me out of my own head.

Daphne was independent alright, but she loved me, and she was a good person. She wouldn't cheat on me with Jackson. The two things were completely unrelated, and I wasn't the kind of guy who was going to jump to conclusions on a weird coincidence.

Still, it took more effort than it should have to push the matter out of my mind.

Three games of pool—and three wins for me—later, I was feeling like myself again. Greg was the best kind of buddy you could ask for. We returned to the table to order refills, and I made a rash decision. I decided to tell him about wanting to propose to Daphne and how she kept pushing me away. He had been married before. I knew he had adored his wife. He would probably have some wise advice, and I could use it.

But right after I told him I had something I needed to get off my chest, he got a text message and his whole face changed.

"What is it?" I asked, concerned. I had never seen Greg look so disturbed.

"Something came up," he said, still staring at his phone. He finally looked up and shook his head, staring at me for a long time, like there was something I should know but that he couldn't tell me. "I'm sorry, man. I've gotta go. Emergency."

He pushed away from the table and left, leaving me alone to wonder what the hell kind of emergency had happened in Rosemary Mountain this time.

I called Daphne's cell, needing to hear she was safe.

She didn't answer. Just texted me back that she was tied up with something and would call me back later.

But she never did.

Chapter Twenty-Eight

Eileen's Journal

I had another vision of the girl, and I don't understand it. She's in terrible trouble. I went to town to see if I could find her again, but I couldn't. I asked around a bit, to see if anyone knew her, but nobody seemed to.

I'm questioning everything. Things are so tense between me and Lonnie. I'm keeping secrets from him, and I feel like everything in my life is falling apart. I hate it all. Maybe he's right and I need to just forget about these visions and focus on our own life.

Daphne

As soon as Joe left, I put the teakettle on. I wanted to drink another cup of mugwort tea and see if I could get anything. Something really bothered me about the way Joe had looked when the journal came up. He had tried to be casual, and to anyone else, he probably would have appeared that way. But I could feel his energy change. He didn't just want to look at the journal to see if it had any clues for the case. He wanted to know what it said about him.

When I'd originally read about the letters in the journal, I hadn't thought much about them, honestly. I had been focused on Eileen's visions of the girl and how they might relate to Don and the church. But now, I was wondering if I had been looking in the wrong place the whole time.

I made sure the curtains were closed over my windows before pulling the journal out from its hiding spot and curling up on the couch with it and my mug of tea. I sipped the tea slowly, focused on my intention, and flipped through the pages of the journal again.

I felt something that surprised me—a feeling of holding back. I got the sense that when Eileen had been writing about Joe, she wasn't writing everything. That feeling grew stronger the longer I sat with it, making me wonder what was behind it.

Then, I saw.

As I turned to the page where Eileen had written about the threatening letters, I saw her going to Joe about them, showing them to him. He read them over, wearing that poker face I knew too well. He told her not to worry, that he would have a talk with Russell. But as Eileen took the letters back and left, she didn't feel reassured—in fact, her worry had grown. I could feel it, strong and thick, coursing through my body just as it had hers.

I could hear the thoughts she didn't write, the thoughts that made her feel guilty just for thinking them.

The thought that she might have just given Joe the perfect way to get rid of her.

I opened my eyes and closed the journal, my heart pounding. If my vision was true, it meant Joe had known of the threat from Russell long before he and I had started investigating. That raised two big questions. First, why hadn't he investigated her death the first time around? If he had known there was a threat, he should have taken her death more seriously.

Second, why had he told me a story about Russell that conveniently left out the fact that he had known about the threat all along? It made me wonder if he was making Russell a scapegoat now. But that didn't totally make sense, either, because if he needed a scapegoat, he could have used Russell to begin with.

None of it made sense, but all of it together solidified one thing. I would no longer trust Joe. With anything.

CHAPTER TWENTY-NINE

She's dead. Becky, the girl from my visions, is dead. I knew it before the news broke; I saw it in a vision—a horrible vision. I was supposed to stop it, and I failed. But now she's dead. She was only nineteen. I'm glad she wasn't a child, at least... Not really, anyway. But I still failed her.

And I'm terrified about what this means for me.

Daphne

As soon as the sun rose the next morning, I walked over to Fiona's house to tell her about the vision I'd had of Joe. I felt guilty for getting her involved yet again, but I also recognized that at least part of that guilt had been put there by Joe himself. It was a brilliant plan by him, really, to isolate me from everyone but him.

Fiona let me in, her face pale, reflecting the same weariness as my own. She poured us both hot cups of coffee, and I told her everything, from beginning to end, leaving nothing out—including how Joe had encouraged me to play like I was dropping the investigation, and how initially I had thought it was to protect her.

She listened quietly, her lips in a thin line. When I finished my story, she just shook her head in sorrow.

"It doesn't look good for Joe, now, does it?"

"No," I agreed. "I don't know what game he's playing, Fiona. He's hiding things, maybe even deliberately throwing me off track. But why? If it was to cover up his own involvement, then why not just pin the murder on Russell twenty years ago? Why now? Or do you think there's a chance he really believes Russell killed her and he's just trying to hide his own lack of investigation?"

"I don't know, honey. I just don't know."

As I thought it over, a new idea began to form. "Maybe he assumed Don killed her and failed to investigate because he didn't want to risk the bribe coming out. But now, Don's dead and Katie said it was someone else, so he's finally looking into it? But is still trying to cover up his own failures? I don't know." I raised my hands helplessly. "I feel so lost in all of this."

Fiona nodded. "I know what you mean." She stared into her cup for a long time, a look of sadness on her face. "I hate to think it of him, but I guess I've always known something wasn't quite right. Back in the day, he wanted to be my beau, you might say. The feelings went both ways. But something always held me back."

"I know Eileen warned you off of him," I said quietly. When Fiona looked up, startled, I explained. "She mentioned it in her journal. That he had asked you out, and she advised you not to go."

"Yes," she said, nodding. "She passed before she could tell me why. I trusted her enough to listen, and it's always stayed with me. Until you came here and all this happened, I sure never thought he was connected in any way to her death, though. I promise you that."

"I know," I said. "I haven't known him nearly as long as you have, and I don't want to believe it, either."

She just shook her head, and we fell into silence. But the silence was soon broken by someone pounding on her front door. We both jumped and looked at each other, still uneasy from the conversation we just had.

Wordlessly, Fiona got up and pulled the shotgun from above her mantle, pointing it toward the doorway.

"Who's there and what do you want?" she called out.

"It's Joe, Fiona. Put down your damn gun." Joe's voice was muffled from behind the door, but it was clearly him.

Fiona held on to the gun anyway and motioned for me to let him in.

I went to the door and opened it. He glared at me, fury all over his face.

"I thought you'd be here." He marched inside and slammed the door behind him. "Fiona, didn't I tell you to put down your damn gun? It's just me."

"What do you want?" she asked, cutting straight to the point, the gun still pointed right at him.

He looked at her first with shock, then something else—guilt? I wasn't sure. But some kind of emotion was going through him, and it wasn't pretty.

"I came to talk to her," he said, pointing at me, his voice gruff.

"Talk then," Fiona said calmly. She pointed her gun down to the floor but kept it in her hands.

He gave her one more look, with that same expression on his face, like he couldn't believe what was happening. Then he turned to me, the fury back in his eyes.

"What did you do?" he demanded.

"Excuse me?" I crossed my arms, feeling brave with Fiona backing me up. I would not take anything from him. Not today.

He repeated the words slowly, enunciating each one. "What. Did. You. Do?"

"What are you talking about?"

He looked at me, still furious, and shook his head. "Katie's dead."

Shock rippled through me. Of all the things he could have said, I hadn't been expecting that one. I could feel my face go pale as my bravado left.

"What do you mean she's dead?" I shook my head, unwilling to believe it. "I just talked to her." My mind was racing and my hands started to tremble. *Please, oh please, let him be wrong.*

He gave me a pointed look. "Do I have to spell it out for you? You talked to her. She's dead now. Slit her wrists in her cell."

I looked into his eyes, hoping beyond hope that this was some kind of sick joke, that he was trying to shock me into stopping my investigation. But I could see the truth of his words on his face. Katie was dead.

"Someone got to her." I paced the room, feeling sick.

Katie was a terrible person, a cold-blooded killer, yet I still felt sorry for her. In some ways, we were alike—we had both been dealt an unfair hand, losing our mothers so young. At least I had grown up with a father. Katie had grown up completely alone. Guilt washed over me like a flood. I had never even considered that going to her would put her in danger. Not really. Even when she'd acted scared during our conversation, I'd thought she was just being dramatic, that she would be perfectly safe locked up in jail.

But now look. She was dead. Another person had died because of me and my impulsive decisions.

"Someone had to have gotten to her," I repeated, still pacing. "Someone was watching."

"Maybe. Or maybe she did it herself, out of fear of something worse. Who knows anymore?" Joe ran his hand wearily over his face, showing his age for once. "The point is, I told you I was handling things. Why the hell did you decide to take things into your own hands? I told you it was too dangerous for you to talk to her!"

I started to defend myself, then stopped. "Wait. How do you know I talked to her?"

"Excuse me?" Now it was his turn to act offended.

I mimicked him, repeating each word slowly. "How. Did. You. Know. I talked to her?"

"Because I know everything that goes on there," he yelled. "I was sheriff for decades. You think I don't still have friends there? I had a guy watching out for Katie. He called me as soon as it happened last night. When I questioned him about it, I found out she had a certain visitor show up asking questions! What were you thinking?"

It was my turn to yell. "I was thinking that maybe, just maybe, you're a dirty cop who doesn't have the slightest bit of interest in finding out who killed my mother because just maybe you were the one to cover it up to begin with! That's *if* you weren't the one to kill her yourself!"

His face changed instantly to shock and grief. "How could you think that?" His voice was quieter this time. Hurt. "I cared about your ma. I've felt nothing but guilt since her death. You know that."

I lowered my voice to match his. "What I know is that I asked you months ago to get an interview with Katie and you never did. What I know is that you stopped answering any of my questions and blew me off any time I tried to bring up the case. What I know is that you lied to me about not having any idea that Russell was writing threatening letters to her again. What I know is that Eileen didn't trust you, and I'm thinking it was a big mistake that I did."

He just shook his head. "Believe what you want to believe, kid. Nothing I say is going to make a difference anyway. But believe it not, everything I've been doing is to protect you." He shook his head again and started to leave, then stopped and turned to me, pointing a finger. "You need to stay out of this. You don't belong here. You don't know what you're dealing with. Take Katie's death as the warning it should be and stay the hell away before you get yourself—or someone else—hurt." He cast a look toward Fiona, pain clouding his face.

I took a deep breath and made my voice as firm as I could. "I'll never stop until the day I take down every single person who had a hand in my mother's death."

He just shook his head again and walked out, slamming the door behind his back.

Chapter Thirty

Eileen's Journal

Am I going crazy? Am I literally losing my mind? Doc Rogers confirmed Becky's death was an accident, a result of a car accident. Surely he wouldn't be involved in a coverup ... would he?

Are these visions even real?

I've never questioned them before. They've always led to truth. But surely this whole town can't be corrupt ... can it?

Daphne

Katie's dead. I kept repeating the words, trying to make sense of them. Or maybe hoping that, if I said them repeatedly, it would somehow turn out not to be true. That someone would come shake me, tell me to stop being so ridiculous. Of course Katie wasn't dead. This was Rosemary Mountain, not some big scary city with a prison full of felons who shanked each other out of boredom.

But nobody came. Fiona just sat across from me with a mournful look on her face while I kept repeating it. Like she knew I needed to say it until it sank in.

Finally, I stopped and looked at her. Really looked at her.

"This is all my fault," I said. I wasn't looking for reassurance to the contrary, which again, she seemed to know, because I could see her fighting the urge to contradict me.

"I have to go," I said next. Where? I didn't even know. All I knew was I had to get out of this house, away from Fiona. Far, far away from her, where the danger that had followed me since I had come to this town couldn't touch her. Not her. It could never touch her.

"Daphne," she started, but I stopped her with a raised hand.

"Promise me," I said, staring at her. "Promise me you will stay far away from this. Fiona, I can't lose you too."

She repeated her promise from earlier, and this time, I believed her, because she saw the fear and grief on my face. She knew this wasn't a game anymore.

Katie Rogers had died in the county jail because she'd talked to me.

I was a curse, a leper, and I needed to get as far away as possible from everyone I loved.

I left Fiona's and went back to my cottage, double checking the locks behind me. If nothing else, Katie's death proved that the man I was looking for was still very much alive. I had suspected as much, but this was certain confirmation. It meant that Don Kistler wasn't behind Eileen's death. Part of me had hoped it had been Don all along, that I would find out her killer was already dead and dealt with. But deep down, I had known that wasn't the case. I had felt the coming danger.

Don certainly hadn't come back from the dead to take out Katie after she talked to me. Once again, I was back to the faceless Mr. Boddy, the one either blackmailing Don or running the show.

Or Joe.

But while I had zero trust left for him, I still didn't believe he was Mr. Boddy. And he had seemed genuinely surprised and upset by Katie's death. I knew he could put on a show and deceive me, but his reaction had seemed real.

I would have to deal with Joe later. For now, all my efforts had to go into finding out once and for all who this Mr. Boddy was.

All of a sudden, it hit me that I had another connection. Someone who just might be interested in helping me. It was a long shot, but it was all I had.

I was preparing myself to go talk to Luke about Mr. Boddy when, once again, my plans were interrupted by a knock on the door. I slipped to the window to get a peek outside before answering, half afraid it was Mr. Boddy himself, finally here to finish me off.

I sighed in relief when I saw it was Jackson. He, at least, I could trust. He was too young to have been involved in Eileen's death, and he had arranged the interview with Katie. Had he wanted to stop me from talking to her, he could have just said no.

So I opened the door for him, feeling grateful to see someone who might be a legitimate help in this investigation until I saw the distress on his face.

"I heard about Katie," I said, pulling him into the house.

He went straight to the sofa and collapsed there, putting his head into his hands. My guilt immediately returned. Not only had I gotten her killed, but Jackson would carry guilt for it as well—and maybe even some kind of punishment since he had recommended going against policy to make the interview happen. Another life I had managed to screw up by being here.

"I'm sorry," I said, knowing it wasn't enough. "I had no idea I was putting her in any real danger. I wouldn't have asked you for the interview if I had known."

He said nothing, just kept sitting there with his head in his hands. My heart broke for him. I went and sat beside him, putting a hand lightly on his shoulder.

When I did, the room went blurry and dark and I found myself in another time and place, a dark room that smelled of cigarettes and beer. A man's voice cackled and asked me wasn't I proud, proud to be his son and to have come from all this?

I yanked my hand away from his shoulder and sat back, shocked.

Jackson lifted his head and looked at me with red eyes. "You just had a vision, didn't you?" he asked quietly.

"H-how do you know about that?" I stammered, shocked.

He dropped his head into his hands again. "We need to talk," he said, his tone muffled.

We might have needed to talk, but Jackson was in no shape to. It was clear he was falling apart. Without even thinking, I got up and went to the kitchen to put on the teakettle. Maybe Fiona was rubbing off on me after all.

I came back with cups of chamomile—a favorite of Fiona's in times like these—and handed him one. He took it but didn't drink from it. It at least got his head out of his hands though.

I sipped my tea and waited patiently, another trick I had learned from Fiona. I was dying to ask him how he knew about my visions and if he could explain what I had just seen. But I waited, biding my time, while he recovered.

"I, uh, haven't been completely honest with you," he said finally.

"Oh, yeah?" I asked, keeping my tone mild, giving him space to talk.

He let out a groan and finally took a sip of his tea. "I know about your sight," he said finally. "I've known about it for a long time." He looked up at me and must have seen something on my face, because he quickly added, "Don't worry. I haven't told anyone. Greg doesn't know. Although, he probably will soon."

My stomach clenched. "How did you find out? And why will Greg know soon?"

"Greg's investigating your mother's death," he said. "Look, I'm not supposed to tell you that. He doesn't want you getting involved."

I rolled my eyes. "It's not exactly like I *want* to be involved, now is it? But let's be honest, nobody cared about her or how she died until I came here and started stirring things up. So I have to be involved, to make sure this gets done."

He nodded, giving me the point. "I don't blame you for that," he said. He stared at his cup for a long minute before taking another slow sip. "I know what it's like to want answers about your past."

I nodded slowly, trying to stay patient even though he wasn't answering my questions directly. He wanted to talk, that much was obvious. I was just going to have to let him get everything out in his own way, on his own timetable.

But when he didn't speak again for a full two minutes, my patience gave out. "You still haven't answered," I said. "How do you know I have the sight?"

He ran a weary hand over his face. "Because ... because I've known about your mother longer than you have, Daphne."

Nothing could have shocked me more. I had a million questions, but before I could even ask them, pieces of the puzzle started falling into place. "Wait, you know I have the second sight. Is that why you didn't mind when I helped with the Adams murder investigation?"

He nodded, slowly.

"And is that why you let me look at the journal in the break room? You knew I might have a vision?"

He nodded again, confirming.

"I still don't understand," I said, pulling myself back to the current issue. "How did you know about Eileen? *What* do you know about Eileen?"

He looked down at the floor. "I know more about your mother than you probably realize."

My stomach started clenching again as I feared where he was going with it. The weight of it all felt so heavy. I just wanted to run away and pretend none of this was happening, none of this was real. But it was real. And here we were, discussing it calmly over cups of chamomile tea.

"There's no easy way to say this," he started.

"I think I know," I interrupted, wanting to put him out of his obvious misery. "Your father is Russell Sharp, isn't he?"

His hand clenched on his mug, and he nodded confirmation. "I'm sorry," he said.

"Why should you be sorry? You didn't hurt her. Did you?"

He kept staring at the floor. "No, but half of me came from him. And now you might hate me for that."

"Jackson," I said gently. "I don't hate you for anything he did, even if..." I couldn't finish the sentence. "And you shouldn't hate yourself for coming from him. Look at you. You aren't him. You aren't anything like him at all." I knew he needed to hear that.

"How do you know?" he asked, his voice thick with pain..

"Because the vision I just had? It was him. And he couldn't possibly be further from who you are as a person."

He looked at me with eyes that seemed empty and haunted. But he seemed grateful to hear my words, even if it was clear he didn't totally believe them. Not yet. But I understood that. Old wounds were hard to heal.

"Now why don't you tell me what you know?" I suggested gently, fearing if I pushed too hard he would break down altogether. It was a strange role reversal, being the one to question the law enforcement officer.

"Well," he said. "I was a kid back then, too young to remember anything about Russell going to prison. But I remember when he got out," he said. His face turned to stone. "He was angry. Cruel." He stopped talking and stared across the room blankly, as if visions of his own were playing out in front of his eyes.

I could feel the huge amount of hurt he carried, even now.

"Anyway," he continued. "He talked about your mother a lot. One of his favorite conversations when he was drunk and angry." Jackson grimaced, obviously struggling with this conversation. "He knew about her being a psychic, or having the sight, or whatever you prefer to call it. Her visions."

He glanced at me, as if unsure how much I could take. "He said some awful things. Blamed her for him being sent away. As a kid, I was kind of in awe of her," he admitted. "I wanted nothing more than to meet the woman who had given me a long break from the hell I lived in when Russell was around. Anyway. One night, he came home late, drunk and happy this time. Didn't hit me or my mom that night. Said Eileen Sullivan had finally gotten what she deserved." A shadow crossed his face. "I knew then that he had killed her."

My heart nearly stopped. "Are you sure?" I asked.

He nodded then shrugged. "The detective in me says no, I'm not sure. There wasn't any proof. Just a gut feeling, a fear in a kid's heart who knew just how cruel that man could be. But yeah, I'm sure. But"—he looked up at me, pained—"I was too scared to do anything, too scared to tell anyone. Even when I ended up in foster care shortly after, I never told a soul. But I also never forgot. I never forgot her name."

His eyes were haunted. "I made it my mission in life to protect and serve. To, I don't know, make up for never saying anything. Make up for fearing him. Like I could somehow even it all out. But then you showed up here, looking for her killer ... and you didn't know you were staring at his son the whole time."

I let out a breath, unsure of what to say.

"I don't know how you can ever forgive me for staying quiet," he said, running his hands through his blonde hair.

"Jackson," I said, "it's not your fault. Number one, you were a kid. Nothing your dad said or did is your fault, okay? You shouldn't own that." My heart broke for him. "And I can't blame you for staying quiet, at least back then. Like you said, you were terrified of him, for good reason."

He nodded glumly. "Greg doesn't even know who I am," he said.

"What do you mean?"

He let out a breath. "A family from Nashville adopted me. New last name, new birth certificate, new social security number. New life. Adoption records are sealed. I've never told anyone here that Russell Sharp is my father. Can you imagine what they'll think? There's not a single person in law enforcement here that doesn't know and despise that man. If they knew I was his son..." He shook his head, misery on his face.

"They know you. You are not your father," I said gently. "Greg's a good guy. He'll understand."

"Easy for you to say," he replied, his tone still glum. "Telling you the truth was the easy part, but, Daphne, I don't know if I'm brave enough to blow up my whole life."

CHAPTER THIRTY-ONE

Eileen's Journal

I had two more visions yesterday. They were of people who died here in Rosemary Mountain last year. I went to the library and did some research. Both deaths were declared to be from natural causes, but I think that's a coverup too. One of them was a young man, and in my vision, he looked like he had been beaten to a pulp. Another was a young girl, like Becky, with a needle in her arm. The question is: why? Why would Doc—and Joe, for that matter—be covering up suspicious deaths?

Emerson

MY SHIFT at work started with chaos. The team needed me to go on a flight almost immediately after walking in the door to transfer a patient to the trauma center in Nashville. It was hours before I had time to breathe, which meant it was late afternoon before I heard the news about Katie's death. The other flight nurses were chatting about it casually, with no idea of how personal it was to me.

My stomach immediately dropped. I grabbed my phone and texted Daphne, who still hadn't called me back since last night.

Nothing.

I called her again.

No answer.

The familiar panic rose again, the fear of being helpless while someone I loved was hurt. *Helpless.* It was the feeling I hated most.

I went to my supervisor. "Do you guys have things covered?" I asked.

He looked up at me with surprise. "Well, yeah, we're good right now. Why? And why do you look like you just saw a ghost?"

"It may be nothing, but I really need to check on someone."

He gave me an odd look. "You've never left in the middle of a shift before. You know that's not how it works here. Even if there's nothing to do, you stay because you don't know what call might come next."

"Please," I said, trying to keep my voice calm. "I'll be less than ten minutes away. You can call me if you need me, and if it turns out everything is okay, I'll come right back. But something happened. I just need to make sure Daphne's okay, and I can't get her on the phone."

He held my gaze for a minute, then nodded. "Alright. I get that. Go check on her, then come back. If something happened, call me. We'll cover for you. Whatever you need."

"Thanks." The panic eased just a little as I headed out to my truck to make sure the love of my life was safe.

I recognized Jackson's truck as soon as I turned the corner toward her driveway at the end of the lane. The panic rose again. *They got to her, too. She's hurt. Something happened.* My heart felt so much fear and pain at the same moment I didn't know if I could take it.

I jumped out of my truck and ran toward her doorway, terrified of what might have happened to Daphne. I never should have gone to work. Never should have left her alone while she was investigating this. Hadn't we all felt the danger? I should have been there, should have protected her.

I ran straight into her living room without knocking, then stopped suddenly, realizing my mistake.

"Emerson! What are you doing here?"

Daphne was shocked to see me, that much was for sure.

But I was shocked too, as the ramifications of what I was seeing washed over me. Daphne hadn't ignored my call and texts because she was hurt. She'd ignored them because she was with *him*. Jackson wasn't here officially. In fact, based on how closely they sat together on the couch, with Daphne's hand on his arm—until she saw the look on my face and yanked it off—I would say he was here on very personal business indeed.

I had felt like a sorry ass for even briefly imagining that Daphne might be Jackson's mystery woman, yet here was evidence right in front of me. I was a total fool.

"What am *I* doing here?" I said, reeling in hurt and disbelief. "Well, I left work early because I heard about Katie and I hadn't been able to get in touch with you. At the very least, I figured you would be a wreck once you heard about her, but beyond that, I was terrified they got to you too. I was afraid you were hurt, or might be. I didn't want you to be alone. But I see you aren't. Alone, that is."

I looked at Jackson and just shook my head, still in shock.

"I should go," Jackson said uneasily, as he stood to his feet.

"You don't have to," Daphne interjected, piercing me through the heart again. She turned to me and opened her mouth, then closed it and looked at Jackson helplessly, like she was waiting for him to give me the bad news. But he didn't say a word.

I looked at them both as we all three stood in awkward silence.

"Maybe I'm the one who should go," I said, my voice strangely stiff. My heart felt like it was shattered into a thousand pieces. "Sorry I barged in without an invitation." I turned on my heels and walked out.

Daphne followed me. "Emerson! Wait!" she called, as I climbed into my truck. She ran over to me. "Don't be mad. Stay. Let's have dinner."

Dinner? Seriously? "It looks like you already have a dinner guest," I answered, my tone still so stiff and awkward I barely recognized my own voice.

"Jackson was just about to leave. Come back in."

"What's he doing here, Daphne?" I waited a beat, but she didn't answer.

My chest ached, but I was determined to stay stoic. "Just tell me why," I said, wishing she would at least give me an explanation.

"I can't," she said, looking down.

I just shook my head. "I've got to go. My shift isn't over." I pulled the truck door closed and backed out of the driveway, leaving her standing there alone.

Although, all she had to do was walk back inside to Jackson.

When it came down to it, I was the only one who was actually alone.

I drove back to work, furious at myself. Hadn't I seen from the start that there was some sort of connection between the two of them? Daphne had always said there was nothing there. I had believed her, despite seeing the interest Jackson always took in her. He had always been overly friendly, overly *eager* to work with her. Unlike Greg, he didn't seem to think twice about involving a civilian in his investigations. There had been red flags there from the beginning.

Daphne had been shocked when I walked in. Granted, I did usually knock. But I had been so worried about her I wasn't thinking straight. And I had walked right into a situation she obviously didn't want me to see.

Had he been there last night, when Greg had thought he was with a lady friend, and when Daphne hadn't answered her phone? Almost certainly. Was it like this every time I was at work? Daphne and Jackson together, knowing I was safely tucked away at the base for twenty-four hours, where I wouldn't see a thing?

My heart couldn't believe it. Couldn't believe Daphne would betray me that way. But I had seen them together with my own two eyes, and she had refused to give me any sort of explanation. Refused to even try to explain the whole thing away.

Maybe she didn't think she had to. Truth be told, we had never exactly had the "exclusive" talk. The idea had never even crossed my mind. To me, once we'd said, "I love you," that was it. We were together. It would never have occurred to me to clarify that I wanted to be the only one.

But Daphne was a hell of a lot younger than I was, and maybe dating was completely different now. Maybe I had been wrong to assume I was the only one in her life. Maybe the reason I could never seem to get her to move forward was because Jackson had been pulling her the other way the whole time.

My heart felt shattered.

I pulled back up to the base and my eyes immediately went to the glove compartment, where her ring was hidden. This time, I didn't even bother pulling it out.

I wasn't sure I ever wanted to see it again. I might just sell the damn truck with the ring still in it.

CHAPTER THIRTY-TWO

I dreamed of her last night, but I don't think it was a dream. I think it was really her. She was begging me to tell the truth about what happened to her.

The truth? What is the truth? I don't even know. The news report said she died in a car accident, that she slid off the road in the rain. But that's not what I saw. In my vision, she died in a motel room, with a needle in her arm. Did they kill her? Why? Would Don really kill someone just to hide his affair? Would Patricia kill her in misguided revenge? I don't understand.

She was so young.

Daphne

EVERYBODY ALWAYS LEAVES ME.

It was a fact I had learned to accept, and there was nothing anyone could say to change it. I was fated to be left behind.

I stood there in the driveway, almost in shock, watching Emerson's truck drive away. I was kicking myself for not explaining why Jackson was there. But I had stopped because it wasn't my secret to tell. It was Jackson's story, and it obviously still humiliated him even though none of it was his fault. I didn't feel right blurting it out to Emerson. But Emerson had obviously jumped to some very wrong conclusions, and I ... I had just let him.

Fate.

I didn't have Fiona's innate understanding of the mysteries of life, but I felt sure that if she really thought about it, she would have to agree with me now. Everybody left me eventually. Maybe it was something caused by my mother's death. Maybe that moment changed my entire future, essentially cursing me to be left behind over and over and over again.

I had no real memories of Eileen. No real memory of losing her, or Rosemary Mountain, or Fiona, or any of it. Yet, as Fiona had once said, it had left an imprint of loss on my heart.

While I couldn't remember that loss, I could remember the one that made me realize the truth, that the ground would always be shaky beneath my feet.

When I was growing up, Mom and Dad had never exactly gotten along. There was always an unspoken tension, something so real it felt like an extra person sitting at the dinner table with us each night. Quiet dinners, where Dad would ask me about my day and everyone would pretend it was normal for a mom and dad to go the entire meal without once looking at each other, much less speaking.

They never fought in front of me. Mom wouldn't allow that. Frankly, I found myself wishing they would. I wished they would just scream at each other, get everything out, have one loud argument that would clear the air and make them finally understand each other, so they could get back to loving each other and we could be a real family.

That's how it was at my friend Celia's house. Her parents argued all the time, about everything it seemed. But there was never any tension at the dinner table there. Her parents winked at each other and stole kisses in front of the sink when they thought the kids had run off to play. Sure, they fought over stupid stuff, like buying the wrong brand of coffee at the store or forgetting to stick something in the mail. But despite all their little arguments and huffs, they loved each other. It was real, so real that even us kids could see it.

Mom never wanted to fight in front of me because she thought it was inappropriate or might harm me in some way, but I couldn't help but think that keeping everything inside was what had made them so different from Celia's parents. If they would have just broken the tension, the unbearable silence, and *fought,* then maybe all that tension would have gone away.

But Mom went away instead.

I was twelve when she left. I remember walking home from school that day, thinking with pity about the girl in my class who had announced that her parents were divorcing. *Divorce. At least that will never happen to me,* I thought. I felt sure of it, the way you feel sure about the sun rising every morning. Sure, Mom and Dad mostly ignored each other, but they were old-fashioned and stable. Not once had I ever heard them mention the word. Divorce didn't seem to be an option in our family. I was sick and tired of the unspoken tension, but I took comfort in this idea of stability. Resilience. Permanence. My parents might not steal kisses in the kitchen, but I had no doubt we would be a family unit forever.

It was with these thoughts in mind that I walked into our house, scheming about how I might get Mom and Dad to actually talk to each other that night. I stopped dead in my tracks when I walked into the living room and found them both there, waiting for me. Mom's giant rolling suitcase, the one I always made fun of, was sitting by her feet.

"What's going on?" I asked, my heart pounding. I felt dizzy, unstable, as if the ground had just been ripped out from underneath me. I think I knew what was happening the very minute I saw the suitcase. I had already blocked out the sight by that point, but it didn't take the second sight to see what was right in front of my face.

"Your Mom and I have decided to get a divorce," Dad stated, his voice as calm and emotionless as if he were relaying what they had chosen for dinner that evening. "You don't have to worry. We have already decided that you will stay here with me. We won't be putting you through any of the chaos that comes from switching houses all the time, living out of a suitcase, or changing schools, or any of that. Things will go on just as they have been, other than the fact that our marriage is over."

I looked at Mom, my eyes full of questions. *It was already decided? Did I not get a say in any of it? No custody battle, like the girl at school was talking about? No parents trying to buy my love with gifts, hoping I would choose them? Nope, just like that, just like *everything* in my life, it had been decided for me. I would stay with Dad, and Mom would move on and live her own life, unencumbered by the kid who could never seem to do anything quite right, who never lived up to her idea of perfection.

The tears I wouldn't let come stung, and my throat throbbed as I swallowed down my feelings.

Why did she not want me?

Mom just looked away, refusing to meet my eyes.

"Okay," I mumbled, unable to voice any of my questions. After all, that wouldn't be proper. We didn't do that in our family.

"Well," Dad said, standing up. "I'll carry out your suitcase." He grabbed Mom's bag and left the room, as if it were as simple as that.

I stood there, willing myself not to cry, trying to accept the new living situation. Dad and I had always gotten along better than Mom and I, that was true. I always felt like a disappointment to her.

In that moment, I realized just how true those feelings were.

I was such a disappointment that she was walking away from our family, walking away from *me*, without a second thought.

She came over and hugged me awkwardly. "Call me if you need me," she said, her voice strained.

Then she walked out the door, leaving me behind.

Just like Emerson was doing now.

Jackson left shortly after Emerson had, knowing he had to face the music with Greg. Even if he couldn't bring himself to tell Greg about Russell yet, he had to deal with the aftermath of Katie's death. There would be investigations and possible lawsuits. The whole thing was a mess. He never said a word blaming me, but we both knew Katie would still be alive if I hadn't gone to talk to her.

Which left me with a lot to chew on. Jackson seemed convinced Russell was behind Eileen's murder, and I had to admit, he seemed like the most likely suspect. Between the threatening letters and the mysterious deaths of his buddies, the evidence was stacked against him.

But why would he kill Katie? How would she have even known to implicate him? I asked Jackson that, to which his response was simply, "Who knows what Katie knows? She claimed to have been secretly investigating this town for years while she figured out a way to get revenge against Don. There's no telling what she uncovered that she hadn't told us yet. And if she knew he committed murder, why wouldn't he kill her? He'll take down anyone who gets in his way."

But I had a hard time imagining Russell as having the power and connections to know what was happening in the county jail. Jackson assured me Russell had more connections than I realized. Apparently, there were perks to being willing to skirt the law, one of them being friendships with people who had dirty work to do but needed to keep their own hands clean. He monitored Russell from a distance and knew he made his living doing other people's dirty work.

Which was another reason to distrust Joe. He easily could have gotten Russell to get rid of Eileen if he'd wanted.

Even so, I still wasn't fully convinced Russell was the man I was looking for. I couldn't shake the feeling that Mr. Boddy was my real target.

I had to keep an open mind though. After all, I had been wrong before. In fact, despite the supposed "gift" of my so-called second sight, it seemed I was wrong more than I was right, at least when it came to sniffing out murderers.

Which was at least partially why I was sitting at home by myself, feeling like I had to face this thing completely alone.

Alone. The theme of my life, it seemed. *Sorry, kid, you're on your own.* That's how it had always been. Why did it hurt so much now?

Jackson was on my side—at least, I thought he was. But working with him felt completely different than working with Emerson, Fiona, Mom, or even Joe. They had been my team. And now? I had sent Mom away in order to keep her safe. It had to be that way, no matter how much I hated it. Joe, I had lost faith in. I couldn't trust him.

Fiona, I had to keep at a distance, because I couldn't bear to risk her safety.

And Emerson had done exactly what I had always known he would —run at the first sign of trouble between us, even though it was just a stupid misunderstanding.

In short, Jackson had left me a complete and utter mess. The only person in the world I wanted to be with was Emerson. But thanks to Jackson, he had walked away.

And I didn't have it in me to beg him to come back.

Chapter Thirty-Three

Eileen's Journal

Doc Rogers came over today to give the kitten another set of shots. I feel so awkward around him now, wondering if he was part of a coverup. I hate having all these suspicious feelings about people I've known my whole life. My neighbors and friends!

Daphne

THE DAY WAS GETTING AWAY from me, and all I really wanted to do was curl up in a ball and cry. My heart and my nerves both felt completely raw, but the investigation still had to continue. If I was lucky, it would at least distract me from the wreck that was my own life for a little while.

I bundled up and headed out the door, choosing to walk to my destination. I needed the shock of the cold air to sharpen my senses, needed to brace myself against the wind and feel something other than the sting of hurt and betrayal, pain and numbness mixed in a cocktail of misery.

The sky was darkening. Soon, the sun would dip fully below the trees, with darkness falling over the woods like a curtain. The old me never would have walked this road in the dark, even if my destination was only one house away. But now? I almost didn't care if something happened to me.

The man I had given my heart to had left me, yet again. It felt like the worst thing that could possibly happen to me already had.

Briefly, anyway.

As I walked the short path to the Kistler's house, the forest came alive with the kind of sounds you only notice in the dark. My brain did exactly what I was hoping it would. It fired off warning signals, reminding me that there were, indeed, worse fates than being unceremoniously dumped by your boyfriend, no matter how in love you were. A broken heart was a painful fate, but a bear-attacked body was an entirely different kind of pain.

My survival instinct was still strong, even if my heart was broken.

My anxiety increased as I neared the house. Luke had been kind to me after his father's death, but he was still an emotionally disturbed man, and Patricia hadn't been kind at all. She was the last person I wanted to face today. But I needed answers, and Luke was the one person who might get them for me.

I walked up the stone steps to their home and lifted my hand to press the doorbell, but stopped when Luke himself stepped out of the shadows.

"What are you doing here?" he asked. He stuck his hands in the pockets of his leather jacket and eyed me suspiciously.

I breathed a sigh of relief, grateful I could avoid Patricia. "I came to talk to you, actually." I stepped toward him, but stopped when he spoke again.

"You shouldn't be here," he said, his voice mixed with accusation and warning. "She won't want to see you."

"I know," I said. "I don't want to bother her, but I'm desperate to talk to you. Can we talk privately?"

He watched me for a moment, then nodded. "Follow me," he said. He turned around and took off, disappearing behind the corner of the house.

I hesitated momentarily, my survival instincts still in high gear.

Nobody knew I was here, and I didn't feel entirely comfortable with Luke. But he had wanted to protect me the last time around, so I took a deep breath and followed him. Still, my hand gripped the metal flashlight in my pocket, just in case.

I followed him along the side of the house, where he abruptly turned the corner again at the back. It was getting darker by the minute, and I was regretting my decision to come here at all. When I turned the corner, I saw his shape sitting on the back steps of a deck, just outside the reach of the dim back porch light.

I walked over and sat down beside him, keeping as much distance between our bodies as possible on the small steps.

"What do you want?" he asked.

I was surprised by his tone. He seemed different somehow. Angrier, but also more confident. Not at all like the shy, lonely, teenage heart inside a man's body I remembered from before.

"I'm looking into my mother's murder," I said, keeping my voice low in case Patricia was anywhere nearby.

He stayed silent.

"I asked you last time if you knew who Mr. Boddy was or if there was anyone possibly blackmailing your dad. Honestly, Luke, it seemed like maybe you knew something. If you do know anything—anything at all—can you please tell me? I need a direction to go in."

He snorted. "How about home?"

"What?"

"You need a direction to go in. How about you just go home?"

This was definitely not the same Luke I had met right after his father's death. He had grown in confidence with his father gone, which was honestly a good thing, but it sure wasn't helping me out right now.

"Luke, I think you know I can't go home until I solve this," I said, my voice low. "Can't you help me?"

Silence, again.

But I wasn't ready to give up. "Can I ask you another question?"

"You can ask. Doesn't mean I'll have an answer for you."

"Do you know anything about how the money works at your dad's church? I know he embezzled money in the past. No matter how it may seem, I'm not trying to do anything that would get you or your mom in trouble, okay?" I put my hand on his forearm, but he flinched, so I pulled it away.

Silence again.

"I went to talk to Matthew," I said, "and I know he had some concerns—"

"You talked to Matthew?" Luke interrupted, turning his face to look at me.

"Yes," I said. "He told me how he was forced out of his position after asking questions about money. I know you wanted him to be the pastor of that church. You told me he was good, remember? That he wasn't like your dad."

"Matthew's good," he repeated, sounding more like the Luke I remembered. "Not like Dad. Not like me."

"Right," I said. "He has the same concerns I have about the money at the church. I'm just trying to figure things out, Luke. See, my mom was looking into the money issue before she died. It might be connected. But your dad didn't kill her. I think Mr. Boddy killed her. I'm just trying to figure out how the money plays into it. If I can trace the money, I think it will lead to Mr. Boddy, and maybe give me some kind of proof to take him down. You could really help me by giving me any information you have."

"Not like Dad," he repeated. "Not like me."

As he said those words, he looked me in the eye and I realized what he was trying to communicate.

"Luke, you're not a bad guy," I said, softly. "You just had a terrible father."

"Don't talk about my dad like that," he said, his voice coming out in a snarl, surprising me. This was the same man who had offered to cover for me when he thought I had killed his father. I certainly hadn't expected him to be offended by my remark.

"I'm sorry," I said, feeling like I was tiptoeing around eggshells I couldn't see. "I didn't mean anything by that. I'm just saying, Luke, I think you're a good person too, and I could really use your help with this."

He stood abruptly and shoved his hands in the pockets of his jacket.

"I'm the man of the house now. It's my job to take care of me and mom. You need to stay away," he said.

"Luke," I started, but he interrupted me again.

"Go home. Forget about all this. You're just going to get more people hurt."

"I don't want anyone to get hurt," I said.

"Then drop it!" he yelled, making me jump. "I can't talk to you anymore. You need to leave."

"Okay, I'm going," I said, holding my hands up in surrender.

His outburst had frightened me and I didn't want to push it anymore. I stood up and walked around the back of the house where he couldn't see me, then leaned against the side, shaking all over. I pulled my flashlight from my pocket and used it to light my way, walking quickly, wanting to get as far away from Luke's dark house as possible. When I reached the road, I breathed a sigh of relief.

The relief didn't last long. Over the noise of my own boots on the gravel, I heard the unmistakable sound of footsteps somewhere behind me. I took a few steps, listening carefully to make sure it wasn't just Luke going back to his house.

But as I heard the footsteps grow closer, I shut off my flashlight to make myself invisible in the dark. Only one thought now—*run.*

Chapter Thirty-Four

Eileen's Journal

I went to the library to do some research on money laundering, just in case there really is more to the money thing than the embezzlement Joe told me about. Then I went to the church and asked who their treasurer is, hoping I could talk to him or her and maybe find out some information. The church secretary was very nice and gave me the treasurer's name. But when I looked him up, he wasn't anything like I expected. I ended up not asking him any questions at all, because something about him seemed off. Threatening.

Daphne

My feet pounded the gravel. I was counting on the fact that I had walked or jogged this road for exercise nearly every day since I had moved here. Despite the darkness, I hoped I knew the path well enough to stay on it and not fall into the ditch on either side until my eyes adjusted.

The footsteps behind me picked up, matching my pace—no, outpacing me. I could hear them getting closer. I took a deep breath and picked up my speed, grateful for every single workout I had done over the past year. My endurance was better than it used to be. I could see my porch light now in the distance. If I could go just a little faster, I could get there in time to get inside and bolt the door.

But the footsteps behind me picked up too, and a flashlight clicked on, illuminating the path in front of me except for my own dark shadow on the road. I fought back a scream and pushed myself even further, running faster now than I had ever run in my entire life.

It wasn't enough.

The light grew brighter, my shadow grew sharper, and the steps got louder, all before powerful arms circled around me, stopping me in my tracks.

I screamed.

A hand slid over my mouth, and a familiar voice whispered roughly in my ear.

"Daphne, what the hell are you doing?"

My body relaxed, even though my heart missed the memo. It pounded even harder as I pushed away from Emerson's arms.

"What am *I* doing?" I asked loudly, turning toward him and clicking on my flashlight, not caring if I blinded him. "You're the one who just chased me down the road and practically tackled me!"

He winced and held his own flashlight down where it wouldn't hurt my eyes. I begrudgingly did the same.

He stepped close to me and spoke in a whisper. "I was out for a nighttime run and saw you sneaking out from the Kistler's backyard. I didn't want to call out to you and get you caught. I was trying to catch up with you so I could make sure you made it home safely, but you took off in a run."

I sighed. "Sorry. I was spooked. I thought you were either a bear or a bad guy, and I wasn't hanging around to find out which."

"You wouldn't have to worry about either if you didn't go out investigating—and trespassing—by yourself at night."

I couldn't see his face clearly, but I knew him well enough to know the expression he was certainly wearing, and I didn't like it.

"I wasn't trespassing," I said, wanting to defend myself. "I was talking to Luke. We were in the backyard so his mom wouldn't hear."

"Ahh, I see. Another date tonight. Got it." His voice dripped with sarcasm.

"That's not fair." Fury bubbled up in me.

He was silent for one long moment, then sighed. "You're right. That was low. I'm sorry."

I could hear the pain in his voice, mirroring the ache in my heart.

"Well, now that we got that settled, I need to get back home." I turned and walked away from him, even though everything within me wanted to do the exact opposite. I would not beg him to come back though. He was the one who had walked away without even giving me a real chance to explain. If that's all it took for him to leave, then I had been right all along and there wasn't a future for us. No matter how much it hurt, a clean break was the best thing.

"Daphne, wait," he said, his voice gruff. "Please."

I paused but didn't turn around. I heard him walking, stopping just behind me, close enough that I could feel his warmth. My entire body seemed to come alive, responding to him the way it always did, even when I didn't want it to. I ached for him to reach out and wrap his arms around me again.

"Just help me understand," he said. "I thought... I thought what we had was good."

"It was," I said, my voice coming out strangled, as I fought back the waves of emotion threatening to wash over me.

"Then why?"

"Why what?"

"Why Jackson?"

I turned around slowly. My eyes had adjusted enough that I could make out his face clearly now, and I made sure I looked him straight in the eye.

"Emerson. Nothing whatsoever happened between me and Jackson. Nothing. He was there to give me information. That's all. I promised him I wouldn't tell anyone what he came to tell me until he tells Greg. It's really personal for him, and I was trying to respect that, so I didn't know what to do or say when you showed up. But what I can tell you is you completely misunderstood what was happening today. He was there about the case. That's all."

Emerson let out a breath and dropped his head. "I am so stupid."

"No, you're not. Well, maybe you are. Emerson, how could you think I would cheat on you? Is that how little you think of me? Really?" It stung to know he could believe that. "Or were you just looking for an excuse to end things?"

"An excuse to end things?" He looked at me like I was crazy. "How could *you* think that?"

I shrugged. "Everything ends eventually. I'm an adult. I get that. But if you wanted to break up, you could have just told me."

He kept staring at me. "You really don't get it, do you?"

"Get what?"

"That I love you, dammit!" He raised his voice in frustration. "I don't want to leave you. Looking for an excuse? How could you say that? All I want—all I've *ever* wanted—is to spend the rest of my life with you. You're the one who's held me at arm's length this entire time, refusing to give me even the tiniest bit of hope for a future."

I stepped back as if someone had slapped me. I opened my mouth to tell him that wasn't fair, but something stopped me. Was he right? Had I held him at arm's length? If I was being honest with myself, then yeah, I guess I had, and not even just with the case. Hadn't I always been protecting my heart, just bracing for the inevitable end?

"I never meant to hold you at arm's length," I said finally.

"But you did." He stepped forward too, his eyes full of hurt, visible even in the low light. "Daphne, every time I bring up the future, you change the subject. Every time I've tried to tell you I want to move forward, you tell me there's no need."

He was pacing now, running his hands through his hair the way he always did when he was frustrated. "You won't even keep a toothbrush at my place, despite staying there at least once a week. When I asked for a drawer at your place, you said no. You're always bringing up me moving back to Wisconsin to be with my family, like you can't wait to get rid of me. Last night, you totally blew me off. Greg told me he couldn't get in touch with Jackson, either, and thought he was with a new girlfriend. So when I saw you with Jackson today, I just thought, well, that's what I needed to know."

He stopped pacing and looked at me again, his voice softening. "You never promised I was the only one. We didn't talk about it. Hell, we never talk about *anything* regarding us. So I started thinking maybe I was an idiot to assume we were as serious as I thought we were. That maybe you don't want what I want."

There was so much hurt in his voice. For the first time, I considered what my actions might look like from his point of view.

"Oh, Emerson," I said. "I never... That's not..."

"On top of that," he continued, "you pushed me away the very minute you got that journal. Like you didn't want me anywhere near it, even though I thought we were partners. You've kept me in the dark the whole time."

"Emerson, I'm just protecting you! I don't want you to get hurt. This is my fight, not yours, and I didn't want you to feel obligated to walk into danger."

He shook his head, disappointment all over his face. "Daphne, my entire life I've made my own choices. Time after time, I've chosen to walk into danger for complete strangers. Strangers, Daphne. Do you honestly think I wouldn't do the same for the woman I love?"

"I ... I don't know what to say," I said, faltering. "I'm sorry. I just—"

"You don't have to explain," he said, stopping me.

"No, I think I do." I sighed and looked around at the dark forest, shivering involuntarily despite my thick coat. "Look, can we go back to my place and talk? Let's not do this here."

He let out a breath and nodded. We turned and walked back toward my cottage in silence as I tried to figure out the right words to say to this man I was no longer willing to lose.

WE WERE STILL silent when we got back to my place. I unlocked the door and let us in, flicking on the lights. The brightness hurt, as my eyes fought to readjust after the time I had spent in the darkness.

I looked at Emerson and saw the pain on his face. He looked absolutely wrecked.

"Come in and sit down," I said, as he stood awkwardly at the door. I hated seeing him stand there that way, like he wasn't sure he was welcome. I had never meant to make him feel that way.

I took his coat and hung it in the coat closet beside mine, where it belonged. I knew that now.

He walked to the couch and sat down, still silent.

"Do you want a drink?" I asked.

"No," he mumbled. "Look, Daphne, I'm sorry I assumed the wrong thing about you and Jackson. Let me just say that right now."

I walked over and sat on the coffee table in front of him, my hands clasped together.

He looked at me, his eyes red. "You're right. I shouldn't have thought so little of you. I just didn't know what to think. I'm sorry for my assumption. And if we have to do a post-mortem, well"—he raised his hands in surrender—"let me have it."

"I'm sorry, too," I said. "Everything you said—I see it now. Other than the case, I didn't mean to hold you at arm's length and shut you out, but I can see that I did." I sighed and shook my head. "When I brought up Wisconsin all those times, it wasn't because I wanted to get rid of you. I just didn't want to get caught off guard when you left."

"But why would you assume I would leave?" he asked. "Didn't I make it clear every single day that I wanted to be with you?"

"Yes, but..."

"But what? Daphne, where did I screw this up? Just tell me."

"It wasn't you," I whispered. "Not really."

"I'm not sure if that makes me feel better or worse."

"Let me explain." I took a deep breath and closed my eyes, trying to figure out the right words to help him understand. "Nobody in my life has ever stayed for long. Not really."

He started to protest, but I held up a hand.

"Just let me finish, okay? I was a toddler when Eileen died. I don't even remember her. But Fiona says that kind of loss leaves a wound anyway. Losing your mother at such a young age feels like abandonment, no matter what the circumstances were."

"That makes sense," he said. "I'm so sorry you went through all of that. But what does that have to do with us?"

"I guess I've always had this fear of abandonment," I confessed. "It didn't help that Janet, the only mom I ever knew, seemed to completely abandon me as well. Again, there were circumstances I didn't know, didn't understand. All I knew was that my mom walked right out of my life, not seeming to care if she ever saw me again. She never fought for me, never gave me any indication that I meant anything at all to her." The pain of it hurt, even now, despite knowing the truth. "I just felt like I was easy to walk away from."

He nodded again and squeezed my hand, letting me know he was listening and giving me the space to continue.

"Even my college boyfriend abandoned me," I said with a painful laugh. "Although, I've never really thought about how I probably pushed him away too. He broke up with me after three years of dating. Quickly married someone else, which shocked me. But you know what? I did the same thing to him. I never let things get serious, never moved forward. I never really let him in or even told him I loved him."

"So, what are you saying?" he asked.

"I think," I said, slowly, "I've just always expected you to leave. I've learned to not hope for anything to last. Not really. So I've always been bracing for it. Does that make sense? That's why I never wanted things to move forward. The closer we got, the more entrenched our lives became, the more painful it would be the day you left. Easier to keep things as simple as possible and just enjoy the moment."

"But I never wanted to leave."

"But you did leave," I pointed out. "At the first sign of trouble. You assumed the worst and left. So, I was right." I attempted a painful smile.

He leaned his head back on the couch and stared at the ceiling. I chewed on my nail, waiting for him to speak.

"I was wrong to walk away without giving you a chance to explain," he finally said, his voice quiet. "But you were wrong too. I left the *situation*. But I didn't leave you. Daphne, I never want to leave you. Not for Wisconsin or anything else."

He reached out and took my hand, wrapping it in his. "For weeks, I've waited for the perfect moment to ask this question. This is definitely not the perfect moment. But maybe that's okay. Because we aren't perfect people, are we? We've made mistakes and screwed this up more than once. But I promise you this. I will never walk away from you again. I will never be that person who walks out on you. Ever. I love you."

I looked into his eyes and felt a flutter of hope. "I love you too," I whispered.

"All I've wanted since we got back together was to marry you. So"—he paused and got off the couch, kneeling down on one knee—"Daphne Sullivan, as imperfect as I am, will you stop running away from me—literally *and* metaphorically—and marry me, so I can love you every day for the rest of my life? For better or worse, in sickness and in health, and even in murder investigations—I want it all. I want to be the one by your side for every bit of it."

I was stunned. "You don't have to," I began.

"Have to?" His eyes got wide. "You really, really don't get it, do you?" He laughed and shook his head. "Daphne, I've been carrying an engagement ring in my truck since the week we got back together. Remember that trip I had to make to Asheville?"

I nodded.

"I bought it then. I've had it ever since, just waiting until I thought you might actually say yes. Now, I'm asking even though I have no idea what you're going to say. But I can't wait any longer. If you don't want me, I respect that. But if the reason you're always pulling away is that you're not convinced I want to be with you every single day for the rest of my life, then give me the chance to make that promise to you."

I stared at him and realized he was dead serious. The heaviness in my heart lifted as I saw the truth. Emerson loved me—truly loved me. Not just for now. Forever. This was real. It was solid and true. No matter how we had screwed it up in the past or how we might screw it up in the future, we would make it. Our love was strong enough to survive us being human.

"Ask me again," I whispered.

He cocked his head and looked at me, then smiled. "Okay. Daphne Sullivan, will you marry me?"

"Yes," I said, unable to hold back my smile. "Yes, I will."

CHAPTER THIRTY-FIVE

Eileen's Journal

Lonnie took me out on a date tonight to reconnect. He says he's been feeling the distance between us. I feel so guilty for everything I've kept from him. I don't know if I should tell him the truth about everything or not. Initially, I kept my investigation to myself because I didn't want him to be angry. Now I'm worried that if he knows what I know, he may be in danger. I keep feeling this sense of danger coming, a darkness that I can't escape.

The owl was hooting again tonight.

Daphne

EMERSON INSISTED we go straight to his cabin to get the ring and to love on Thor, who was apparently missing me almost as much as Emerson had been. We hopped in my car and drove down to his place, both grinning like kids the entire way. That was the thing I loved most about this man. No matter what was going on in my world, he could make me forget it all. The world could fall, but if we were together, everything was okay.

We pulled up beside his truck. He immediately hopped out and went to the passenger-side door, retrieving a little black box from his glove compartment. My heart rose in anticipation. I had believed him when he'd told me about the ring, of course, but hearing about it was different seeing it in person. The reality of what was happening made my heart beat just a little bit faster, and I couldn't contain my smile.

He stuck the box in his pocket and took my hand, leading me up to his front door. I could hear Thor whining on the other side, eager for us to open it and come in. When Emerson opened the door, Thor ran out and came straight to me, nudging my hand onto the top of his head. I crouched down to his level and rubbed him behind his ears, letting him give me a gentle kiss.

"I missed you too, boy," I murmured.

I looked up and saw Emerson leaning against the doorframe, watching us with a look of complete satisfaction on his face. His girl and his dog. His emotions were so strong I could practically feel them in the moment. We were all he wanted, all he needed. I met his eyes, hoping he could feel the same love from my heart.

I finally let Thor go and walked to Emerson, kissing him lightly on the lips before heading into the cabin. He followed me in, trailing his fingertips along my back the way I loved, then closed the door behind us.

"I don't know why I'm nervous," he said, pulling the box from his pocket.

"Me either, since I already gave you my answer," I teased.

"I just hope you'll like it."

I couldn't help but smile. His nerves were real, and I thought it was adorable. He was usually so confident.

"I'm sure it will be perfect," I assured him.

"I hope so."

He opened the box, and I immediately gasped. The ring, an emerald set in gold, surrounded by a circle of small diamonds, was more beautiful than I ever could have imagined. It was so unique, so utterly *me*. I couldn't have chosen anything more perfect if I had picked it out myself.

"It's absolutely beautiful," I whispered, entranced by the beauty of the jewels.

He slid it carefully onto my finger, where it sparkled underneath the lights. "I took a chance," he confessed. "I know diamonds are the norm. But, Daphne, there's nothing ordinary about you. When I saw the emerald, I thought of your green eyes. 'That's the one,' I thought. But if you would rather have something more traditional, we can trade it out."

"No," I breathed. "It's absolutely perfect. I love it."

He brushed my hair away from my face and pressed his lips to mine. "I love you," he said, when he finally broke the kiss.

It was a perfect moment, which of course meant it couldn't last.

WE OPENED a bottle of wine and had every intention of spending the evening celebrating, but my phone rang, interrupting our evening.

"It's Greg," I said, as I met Emerson's eyes. Greg didn't call me for social reasons. If Greg was calling, something was wrong.

Emerson set his mouth in a firm line and nodded, all business again.

"Hello?" I asked, answering the call.

"Daphne, it's Sheriff Morrison," Greg said. "Listen, I need to ask you some questions, but I'd rather do it outside the office. I know it's late in the day, but I'm just now wrapping things up. Can I swing by your house?"

Emerson put his hand on my thigh and raised his eyebrows, then looked pointedly at the foot I was twitching back and forth.

"Nervous habit," I mouthed.

He just handed me my glass of wine.

"I'm happy to answer your questions, but I'm not home right now," I said. I shot Emerson a questioning look. He nodded, letting me know it was okay to invite Greg to his place. "I'm at Emerson's right now. You're welcome to come by."

"Even better," Greg said. "I'll head that way in about thirty."

"See you then," I said before ending the call. I put my phone down and began chewing my fingernail—yet another nervous habit.

"What's up?" Emerson asked.

"Greg's coming over. Says he wants to ask questions, but not at the office."

Emerson raised his eyebrows. "So, not officially, then."

"I guess not. What do you think it's about?"

"Katie."

"Yeah," I said, sighing. "He won't be happy about that." I reached for my wine and drained the glass, needing a little liquid courage before the conversation where I would almost certainly get chewed out for requesting the meeting. On the other hand, Greg had approved it, so it wasn't like I was the only one culpable for the whole thing.

"Emerson," I said, sighing again.

"Yeah, babe?"

"Are you sure you want to be involved in this investigation?"

He just gave me an annoyed look.

"Okay," I said. "Then I need to fill you in on everything, and we can decide together how much to share with Greg."

"Alright. I'm listening." He sat back on the couch and turned all his attention toward me, ready to hear the whole story.

I told him everything that was in the journal, what I had learned from Matthew and Luke, and about my confrontation with Joe. I even told him Jackson's story. He could be trusted with Jackson's secret until Jackson finally got up the courage to tell Greg the truth. Never again would I hide anything from Emerson. He wasn't just my boyfriend anymore. We were going to be husband and wife, and I wouldn't keep anything from him. I was done with that.

Emerson listened quietly, only interrupting to ask questions.

"So?" I asked when I finally finished. "What are your thoughts?"

"I don't know," he admitted, rubbing his beard in thought. "I'll be honest. If I didn't know you and your, well, gifts, I think I would read Eileen's journal and assume she had schizophrenia. From what you're saying, she doesn't come across as credible."

I tampered the immediate indignation, because I had to admit he had a point. "Yeah," I finally said. "But I don't believe that."

"I don't, either," he clarified. "Because I *do* know you and your gifts. Besides, Katie's death seems to confirm there was legitimately something to fear."

"Right," I said, relieved he believed in Eileen.

"But if she didn't come across as credible, then where's the motive?" he pointed out. "From what you're saying, it sounds like she uncovered someone's business and might be a threat from a financial or legal standpoint. The deaths, needles, and money laundering... Altogether, it sounds like drug trafficking to me. There's big money there. If she could prove anything, I don't doubt she would be in danger. But if all she had were visions, who on earth would believe her?"

"That's a good point," I admitted. "But Joe trusted her visions. He went after Russell based solely on Eileen's word, and Russell ended up serving time in prison. So, visions alone could have made her a threat."

Emerson's face showed doubt. "In Russell's case, there were two witnesses who backed up what she said. So it wasn't just based on her word. I don't know. I think it's doubtful she would have been able to take down a drug trafficker based on a few visions. That leaves a real lack of motive. Without a motive, there's no crime. The journal kept mentioning Don, but you've moved on from considering him a suspect, right?"

"Yeah." I adjusted myself on the couch and reached again for my glass of wine, thinking it over before I replied. "For one thing, Katie said it wasn't him, and I believe her. I think she would have told me if he had done it, if only to convince me his murder was justified. For another thing, if it was him, then who would have killed Katie for talking to me? Like you said, where's the motive? If she was going to incriminate a dead man, who would have a motive for killing her? It has to be someone who's alive."

"Yeah." He rubbed his beard again, deep in thought. "Maybe Jackson's revenge theory is right. Maybe it really was his dad."

"I don't know," I said, shaking my head. "That doesn't feel right to me."

"Revenge is a legitimate motive. After all, that's why Katie killed Don," he pointed out.

"I know it's a legitimate motive. And you're right. We may not have another one right now." I buried my face in my hands and sighed. "Ugh. I just don't want it to be Russell."

"Why not?"

I paused, unsure how to express what was in my heart. "Look, I'll be grateful if we can get justice, no matter what. If it is Russell and we prove that, then we'll get a murderer off the streets, and that's a good thing, right? But"—I looked down and twisted the sleeve of my shirt—"I really need it to be connected to Don somehow." I said the words so quietly I wasn't sure he heard me at first.

"Why do you need it to be connected to Don?" He asked it quietly, sensing my struggle.

I looked up at him with tears in my eyes. "Because I need all of this to be worth it. If it turns out Eileen's death had nothing to do with Don and the shady business at the church, then what was the point? Don died. He *died.* In my front yard. Fiona lost trust in Joe, her best friend for decades. This quest has ruined so many lives, and if it turns out I opened all these cans of worms and none of them even had anything to do with it?"

He reached over and took my hand in his. "They needed to be opened. Fiona needed to know the truth about Joe. Don may not have deserved to die, but it's not like he was a saint. He ruined plenty of lives himself and he can't do that anymore. Besides, his death wasn't your fault. You have to stop blaming yourself for it."

"Says you of all people," I commented, giving him a pointed look.

"Yes, me of all people. I know what I'm talking about." He paused for a minute, then grinned. "Want me to make you some hawthorn tea?"

I started to laugh but stopped when we heard the knock on the door. Greg was here, and tea would have to wait.

CHAPTER THIRTY-SIX

EILEEN'S JOURNAL

Lonnie keeps pushing me to tell him what's wrong, but I can't. It might put him in danger. I'm getting more and more scared. I keep feeling like someone is watching me when I'm in town. That feeling that sends chills down your spine, where you just know someone is there watching. Joe's also been acting strange around me, which really makes me worry. I asked him about it and he said he's not the one acting strange, that I'm being strange and that he's worried about me.

Joe

I RUBBED my hands together and blew on them to keep warm as I waited for him to arrive. It was dangerous, meeting out here like this. It wasn't good to run the chance of being seen together. Nor did I like being in such a vulnerable position, as far as he was concerned, meeting in the dark in the woods without backup, but desperate times and all that.

He arrived ten minutes late, puffing on a cigarette like he didn't have a care in the world. I knew better than to comment on the time. You didn't correct Mr. Boddy.

"Good to see you, Joe," he said, taking a puff and exhaling the smoke in my face. I refused to cough on it, even though I couldn't stand the smell of the things.

"Wish I could say the same," I said.

"Bad news?" He raised an eyebrow.

"You could say that. Look, I've protected you for a long time. You know that. But Daphne's bound and determined to figure out what happened to her mother. If she keeps digging, there's a good chance she's going to come across something that proves our particular relationship. So, what I'm asking is, are you going to protect me this time around?"

He took a few more puffs, his face as placid as ever. "Are you asking me to get rid of the girl?"

I could feel myself go pale. "No. Absolutely not. She doesn't get hurt. No matter what."

"Then what exactly are you asking from me, Joe?" His dark eyes went narrow as he stared at me.

I couldn't help but swallow nervously. "I've paid my dues. I'm just asking that you protect my name, that's all. If she uncovers your little operation, keep my name out of it. Deny I ever knew anything about it. Come up with a way to explain how you got it past me without me knowing. Throw someone else under the bus for all I care. Just keep me clean. That's all I'm asking. I'm an old man who's already lost everything except his reputation. Just let me keep that. Please."

He took a few more puffs, his narrow eyes boring into me. "You may be asking too much," he said finally. "If she uncovers my 'little operation,' as you call it, do you really think anyone will believe I got away with it for so long without the help of the law in my corner?" He raised an eyebrow.

"People believe what they want to believe. You and I know that much for sure."

He puffed again, then dropped the cigarette and ground it out underneath his leather shoe. Italian leather. Probably cost a small fortune. Not the kind of thing most men wore out into the woods, but this was Mr. Boddy after all. He wasn't like most men.

"I don't think you have anything to worry about. What could she find?" He shrugged. "Unless she has the skills of her mother...?" His eyes bored into me again.

It was a question, and the look on his face demanded an answer.

I shook my head no. "Nah. She has a touch of the sight, but nothing like Eileen. As far as I know, all she's seen of our business was a meeting between me and Don, and that was easy enough to explain away. She's pretty easy to handle. She's one of those types that's always wanting to see the best in everyone."

Mr. Boddy lifted his lip in amusement. "Still, not a fun conversation for you, I'm assuming."

My temper flared a bit, but I tamped it back down. "No, not a fun conversation. But if that's all she has, she has nothing. Still, she's persistent. You should know that."

"I'll ask you again, then. Do we need to get rid of her?"

I hesitated, only briefly. I had a genuine fondness for Daphne. Beyond that, murder was against my moral code, plain and simple. But self-preservation wasn't, and part of me was just the slightest bit tempted to let him handle things his way. It would make my own future certain and everything could go back to normal. I had paid my dues, both to him and to society as a whole. I had given a lifetime to law enforcement, keeping people safe even as it destroyed my family. And there was no real harm in my arrangement with Mr. Boddy. It was only a bit of supplementary income to look the other way on essentially victimless crimes. Most of the time, anyway. Sometimes there were victims, and that was harder to look past. But they were rarely innocent victims; they were people who knew very well what they were getting into. People who played with fire were bound to get burned every now and then.

"No," I said when the temptation passed. "No more murder. Besides, that would just draw more attention to both of us." I gave him a pointed look. "Her boyfriend is buddies with the current sheriff."

Mr. Boddy nodded. "Sheriff Morrison can be bought. That's something you should have taken care of a long time ago, isn't it?" His tone let me know how disappointed he was that I hadn't already secured Sheriff Morrison's silence.

"I don't know," I said carefully, always slightly uncomfortable when disagreeing with him. I never knew how he was going to react to that. "I'm not sure we can buy him. None of the feelers we've put out in that direction have ever gone anywhere. He's his own man, that one."

Mr. Boddy shrugged. "You know how it is. If money doesn't tempt him, I have other ways of convincing people to go along with what's in their own best interest. It's past time we taught Sheriff Morrison how things work here in my town."

My blood ran cold. I knew exactly what some of those ways were. "You're going to make him an offer he can't refuse?" I said, attempting to laugh.

He chuckled. "Funny. All men have a weakness, Joe. If needed, I'll find his. I plan to continue my reign over this town for a long, long time. Remember that. I won't allow Daphne Sullivan or Greg Morrison to come against me. If that means a little more bloodshed, then..." He shrugged, as if it were nothing.

"I'll pretend I didn't hear that," I said pointedly.

Mr. Boddy just grinned. "Don't worry, Joe." He clamped a hand on my shoulder, making my blood run cold again. "Consider it taken care of."

CHAPTER THIRTY-SEVEN

Eileen's Journal

I took Daphne over to Fiona's today. Fiona's house always feels so safe, like nothing can touch us while I'm there. Fiona asked what was worrying me, but I couldn't bring myself to tell her. She sent me home with some tea, of course. She's such a blessing to my life.

She told me Joe had asked her out on another date. Ever since his wife left, he's looked at Fiona differently. I know she feels something for him, too. Before all of this, I hoped they would find their way to each other. I love Fiona and want her to have someone in her life.

But now? With what I've seen? I'm terrified at the idea of her getting involved with him. I couldn't tell her the truth, but I urged her to say no. She knows me well enough to know I wouldn't say that unless there was something behind it.

She seemed disappointed, maybe even heartbroken, but I know she'll heed my warning.

I can't bear to think of her as being in danger.

Daphne

GREG HUNG his hat and jacket on the pegs beside Emerson's door and warmed his hands by the fire before taking the seat across from us. The tension in the room was so thick you could cut it with a knife. I bit my lip and waited for him to speak, wondering how angry he was going to be at me over Katie's death.

But when he finally spoke, he didn't seem angry at all. If anything, he seemed exhausted. Weary. As fed up as I was with everything happening in this town we both had grown to love, the town we both wanted to protect.

"I'm going to cut straight to the point," he said, leaning forward, his hands clasped together. He shook his head. "Daphne, there's not a damn thing in your mother's report that suggests murder."

I opened my mouth to protest, but he stopped me.

"Hold on now. I said there was nothing in the report. But your coming here and looking into it has obviously stirred the pot. I watched that interview with Katie. I saw her fear. And obviously, that fear was well-founded."

I nodded. "Katie's death... It wasn't suicide, was it?"

He grimaced. "I sure as hell don't think so. That would be one big coincidence, wouldn't it? Just like your mother's, it was staged to look like one. But no, I don't believe it was. At this point, my gut tells me both women were murdered, and likely by the same person. I'm hoping you can help me figure out who that person is."

My heart pounded as I nodded. I didn't know if Jackson had told Greg about my sight. I wasn't sure if I was ready to give that up if he hadn't—or what Greg might think about it. It seemed like a safe bet he would be skeptical, to say the least. Maybe even skeptical enough to decide, again, that I was just crazy. So I planned on keeping that card close to my chest as long as possible, unless he already knew.

I stayed silent, waiting for him to speak.

"I've been working here for just over a year now," he said finally. "The first real outsider to hold the position. I've had to walk a careful line because of that. The people here, they're loyal to the old timers. You both know that." He tipped a head toward us, waiting for us to confirm.

All three of us were relatively new to Rosemary Mountain, and we had all experienced just how hard it was to be accepted here.

"Joe Hemsworth is practically royalty in this town," he said, shaking his head. "I've had more than my fair share of trouble from people with no respect for the badge unless he's wearing it. That goes for citizens and deputies alike. No sheriff since him has lasted long, not even the ones who grew up here. It's been an uphill battle since day one."

He paused, rubbing his chin. "I've had some red flags ever since I took over. Little things that bothered me. Some patterns, some oddities. Things that make me wonder if the department hasn't always been run on the up-and-up, so to speak. But I've had to be careful, see? Can't really question Joe or his leadership. Certainly can't investigate him, at least not openly. I'd be out faster than you can believe if I did."

My heart pounded harder. "So you think Joe is the one behind all this?"

He shook his head. "Nah. I think Joe's been covering for someone else."

"So, what red flags have you seen?" I asked, wanting to hear his side of things.

He looked at us, long and hard. "This conversation stays here, understood?"

We both nodded. I reached for Emerson's hand automatically, squeezing it for strength.

"Rosemary Mountain is a small town," Greg said. "Quaint, cute, a place people love to visit. But also the kind of place a lot of kids hate to grow up in. Seems you've gotta reach a certain age to really appreciate this kind of place. And like a lot of other small, rural towns, we have a lack of entertainment options, which means we have a problem."

"Drugs," Emerson said with a nod.

"Exactly." Greg met his eyes and nodded with a grim smile. "Common problem for small towns. People used to think drugs were an inner-city problem, but drug use and overdose are actually higher in rural areas. Starts younger and younger too."

"Yeah, I've seen that more than I care to," Emerson agreed.

I bit my lip and stayed silent, not wanting to divulge yet what I had read in Eileen's journal.

"It's a real problem here in Tennessee," Greg said. "We're something of a transit state for drug dealers, because of all our interstates. Heck, a few years back, dealers started coming here from Detroit, because they could do better here than there."

"Wow," I said, frowning. "I didn't realize that was such an issue."

"Yes, ma'am," Greg said. "Plus, there was this big fiasco a few years back where an investigation showed that law enforcement here in Tennessee was more focused on seizing drug money after the deals than actually getting the drugs off the streets. Turns out, letting the drugs go then seizing the money is a lucrative way to fund departments." He raised his eyebrows. "That's above my pay grade, but I'll tell you, I don't like it one bit. And while we've made some progress here in Rosemary Mountain, catching low-level dealers, I've felt like there's a bigger fish to fry. Red flags, you see," Greg said, exchanging looks with Emerson.

"But," he continued, "our big fish seems to be awfully protected. Catch a low-level guy, normally you've got a chance of getting some info out of them. Offer him a deal. Release for information." Greg shrugged. "That doesn't work here. Everybody's scared to death to talk, just like Katie. That's been an issue for me all along, but now it's a major problem 'cause I've got a suspicious death in the county jail. So not only does this big fish have all his dealers scared to death to talk to us, he also has eyes in my jail, which brings me back to my problems with Joe Hemsworth."

I nodded. "I have reasons for being uncomfortable with Joe, too," I admitted. "But there's another suspect you should know about. It's not my story to tell though."

He held up a hand. "If you're talking about Jackson's scumbag sperm donor, Jackson told me all about that a little while ago. I'll be looking into that, but my gut says we're looking closer to home."

"Mine does too," I said, relieved. I looked at Greg and decided to trust my gut again. "There's something else you should know."

He raised an eyebrow in question.

"Remember how back when you were investigating Don's death, you caught me in his office and I told you I was looking for evidence of a Mr. Boddy?"

His face changed as he fought back what was either a grimace or a smile. "I remember."

"Look," I said, leaning forward and letting out a long breath. "I promised I would keep her out of this. So I'm begging you, please keep this between us. But you're trusting us, so I'm going to trust you. Okay?"

He leaned forward, matching my posture. "I'll try my best," he said.

"I learned about Mr. Boddy from Christie. She was sort of dating Don."

Greg frowned. "Christie?"

"Yeah," I said. "You know, Christie. The blonde waitress at Marco's who just had a baby. I talked to her the night we had pizza there. She told me the reason you couldn't find Don's cell phone was because she has it." I blushed, feeling as guilty for just now telling him this as if I had taken the cell phone myself. "That cell phone is the one that had the messages from Mr. Boddy. Greg, I'm pretty sure Mr. Boddy is your big fish *and* the one who killed my mother. Christy is going to give me the cell phone so I can find him."

Greg's jaw nearly hit the ground.

"I know I should have told you earlier," I said, seeing the shock on his face. "I'm sorry. I thought I was doing the right thing by keeping her secret."

"Daphne, are you talking about Christie Jameson? Nineteen years old?"

"I think so," I said, a little confused. "I actually don't know her last name, but yeah, she's about nineteen."

"Yeah, it's Christie Jameson," Emerson confirmed. "Why? What's wrong?"

Greg ran a hand over his face, pale now. "Christie's parents reported her missing about two hours ago."

Chapter Thirty-Eight

I went to town today, wanting a nice outing for me and Daphne, a day to take my mind off of everything going on. Instead, I found the truth in the place where I least expected it. It all makes sense, and it breaks my heart.

In the end, it all comes down to money. Money and power. That's all they care about. Who cares if someone gets hurt, or even dies, in the process? Just as long as the money keeps rolling in. It makes me want to scream.

I don't know what to do. It's so much bigger, and scarier, than I thought. I can't go to Joe. As far as I know, he's only guilty of taking that one bribe. But that bribe taints him. It's a liability, because it will come out in the investigation. Would he be willing to give up his entire career and potentially face charges himself in order to take down these criminals? I want to say yes, but truthfully, I don't know ... and I have to admit there's a possibility he's aligned with them.

I don't know who I can trust. I don't want to tell the wrong person.

State police maybe? Or bigger? I don't know. But I need to figure out who to go to with this.

Daphne

My stomach dropped when Greg said Christie was missing.

"What do you mean missing?" I demanded.

Greg shook his head, still as white as a ghost. "Her parents called the station earlier. Said she was supposed to come over today with the baby. She never showed. Wasn't answering her cell and wasn't at work."

My face was ashen. "We have to find her! Who's looking for her?"

"Nobody," he said. "She's an adult, she doesn't live with her parents anymore, and it's been less than twenty-four hours."

"But—"

"I get it," he interrupted, his face grim. "This is different. Now that I know the rest of the story, I agree with you. We've got to find her." He paused, obviously torn with how to handle the situation. "I've got to tell you, I don't know as I feel comfortable calling in the cavalry. I'm not yet sure who all is in this guy's pocket."

"You're right," I said. There was only a handful of people I could truly trust, and everything within me said we needed to limit the search for Christie to them. I thought for a second, then decided to take a chance. I looked to Emerson, who met my eyes and seemed to know exactly what I was thinking. He squeezed my hand and gave me a little nod, letting me know I had his support.

"Listen," I said, drawing in every bit of strength from Emerson beside me. "Two things. One, I know you don't know who to trust, but I think you can trust Jackson."

Greg nodded in agreement. "I do trust him, despite his apparent lack of trust in me. Jackson's been my right-hand man up there for a lot of reasons, and his childhood doesn't change that."

I let out a breath, relieved. "Okay, part two. I think I can help."

"I appreciate the offer, but unless your help is information about where we might find Christie, I think you better just hang tight. *If* we're dealing with a potential drug lord, the last thing I need is a civilian out investigating or trying to intervene." He gave me a pointed look.

"I know that's what you think," I said. "But there's a reason I think I can help."

He waited, a skeptical look on his face.

I looked to Emerson again for reassurance and found it in his eyes. I turned back to Greg. "There's something about me you should know," I began. "Something that's hard to explain and probably won't make any sense to you at all. But it's true, and it can help. My mother died because she was dangerous. She saw things, knew things. She had what Fiona calls the second sight. Visions. She actually worked with Joe on several of his cases, including the one that put Jackson's father in jail. I don't know if Jackson told you that part or not."

I tried to ignore the skepticism on his face. "She passed the gift on to me," I said, confessing to him the one thing I swore I'd never tell him. "It's not as strong as hers, but lately, I've been getting more. I'm learning how to use it. And everything within me says that I need to go to Christie's house. That, if I go there, I'll ... I'll be able to see what happened to her." I swallowed hard, knowing how crazy the whole thing sounded.

Greg gave me a long, hard look, saying nothing.

"It's true," Emerson said, slipping his hand out of mine and wrapping an arm around me as if he could protect me from Greg's judgment. "I didn't believe it at first, either, but I've seen it in action. It's what made her realize her mother was murdered in the first place. It's how she knew Julie was Wes Adams' girlfriend back during that whole thing. It's even how she's known, for some time, that Joe took bribes from Don Kistler when he was sheriff."

At this, Greg stiffened, shocked. "Bribes? Are you sure?"

I nodded. "Yes. Joe confirmed. There's more I can tell you about all of that, and my mother, and maybe even your drug issue. But right now, we have to find Christie. I can feel it. We don't have much time."

Greg looked to Emerson then back to me and sighed, running a weary hand over his face. "Why is nothing ever easy with red-headed women?" he muttered under his breath. "Fine. Let's go. I'll call Jackson on the way."

"One more thing," I said, as he stood. "We need to take Fiona."

It was a certainty I could feel deep in my soul. I hated it. I wanted to protect her, wanted to keep her far from all of this—but everything within me said I couldn't do it without her. Christie was in grave danger, and Fiona knew her better than any of us. Besides that, I could practically hear Fiona's voice whispering to me. We were stronger together. We had to do this as a team.

"Out of the question," Greg said. His tone let me know he had no intention of negotiating.

"I need her," I said. "I don't know why, but I do." I wrapped my fingers around the locket Fiona gave me and looked back at Emerson. "We're stronger together," I said, echoing Fiona's words.

Emerson looked at Greg. "I think you should listen to her."

Greg closed his eyes and stood there. I could almost hear him counting to ten inside his head, praying for patience.

"Call Jackson," I said. "Emerson, you go pick up Fiona. Tell her why I need her. I'm putting on the teakettle."

"Tea? We're running out of time to find Christie, but you're taking the time to make a pot of *tea?*" Greg was furious.

"Yes," I said. "It will just take a minute. It helps me see what I need to see."

He stuck out his jaw and took another breath, then stalked off to call Jackson.

"He took that well, I think," I said.

Emerson chuckled. "Yeah. I think he did."

"Go get Fiona," I said, sobering again. "I don't know why, but we need her. I'll be ready when you get back."

He stood up and pulled me to him, wrapping his arms around me and burying his head in my hair. "You're incredible, you know that?" he murmured.

"You are too." I meant it. It was amazing how he had backed me up, and how after everything we had been through, he was still by my side completely.

"I'm sorry this is how we're spending our engagement night," I whispered.

He pulled back and looked me in the eye, lifting my chin. "Don't be. Remember? I want it all."

I lifted onto my tiptoes and kissed him. "I love you. No matter what happens or how all of this turns out, I need you to know that. I love you, Emerson."

"This is all going to turn out fine," he said. "We're all going to be okay. And I love you too."

He hugged me once more, then pulled away and grabbed his jacket, heading out the door to get Fiona.

I gave myself two seconds to breathe before heading into the kitchen to start the tea. I wished I had his confidence. Because the truth was that my gut was screaming loudly right now, telling me three different things. First, I was running out of time to find Christie. Second, I needed Fiona with me.

And third, that whatever was going to happen tonight was going to change things in a way I couldn't possibly predict.

CHAPTER THIRTY-NINE

Eileen's Journal

I think I screwed up. I went back to the library to do some research on who I could contact in law enforcement, trying to find someone outside of Rosemary Mountain. There was a man who seemed to be watching me. I think he saw my screen. He gave me a look that made me feel like a marked woman.

I'm terrified.

Emerson

I left Daphne with reassuring words, but truth be told, I wasn't at all sure we would all come out of this okay. It felt like we were going into battle, and battle meant one thing—casualties. All I could do was promise myself I would do whatever it took to make sure Daphne wasn't one of them.

Fiona was standing on the front porch, wringing her hands, when I pulled up. I jumped out of the truck and ran up to her.

"I wondered who was coming," she said quietly, worry etched on her wrinkled face. "Is Daphne okay?"

"Daphne's fine," I said, placing a hand on her arm to steady her. "Christie's missing. Daphne talked Greg into taking her to Christie's apartment. She told him about the sight. She says she needs you, too."

Fiona nodded, clearly understanding the gravity of the situation. "Let me grab my bag," she said. She disappeared into her cottage and returned moments later. She locked the front door and followed me to the truck, waiting until we were safely in the cab before asking more questions.

"How's Christie wrapped up in this mess?"

I quickly explained about Mr. Boddy and the phone.

She just shook her head. "Poor Christie. That girl has a knack for getting into trouble, that's for sure."

"She does," I agreed.

"I've got a bad feeling about this," Fiona admitted.

I looked over at her. "I do too," I confessed.

She nodded, then turned her face to look out the window.

I could hear the distinctive hoot of an owl, close enough to be heard even over the sound of my truck on the gravel road.

Fiona just shook her head and repeated her words. "Yes, a mighty bad feeling about this…"

CHAPTER FORTY

Eileen's Journal

Lonnie has a fishing trip scheduled for this weekend. I asked him to cancel it, to stay with me. He chalked it up to anxiety. Anxiety! Said he had been so worried about me lately that he talked to Doc about me. Doc said I probably just had some "postpartum blues" and that he could prescribe some sleeping pills. Postpartum blues! Daphne is three years old, for goodness' sake!

I almost told Lonnie the truth. I opened my mouth and came so close. But then I stopped myself. I told myself it was because I was keeping him safe. But truthfully? Part of me knows, if I tell him the truth, he'll insist on us leaving Rosemary Mountain. He would never feel safe here again. He couldn't bear to think of me and Daphne as even being in hypothetical danger here. And I can't bear to think of leaving. Leaving Fiona and this cottage and land that I love so dearly? Raising our daughter in the city somewhere?

So I didn't tell him, and now he's gone, and I'm wondering if I made a huge mistake.

Daphne

I WAS READY, with a travel thermos of mugwort tea in hand, when Emerson and Fiona arrived. Fiona walked in, her face grave, but her eyes brightened as she spotted the ring on my hand.

"Congratulations, my dear," she said quietly, squeezing me in a hug. "Many, many blessings on you both. Soon, we'll all be celebrating."

"Yes, soon," I said, looking at Emerson. It was clear none of us quite believed it. Tension hung over our heads, worry for what was coming, though none of us seemed willing to say it.

Greg appeared, apparently having been waiting for Emerson's return to step back into the room, as if avoiding being alone with me. Not that I could blame him. I had dropped a lot on him tonight, and I was well aware of how crazy it all sounded. I was just grateful he was willing to at least give me a chance to help find Christie.

None of us said much as we loaded into Greg's truck and headed into town. It seemed we were all too worried. We weren't in the mood for small talk, but we also wanted to avoid the elephant in the room. Greg opened his mouth several times, but then clamped it shut and shook his head, as if he still couldn't quite believe we were in this situation.

As we pulled off of Lonely Oak Road onto the main highway, I saw a flash of lightning in the distance, followed by the low rumble of thunder. I looked at Fiona, who just shook her head.

"Storm's coming," she muttered. We both knew she wasn't talking about the weather.

Greg finally broke the silence, asking for directions to Christie's apartment. I had never been there, but Fiona was well acquainted with it, having served as Christie's midwife. She rattled off the address to him and explained that Christie lived in a makeshift apartment over Marco and Sophia's garage. They had taken her in when her parents had kicked her out of the house for getting pregnant out of wedlock.

The house was dark when we pulled up. I knew Marco and Sophia worked long hours at their restaurant and were rarely home. But it didn't matter. Greg didn't hesitate to break in. Christie had been reported missing and didn't answer the door; that was just cause in his mind.

We ran up the stairs to her apartment entrance. The door stood ajar. Greg pushed it open and flicked on the lights. Before I could even see inside, I felt sick. I knew this feeling, this cold energy of intrusion, of a sanctuary violated and no longer safe.

"Ransacked," Greg announced, holding the door open so we could all come in.

All of Christie's drawers had been searched, left open with clothes spilling out. Boxes were pulled from the top of her closet. The mattress was half off the bed, like someone had searched beneath it. Everything had been touched, moved. My eyes filled with tears. I knew exactly how this felt, and my heart ached for Christie. Her home would never quite feel the same after this.

We heard loud footsteps coming up the stairwell behind us. Greg quickly drew his weapon and moved in front of us, but he put it down when he saw it was just Jackson. He started to give Jackson a rundown, then stopped and looked at me helplessly when he got to the part about why I was there. It was clear it embarrassed him to stoop to such tactics.

"It's okay," I said. "Jackson gets it. He's used me on an investigation, too."

Greg looked at Jackson, who turned slightly pale under his gaze.

"You've, uh, worked with Daphne before?" Greg said, coughing slightly.

Jackson nodded uncertainly. "Yes, sir."

Greg just shook his head. "I see everyone's been keeping secrets from me," he said dryly. "But we'll deal with that later. Finding Christie is the only thing that matters now." He looked at me as if waiting for instantaneous results. As if it were that easy.

"I need a minute," I said. "A few minutes in here to just sit and focus and try to see what happened."

He didn't look happy, but he nodded his agreement. "Fine. Jackson, I need you to go interview Christie's parents. Find out anything you can that might help. I know this is your first missing persons case, but you've trained for this. You know what to do, what to ask."

Jackson nodded. "Yes, sir." He spun on his heels and headed back down the stairs, looking grateful to still be Greg's right-hand man.

"Emerson," Greg said, calling him over. "You're the best tracker I know. Let's go back into the yard and look for anything that might give us a clue as to who ransacked this place and where they might have gone."

Emerson nodded. "Are you going to be okay up here?" he asked, before leaving.

I nodded and gave him my most reassuring smile. He reached for my hand and gave it a squeeze, holding my gaze like he didn't want to walk away. Like he was waiting for me to ask him to stay. But when I didn't, he finally dropped it and headed out after Greg.

I sat down on Christie's bed, finally exhaling. "Fiona. What if I can't do this?"

"Shhhhh," she said, coming to sit beside me. "Just do your thing. It'll come to you."

I leaned over and picked up a pillow that had been unceremoniously thrown on the floor and pulled it toward me, closing my eyes as I focused my intention on seeing what had happened here this evening. Images were just starting to come to me—images of Christie surprised, scared, pulling away from a gloved hand—when I felt Fiona suddenly stand up.

"What are *you* doing here?" she snapped.

I opened my eyes and saw Joe standing in the doorway. I immediately jumped up and stood in front of Fiona, not willing to let him close to her.

"You shouldn't be here," he said, stepping forward.

As he stepped into the light of the room, I saw the gun in his hand.

Chapter Forty-One

Dear Lonnie,

I'm afraid something terrible is going to happen to me, and I don't know how to stop it. I was going to pack Daphne up and head to my parents' house this weekend since you're gone, but my car won't start. Someone tampered with it. I can feel it. I can feel the energy around it. I walked to Fiona's, but she's not home. I don't know what to do.

Hopefully, this feeling will pass and you'll never have reason to see this note. But if something happens to me... If you come home and I'm not here ... take Daphne and run. Keep her safe. Never bring her back here.

Don't trust anyone here. Lonnie, I know you think it's postpartum blues, but it's not. My worries are real. This town is corrupt, and it isn't safe here.

I hope this feeling is wrong and that we can make a plan together when you get back. But if something happens to me, know this, darling. I love you with all my heart, and I am grateful for every moment we had together. You have given me such a wonderful, beautiful life. Take care of our daughter and know that I'll always be watching over you both.

Love,

Eileen

Daphne

FIONA MUST HAVE SEEN Joe's gun too, because she pushed me aside, brandishing her own pistol.

"Whoa," Joe said, lifting his free hand. "I'm not here to hurt you. Really."

Keeping his eyes fixed on hers, he proved the point by sliding his pistol into its holster and holding up his other hand.

"Then why are you here?" she asked, lowering hers as well.

"I'm here to keep you safe, you stubborn woman," he said with just a hint of a smile.

I immediately felt torn. Joe was not a good guy. Yet he was. I had never met anyone so contradictory in nature, and it left me off balance, not knowing what to think of him.

"Some nerve," Fiona sniffed. "I've been doing a mighty fine job of keeping myself safe, thank you very much. And you have an awful lot of explaining to do, Mr. Joe Hemsworth."

"I know," he said, still holding up his hands. His eyes were full of pain. "Look, I've made some mistakes. I'm not going to lie about that. But right now? I'm trying to make them right. Look, you two have to go, okay? You're not safe here."

"Christie's missing," I said. "We're here to help find her."

He shook his head sadly. "If Christie's missing, there's nothing you can do for her now. But there's still time for you to walk away from this. You've got to listen to me."

"Why should I listen to anything you have to say?" I asked, the bitterness spilling out. "For the life of me, I still can't figure out your game."

"There's no game," he said. "Look, I know nothing I say is going to matter to you at this point. But, Daphne, you're in danger. I've tried to protect you, tried to throw you off course, but you're like a damn dog with a bone. Mr. Boddy knows you're getting close. He'll come after you. Daphne, please, listen to me. You don't have to end up like your ma. But if you keep pursuing this, it's going to go badly for you."

He stepped forward, close enough that I could see the pleading—and the truth—in his eyes. "You don't know Mr. Boddy. He's powerful. He's got friends everywhere. There's no going against him and winning. Trust me. I don't like it any more than you do, but the only option is to just get out of his way. So come on. Let's get out of here."

I shook my head. "Joe, you may believe that. But I don't. I believe in justice." It rose up in me, even now. "I will not walk away from this." My voice shook, but I felt stronger inside than I ever had. "Mr. Boddy doesn't get to keep hurting people. We're going to find Christie, and we're going to take him down."

"There is no taking him down!" For once, Joe lost that endless patience. He turned to Fiona, casting his pleading eyes on her. "Fi, talk some sense into her. I know what I'm talking about. You cannot go up against him and win. Now, I've got to get you two out of here before it's too late! There's no time to be stubborn now!"

Fiona shook her head and moved closer to me. "I'm with her, Joe. Justice has been a long time coming, and we're not walking away now."

Joe reached out and grabbed my arm, apparently intent on dragging me out of there. But when he touched me, the room faded away again, and I immediately dropped into a vision—a vision of Joe and Mr. Boddy meeting together, only hours before.

He dropped my arm like a hot coal. "You saw," he whispered, staring at me.

I nodded slowly. In that moment, all the clues fell into place. The drugs, the power, the blackmail, the money, the money laundering, the people in his pocket. Mr. Boddy wasn't just a drug lord. He was a modern-day version of The Godfather. A real-life Sicilian crime boss who controlled everything and everyone around him.

Mr. Boddy was none other than Marco himself, the muscled family man from Sicily that I had adored since I had met him on my very first night in Rosemary Mountain. I had moved here looking for my mother's killer and never imagined my first meal here had been prepared by the man who'd murdered her.

I sat down heavily on the bed, in shock.

"Do you see now why we have to go?" Joe said, frantic. "He doesn't mess around. I've seen what his people do. He's protected, Daphne. There's no taking him down. All we can do is protect ourselves now."

"Hold up," Fiona said, irritation in her voice. "Seems I've been left out of the loop. Who is this Mr. Boddy after all?"

"I'm afraid I am, my dear," came his voice, from the doorway.

I jumped and grabbed Fiona, as a loud noise rang out and Joe toppled to the floor, dead.

Marco stepped out from the shadows, a look of disgust on his face as he surveyed the room, before his eyes finally landed on Joe's body. One of his men had already swooped in, taking Fiona's pistol from her as smoothly as if they had practiced it, before disappearing again out of the room.

"My apologies for the mess," he said smoothly, in his strong Italian accent. "I'm working with some new boys who haven't yet learned the art of discretion."

I saw a tall form standing back in the doorway. The darkness masked him, but even so, I knew. It was Luke. My heart fell and rose at the same time. Heartbreak for him and what he was doing now, and hope—hope because deep down I believed Luke had goodness in his heart. Maybe, just maybe, Luke would protect us.

Marco snapped his fingers, and Luke walked into the room like a dog, with his head down. He refused to look in my direction.

"Where's Christie?" I asked. I refused to show fear, no matter what Marco was used to.

"Your little friend is fine," Marco said, waving a hand. "She simply needed to be educated on her role within this family. She has been a child, protected. It is time for her to grow up."

My blood ran cold as I wondered what that meant for Christie. It didn't sound good.

"Unfortunately," he said, looking me over, "I'm afraid we don't have a role for you in the family. Your particular values don't, shall we say, mix well with our own." He shrugged, as if he were doing nothing more than turning me down for a business opportunity.

"Is that why you killed my mother?" I asked.

Marco pulled a cigarette out of his pocket and lit it, taking a long drag before answering my question. "Your mother," he said, "refused to be educated on how this town works. I gave her an opportunity to work for me."

He grinned suddenly. "Can you imagine what we could have done together with her abilities? The money we could have made." He shrugged again, then smiled coldly. "But she thinks I have no morals. I have morals. My morals are loyalty. Family. I have given my family a good life. I protect those who are loyal to me. She could have given her family a good life too, but she chose differently."

"So you killed her because she wouldn't work for you? Wouldn't help you get away with selling drugs?" I was shaking with fury.

"People like drugs. Drugs make them happy and take away their pain for a little while. If I can make a good living off of that, provide nice things for my family, what's the harm?" He shrugged again.

"People were dying," I said, still shaking. "What's the harm? They were *dying*."

"Everyone dies, *piccolo ragazza*. I gave your mother a choice. Drop her misguided sense of morals and work for me, like everyone else in this town. Or don't." He shrugged again, as if he were being completely fair. "Your mother is one of the few people who have ever told me no. I didn't like that, at all. She had no respect. So I gave her another choice. One she couldn't say no to."

"What choice was that?" I asked, my voice quivering. I wanted to control it, but I couldn't.

He shrugged. "Simple. I took you, my dear. Sweet, innocent little Daphne. And then I gave her a choice. She would either take the pills I offered and have a painless death, knowing you were safe. I am, after all, a man of my word. Or she would live a life of guilt and pain, knowing we had sold her daughter to the highest bidder when she could have prevented all of it."

His words shocked me. Tears filled my eyes.

"You threatened her with me," I whispered. "You're a cruel, horrid man."

"Yes," he said, shrugging. "I suppose you think so. Self-preservation, my dear. I knew she would make the right choice. Family is everything. She and I agreed on that, at least. And I kept my word. A painless death for her, safety for you."

My head dropped, tears falling, as I thought of my mother, who had been offered the worst choice imaginable. She had given up her life, hoping it would protect mine. She had never chosen to leave me. She had been forced to, by the heartless man standing in front of me.

"Now, I'm afraid," he said, "I won't be offering you a position within the family. I already know your answer." He looked toward Luke. "I trust you to handle this. Make sure you dispose of her body properly. We need no more questions. We have enough of a mess to clean up already," he said, eyeing Joe's body with disgust.

Marco looked toward Fiona with fondness in his eyes. "I've always liked you, Fiona. We've always gotten along, you and I, haven't we? Shall we come to an agreement? Or are you going to choose death, too?"

"I'm with Daphne," she said stubbornly.

His expression filled with regret. "Well, I am disappointed but not particularly surprised. Luke, that gives you two to take care of. Are you up for the task, or do I need to call in Billy?"

"I can handle it, boss," Luke said, still looking down.

"Excellent." He patted Luke's face proudly.

I saw the flash of warmth in Luke's eyes. This kid in a grown man's body who had always hungered for love and acceptance had finally found it in a criminal organization. I realized then that getting through to Luke would be harder than I had expected, but I still had to hope. There was a seed of goodness inside him. I was sure of it.

Marco stood and watched as Luke tied up Fiona first, apparently wanting to make sure Luke really could handle it. I understood why. Fiona had a reputation for being feisty, and had it only been us and Luke in the room, we certainly would have tried to overpower him. But not even I would dare try that with Marco watching.

When Luke had us both tied up, Marco nodded his approval and gestured for Luke to take us out of the room first.

"Ladies, please don't try to run," Marco said coolly as we passed him. "Getting shot in the back is quite painful, not to mention the mess. I'd prefer to spare you both that. But make no mistake, we won't hesitate to shoot if you run."

Neither Fiona nor I said anything in reply, but we exchanged glances and it was clear we were both thinking the same thing. We wouldn't run. We would take our chances with Luke once we were away from Marco.

Marco followed us outside. I tried to be discreet, but I couldn't help but look around quickly, hoping Greg and Emerson were nearby and would come to our rescue.

Unfortunately, Marco noticed and smirked. "I'm afraid the men you are looking for have already been dealt with. They were, perhaps, unaware that I have bodyguards stationed around my house at all times. Perhaps you will meet again in the next life."

His words were a dagger through my heart. A sob escaped before I could stop it. *No. Not Emerson.* Nothing he could have said would have broken me more. I looked at Marco, then Luke, with tears flowing from my eyes. I felt stunned beyond belief, shattered beyond repair. Luke looked away, refusing to meet my eyes, but Marco just shrugged again.

"There, there," he said. "It will all be over soon. Sleep well, ladies."

Luke opened the back door to a car, motioning for us to climb in. Fiona went first, and I climbed in after her, somehow feeling both numb and in the worst pain of my life.

Emerson was dead.

And soon I would be too.

CHAPTER FORTY-TWO

Daphne

Lightning continued to flash in the distance as Luke drove us out of town, toward the mountain. I slumped back in my seat, tears falling as I thought of Emerson.

Fiona nudged me. When I looked toward her, she gave me a piercing stare. She didn't say a word, but she didn't have to. I could see it written all over her face. *Don't give up. We can still fight.* I nodded numbly. But I was losing faith. Joe, Greg, and Emerson were all dead, and we were stuck with Luke, who was clearly eager to prove himself to Mr. Boddy. Any hope I'd initially felt about getting him on our side was long gone.

Luke drove us up a twisty road I hadn't yet been on. I kept my eyes open for houses, other cars, or anyone we could signal, but we appeared to be in the middle of literally nowhere. This road seemed rarely traveled, with no sign of human activity that I could see.

After a while, he pulled off onto yet another rural road, this one even less maintained than the first. The road quickly came to a dead end, where he stopped the car and told us to get out.

We obeyed, and my senses quickened as I looked for an opportunity to escape. But I couldn't see one. We could run into the woods, sure, and if we managed to stay together, Fiona could probably get us through the night. But Luke had a gun pointed straight at us. I didn't like the odds of running for cover.

"Luke," I began. "You don't have to do this, you know."

He looked at me like I was stupid. "Yeah, I do. I work for Marco now. I don't have a choice."

"You always have choices," I said. But I could see from his face that nothing I said was ever going to make him believe that. He had spent his entire life feeling trapped. Nothing was going to change that now.

He shoved a flashlight into Fiona's bound hands, grabbed additional ropes from his trunk, then motioned the gun toward the edge of the woods. "Walk," he said, waiting for us to obey.

I hesitated, but Fiona just sighed and walked to the tree line, quickly making her way down a trail I hadn't even seen. I followed her, realizing she at least knew where we were. That knowledge gave me the tiniest spark of hope. If Fiona knew the terrain, she might have a plan.

I followed her down the trail, with Luke falling in line behind me, still pointing his pistol directly at my back.

"Where are we going?" I asked. I wasn't at all sure I wanted to hear the answer, but if I could get Luke talking, maybe it would at least be a distraction.

Luke didn't answer though. After a pause, Fiona answered for him.

"Dead Man's Cave," she called out from the front. "Isn't that right, Luke?"

He grunted, the only acknowledgement he would give.

"Dead Man's Cave?" I asked. The name sent an icy chill down my back.

"That's right," she said. "It's a downright beautiful cave up here, in good weather at least. A favorite exploration place—and make-out spot —for teenagers. At least it used to be. Problem is, it floods. Heavy rains come, the passages flood. Over the years, more than one person has drowned here. All assumed to be unsuspecting hikers who didn't know better, or idiots who came up here without checking the weather, or just poor saps who got caught in a freak downpour that nobody knew was coming."

She went quiet for a minute.

"Luke, I'm guessing we were assuming wrong, at least about some of those poor folks?"

Luke stayed silent, but I realized what she was saying. It would be an easy way to cover up a crime, and it would avoid the "mess" Marco seemed to detest.

"Yeah, I'm guessing I know Luke's plan," Fiona continued, seemingly unafraid of riling him up. "Probably going to tie us up in that cave and just wait for the water to rise, aren't you, Luke? Storm's a comin', that's for sure." She just shook her head.

"Drowning isn't that bad," Luke finally said in a quiet voice, confirming her suspicions. "It's over quick."

His words chilled me to the bone, but it also gave me another way to appeal to him. He was trapped alright, but unless Marco had specifically told him to deal with us here, it meant he had chosen a relatively hands-off way to kill us. Drowning seemed like a horrible way to go from where I was sitting, but he had chosen what he considered to be a humane death. It meant he still had a heart. Maybe I could reach it.

"Luke," I began. "I know you feel trapped. I know that. You're probably scared of what Marco will do to you if you don't follow orders. But I also know you. You're not a bad guy. You are *not* your dad. Luke, I don't believe you want to kill us, because in your heart, you're good too, like Matthew. We can help you. Together, we can take Marco down. You'll see. You don't have to be trapped anymore."

His temper flared. "You don't know anything!"

I forced myself to remain calm and ignore the gun he was still pointing right at me. "I know you've had a really hard life and you probably don't see a lot of options, but—"

"But *nothing*!" he yelled. "You don't understand. This is my job now. There's no escaping Marco."

I could feel the despair and the fear in his voice. "Luke—"

"*Shut up*! Don't talk anymore. Just walk." He pressed the gun into my spine, reminding me of who was in charge here.

I clamped my lips shut and kept walking, praying for another way.

We continued tramping through the woods. I soon heard water trickling, and before I knew it, we were walking beside a small stream. The trees had parted, and the moonlight reflected off the water, briefly illuminating our path. Within minutes, clouds covered the moon and our only extra light was the occasional flash of lightning in the distance, a reminder that the storm—and the flash floods that would surely accompany it—were coming soon. We continued to head upstream, and before long, Fiona's flashlight hit upon the small mouth of a cave at the top.

"We're here," she said, as Luke and I caught up to her.

He nodded, motioning with the gun. "Inside."

From where we were, I wasn't sure how we would even get inside, but as we got closer, I realized the entrance was bigger than I had realized. We had to stoop at first, but just a few feet inside, the cave opened up and we could stand in the small cavern. Fiona moved the flashlight around, giving me a look at our surroundings.

"There," Luke said, pointing his own flashlight at some boulders sitting in the middle of the stream that ran through the cave.

"What do you mean, 'there'?" Fiona asked, a twinge of sarcasm in her voice.

"Go, sit there by the boulder," Luke said. I could tell it pained him a little.

"Luke," I began, thinking I might try to appeal to him one more time.

He cut me off immediately. "Shut up," he said, refusing to look at me. "I mean it. Don't talk to me. Just go sit there."

Fiona shot me a warning glance and immediately moved to comply. She shuffled through the shallow water of the stream and plopped down in the water, leaning up against one of the boulders. How could she just give up like this? I looked at Luke, still holding the pistol, and wondered if I could take him down myself. There was a good chance I would get shot in the process, but it might give Fiona time to get away. I didn't care what happened to me anymore, but I had to at least give her a chance.

The faint sound of rain filled the cavern.

"Come on, Daphne," Fiona said. "Let's get on with this. The rains are coming. Luke needs to get out of here." There was a slight warning in her voice.

I couldn't understand why she was complying, but all I could do was trust her. Maybe she had a plan. Maybe she was going to knock him out when he tied us up. Maybe ... maybe anything. I looked at the gun and realized I didn't have much of a choice anyway. Even if I successfully tackled him, I couldn't do much damage with my hands bound before he killed me.

I trudged through the stream, noting that it had already risen at least two inches. I looked at Fiona, who gave me a reassuring smile.

"There, there," she said. "It's alright now. At least we're together in the end. Sit there, across from me, so we can have one last good chat. Luke, since we're cooperating, you will leave the light for us, won't you?"

He looked at her then nodded, taking her flashlight and sitting it carefully on one of the taller boulders so it would give us some light in the cavern.

I sat down across from Fiona, like she'd said, and watched as she sat calmly, allowing Luke to tie her to the boulder. The sound of rain came heavier, and the water rose again. Everything in me felt numb as Luke moved to me and tied me up too, wrapping rope completely around me, lashing me to the boulder at my back.

Luke backed up and looked at both of us with sadness in his eyes. "I am sorry," he said softly.

"Don't be sorry," I said. "Just help us! It's not too late."

But he held my gaze a moment, then dropped his eyes and turned, walking away from us.

As soon as he stepped away, I began straining at the ropes, hoping to get loose, but they were solid. I could move my hands, so I pulled and tugged where I could, but all the knots were behind me and he hadn't left me any wiggle room. Meanwhile, the water was continuing to rise. Fiona sat there, quietly watching Luke make his way out of the cave as if she had accepted her fate. Despair filled my heart, and I finally cried out.

"I'm so sorry, Fiona," I cried. "This is all my fault. I knew I shouldn't have gotten you into this. I'm so, so sorry."

I hung my head and started sobbing, racked with grief, guilt, and fear. I couldn't believe it was going to end this way. My worst fears had come true. I had gotten Emerson, Greg, and Joe killed, and now Fiona and I were going to die too. Joe had been right. There was no going against Marco and winning. I never should have started this fight, never should have thought I could somehow be the one to get justice after all these years. All of it was for nothing now. Marco would go free, and we were all dead.

"If you're done," Fiona said dryly, "could you be a dear and help me?"

I looked up at her, tears still running down my face. "What?"

She wiggled, pushing her foot closer to my hand. "There's a knife hidden in my boot," she said. "I can't reach it, obviously. See if you can get your hand in there and cut us loose. Hurry now. This stream is going to be a raging river here in a minute. Luke stayed around too long to give us the window of time I was hoping for."

I stared at her for half a second before laughing in joy. Of course she had a hidden knife. She'd had a plan all along. Fiona Flanagan would never willingly walk to her death without a plan of escape.

I strained my arm, stretching my hand so I could get my fingers inside the top of her boot. I quickly found the knife and eased it out, slicing my finger in the process. It didn't matter though. A cut was nothing compared to drowning.

"Be careful. Don't drop it," she warned.

I nodded, afraid to speak. If I dropped it, it would be gone instantly, washed away in the stream, which was getting faster by the minute. I carefully got my grip around the knife before pulling it completely out of her boot, breathing a sigh of relief.

"Can you cut yourself free?" she asked.

"I'll try," I replied, already working to bend my arm underneath the ropes. After a minute of effort, I was able to get the bottom rope cut, which gave me the momentum and movement to keep working up. Soon, I was free. I immediately moved to Fiona and cut her free as well, feeling unbelievable relief. We were going to live after all.

"We've got to hurry," Fiona warned as I helped her stand. The water was already halfway up our calves and moving faster by the moment. She grabbed the flashlight and started moving downstream toward the mouth of the cave.

I followed her, still overjoyed, but in my relief, I failed to pay attention to my footing in the treacherous water. I slipped on a rock and slammed down hard, feeling my leg snap as I did. The rushing water swept me away, washing me downstream until I was stuck, pinned against a boulder. I was an animal caught in a trap, frantic and scared, unable to free myself.

Fiona rushed to me, trying to pull me up, but her efforts were futile. The leg I'd fallen on was useless, shattered, and the rushing water had me completely trapped. Fiona pulled desperately, yelling at me to get up. I used everything within me to try to move, clawing with my arms and pushing with my good leg, but it was no use.

Our eyes met, the truth of the situation reflected in both of them.

"Go," I said, my voice strained. "Go get help. I'll be fine until you get back."

It was a lie, and we both knew it.

She shook her head no. "We've got to get you out of here. Come on. Try again!" She pushed helplessly against the boulder that had me pinned. The water continued to rise, and I couldn't let her waste another minute on me.

"Fiona," I said, grabbing her sweater and forcing her to look at me again. "You have to go. Please. I need to know you made it out of here."

She looked back at me, tears filling her own eyes now. She shook her head no, but when I repeated my plea, she finally nodded.

"There's a hunting cabin not far from here," she said, "off the beaten path. A man named Murphy usually stays there this time of year. I'll go for him. I'll hurry. You just hang on now, okay?"

I nodded, but we both knew the truth. There wasn't time to go for Murphy. The water was rising, and soon I would drown, just like Luke had planned.

"Fiona, thank you. For everything." There weren't words to explain what she meant to me, or how grateful I was to have found her again. But I knew she understood.

She touched her forehead to mine, then hurried from the cave, leaving me alone in the darkness.

CHAPTER FORTY-THREE

Daphne

ALONE IN THE DARK, I FELT NUMB. I HAD FAILED EVERYONE—
Eileen, Emerson, Fiona. Greg. Christie. All this loss of life, and for
what? There would be no justice. Marco would continue ruling Rosemary Mountain, killing anyone who stood in his way.

My last remaining hope was that Fiona would make it. And maybe,
just maybe, she could find a way to bring justice to Marco. If not, maybe
she could at least escape him. Go somewhere new, start over. A horrid
price to pay at her age. But at least she had a chance to live. I was so
grateful for that.

The water was up to my chest now. It wouldn't be much longer. I
hoped Fiona wouldn't carry any guilt for being unable to save me. None
of this was her fault, and I prayed she had the wisdom to know that. I
didn't want her to feel even one minute of guilt for any of it.

I don't want to die. That was the truth. Even knowing it was hope-
less, everything in me wanted to fight, to push, to free myself. I tried one
last time, pushing as hard as I could with my broken leg. Sharp, almost
unbearable pain shot into my hip, but I didn't budge.

The water rose to my shoulders. I closed my eyes and saw my mother's face, warm and welcoming. She was proud of me, even though I'd failed. I would be with her soon, with her and Emerson, in whatever came after this world. I wasn't sure what that looked like, but I felt certain we would be together. I clung to the rock and tried to breathe, tried to maintain some sort of dignity here at the end.

Suddenly, the cavern was flooded with light, and I heard shouting. I lifted my head, wondering if I had already died, because the voice I heard was the one I longed to hear more than anything else in the world. *Emerson.*

"Daphne!" The beam of his flashlight fell on me as he ran toward me.

"Emerson!" My eyes filled with tears again—happy tears this time.

He splashed through the water, reaching me, and I wrapped my arm around his neck, crying out in joy and relief.

"I thought you were dead!" I cried out.

"I nearly was. But no time for that now. We've got to get you out of here!"

I nodded, hoping beyond hope he would be strong enough to move the boulder. "I'm stuck," I said. "My leg... I think it's broken. I'm trapped."

Emerson pushed against the boulder, but it was futile. He wrapped his arms around me, trying to tug me free as I pushed against the rock, but still I didn't move. Suddenly, he dove underwater, using his hands to feel, to push, to pull.

"I can't move it," he said when he resurfaced, panic in his voice. "It's not moving. Your leg's wedged underneath somehow."

The water was rising faster now, and I was straining to keep my head above it.

Hope faded as I realized that, even with him here, there was no rescue for me. There just wasn't enough time. Even if they amputated my leg to free me, it would take too long. My time was up.

"You have to go," I said, crying again.

"I'm not leaving you," he said, grabbing my face in his wet hands. The water was raging higher now, pushing harder as the force of it pressed us both against the boulder.

"You have to," I cried. "You'll drown too. Go. It's okay." I was sobbing now, but not from fear. Saying goodbye to him was the hardest thing I had ever done, but I was so grateful he was alive. All I needed was to know he would be okay. I kissed him and held him close one last time, even as a sudden rush of water washed over our faces, leaving us gasping for air.

"I will not leave you," he said fiercely, refusing to let me go. "I've left you before, and I promised you I would never do it again. You can't give up. I'm not going anywhere. We'll find a way." He pushed against the boulder again, another futile move, as I begged him to leave.

I grabbed my mugwort necklace, praying that Emerson would leave and be safe. I saw my mother's face again, her warm smile. She looked at me with pride and sadness, then said goodbye and turned away from me. As she walked away, the cave rumbled. A massive swell of water hit, submerging us both, suddenly jarring the boulder out of place. My head came up, and I gasped for air as the rushing water washed us out the entrance of the cave. Emerson grabbed on to me and swam for both our lives, somehow managing to grab the bank. He heaved me and my shattered leg out of the stream, onto the safety of land, then collapsed as we both coughed up water and took painful, beautiful breaths of air.

"Are you okay?" he asked, rolling toward me, checking me over with his hands, as shocked as I was that we were both alive.

"I'm okay," I gasped. "What... What happened?"

He looked back toward the dark cave entrance. "I think one of the limestone walls gave way, and all the water behind it came out at once." He shook his head. "Daphne, I was so scared. I thought..."

"I know," I said, grabbing his hand. "But we're okay. We're really okay." I reached up again, holding the necklace in my hands, and remembered Eileen's look as she'd walked away. "I think it was her," I whispered.

There was no way I could walk, so Emerson put me on his back and carried me down the trail to where Greg's truck was parked. The pain was excruciating, but I didn't mind it. It meant I was alive.

We were both too exhausted to talk much, but he managed to explain that two of Marco's men had ambushed him and Greg, but

Marco had apparently given orders to not harm them. Yet. From what Emerson could gather, Marco's plan had been to talk to Greg personally and come to the same kind of arrangement he had with Joe. But Greg and Emerson had used Marco's orders to their advantage and had overcome their captors and escaped. They had tracked my cell phone, which Luke had stupidly kept in his car, and arrived at the trailhead just as Luke was returning. Luke refused to tell them where Fiona and I were, so Emerson had set off on the trail alone, using his tracking skills, while Greg held Luke and called Jackson in as backup.

Greg was pacing the trailhead, rain be damned, when we arrived. Visible relief flooded his face when he saw us.

"Thank God," he breathed, shaking his head. "Jackson's almost here. Where's Fiona?"

"She went in search of a man named Murphy," I said.

Greg grimaced. "Old Man Murphy. That's just what this night needs." He shook his head in annoyance, but I could tell he was relieved Fiona was okay.

Meanwhile, we had Luke in custody, but we were all anxious to find Marco—and Christy. Greg had apparently been trying to get Luke to talk the entire time he was waiting for Emerson to return, but Luke refused to say a word.

"Let me talk to him," I said.

Greg shot me a look. "You need emergency medical treatment ASAP," he said, shaking his head.

"It's on the way, isn't it? If I'm going to wait here for them to arrive, let me talk to him in the meantime," I insisted.

Greg didn't have it in him to argue with me anymore, so I talked Emerson into carrying me over to Greg's truck, where Luke was handcuffed in the back seat. Emerson placed me in the driver's seat, taking care not to jar my leg too much. Then he walked around to the passenger side and climbed in. He refused to leave me alone with the man who had just tried to kill me. I didn't mind. We had both nearly lost each other tonight; neither one of us wanted to take any more chances.

"Luke," I began. "I know you're terrified of Marco, but you've got to help us."

He glared at me. "I don't have to do anything. You saw what he did to Katie. He got to her, even in jail. And she wasn't even part of his family. You wouldn't believe what he does to his own people if they turn their backs on him. I'm a dead man if I talk about him."

"I'm pretty sure you're a dead man either way," I said. It wasn't a ploy. If Marco had killed Katie, a woman who wasn't even connected to him, because of what she *might* know, there was no way he would let Luke live.

"He'll protect me if I'm faithful," Luke said, his jaw set.

"You screwed up, Luke," I said, deciding to take a different tack with him. "They gave you one job, and you failed. I'm alive. Fiona's alive. And we have one mission—taking Marco down. Do you really think he's going to go easy on you for letting us get away?"

I could see the fear in his face, but he still refused to speak.

Suddenly, it didn't matter. Because as he sat there thinking over his mistakes, I saw them too.

I looked at Emerson. "Get Greg. I just had a vision. I know where Christie is."

Chapter Forty-Four

Daphne

A week later, I was finally released from the hospital. It had taken more than one surgery to fix my shattered femur, and I had weeks of recovery still ahead of me. But I was alive, and so were Emerson and Fiona. That was all that mattered.

The day I got out of the hospital, Emerson drove me straight home. When we pulled up to my cottage, all lovely and green on what felt like the first true day of spring, I saw Mom and Fiona standing together on the front porch underneath a welcome home banner. Emerson had built a ramp for the wheelchair I would need for a few more weeks, and there was a new table and chairs on the porch, covered in what appeared to be a beautiful lunch spread.

Emerson came around to my door and helped me into the wheelchair, then wheeled me up onto the porch. I couldn't stop smiling, so happy to see everyone.

"Mom, what are you doing here?" I asked. "I thought you went home yesterday."

"I lied," she said, smiling. "I know you don't really need me here, with Emerson and Fiona helping you, but..."

"It's nice to have you here," I said, returning her smile. She squeezed my hand then busied herself at the table, straightening items needlessly and pouring glasses of lemonade.

"What is all this?" I asked.

"A party, silly," Fiona cackled, handing me a cupcake. "Eat. You're too skinny."

"Hospital food is terrible," I commented before immediately diving into the cupcake. As usual, it was delicious. "You're an incredible cook, Fiona."

"Thank you, but Janet made those."

I looked over, impressed. "Baking again? Wow."

Mom just blushed and kept fiddling with the tablecloth. I realized why when Greg's truck pulled into the driveway. I looked over at Mom, who was studiously keeping her eyes fixed on the table, as if rearranging the forks was the most important thing in the world. I couldn't help but grin. Maybe Emerson was right. Maybe it wouldn't be the worst thing in the world if they got together.

Greg and Jackson both climbed out of the truck, gifts in hand. They walked up and handed them to Mom, who blushed as she said hello. Then she turned away quickly to place them on a separate table I hadn't noticed yet.

"Gifts?" I asked, still confused about what was happening.

"It's an engagement party, Daphne," Mom said. "Or did you forget about that?"

I looked down at the emerald sparkling on my finger. "No, I definitely didn't forget about that." I looked up at Emerson, who grinned at me with that warm grin I loved so much. "I'm just surprised! But..."

"But what?" Fiona asked.

"Well, I hate to ruin the party mood, but since everyone's here, can you fill me in on what's happening?" I looked from Greg to Jackson, then back again.

Nobody had given me much of an update in the hospital, due to the doctor being adamant that they shouldn't work me up. Of course, the only thing working me up was not knowing where everything stood. Emerson had given me the basics, of course—yes, Joe was dead. He had died instantly from a gunshot wound to the head. They'd found

Christie, and she was safe, all things considered. Luke was in custody. But that was all Emerson seemed to know, and it still didn't answer my biggest questions. Would there finally be justice for Eileen after all these years?

Greg glanced at Emerson, who nodded. I just rolled my eyes. This fragile patient treatment had to end soon or I would lose my mind.

"Well," Greg said, "we know what we're dealing with now. As hard as it is to believe, Marco was a legitimate Sicilian crime boss, hiding right here in Rosemary Mountain. He moved here back in the nineties, when their heyday was over. He was content playing small compared to some of the big guys, which is probably why his operation went undetected for so long. Well, that and he was exceptionally good at getting people in his pocket."

I shook my head. "That's crazy. I mean, I know that kind of thing is real, but you just don't expect it here, in a place like Rosemary Mountain."

Greg nodded. "Yep, which was another point in his favor. Their chief business was drugs—no surprise there, although they dabbled in other crimes as well. The pizzeria was used to transport their product. It and the church were both used for money laundering. From what I gather, Don didn't have any connection to Marco until he moved here in shame after getting in trouble at his previous church. Marco saw a golden opportunity. He waited for Don to mess up again, then black-mailed him with it in order to take over that church and expand his money laundering capabilities. And since Marco kept Don supplied with women and money, I think they both enjoyed the arrangement."

I glanced at Jackson, who was standing a bit separate from everyone. He still hadn't made eye contact with me since arriving.

"Russell Sharp... Was he involved?" I asked.

Greg glanced back at Jackson too, who met his gaze with an embarrassed look. "No. Turns out he has a solid alibi for the night Eileen died. He was spending the night in the county jail for disorderly conduct. As far as we can tell, he didn't have any connection to Marco's operation. I feel certain Joe was just using him as a patsy to throw you off Marco's trail."

I looked back at Jackson, who still looked highly uncomfortable. My heart went out to him. I knew it was going to take him a while to be okay with everyone knowing his history. He had been so scared of those demons for so long. I only hoped he soon learned that none of us cared who his biological father was. We cared about Jackson, not Jackson's past.

"What about Reverend Pierce?" I asked, turning my attention back to Greg.

Greg nodded confirmation. "Another move by Marco. Pierce skipped town as soon as we took Marco into custody. He was definitely a member of the organization. Word is Matthew is being reinstated as pastor, along with a completely new board of his choosing. He's dismissed everyone who had anything whatsoever to do with the finances or hiring in the past."

"Well, that's one relief," I said. Matthew seemed like a good man. I hoped he would be successful in cleaning up the mess made before him.

"Luke still won't talk," Greg continued. "Not surprising, but I'm hopeful he'll change his mind eventually. Doc Rogers is facing charges for covering up deaths for Marco. He actually *is* talking. I think after Katie's death, he doesn't even care what happens to him now. He just wants someone to pay. And in good news, we searched Joe's house. Joe kept a lot of evidence around, which is how I've been able to learn as much as I have. I guess Joe was hedging his bets. We were able to find out the names of several people in Marco's employ, some of his drug trafficking contacts, and more."

"More?" I asked.

Greg looked me in the eye. "Joe made a tape years ago. A recording. It has Marco talking about Eileen's death after the fact. Marco handled it himself, and we have audio proof of that. Joe knew nothing about it beforehand, but he agreed to help him cover it up."

I let out a breath. So it was done. We knew for sure who killed Eileen, we had proof, and justice would be served. Joe had known the truth all along and had hidden it from me. I was still angry about that, but I also understood it. He had feared Marco, too. In the end, I wanted to believe he really was trying to protect me and Fiona.

I was relieved, but Greg looked distinctly uncomfortable. I stared at him for a minute, my relief vanishing.

"What are you not telling me?" I asked.

Greg let out a breath. "Marco's in FBI custody now. He may be a big fish in Rosemary Mountain, but he's small beans in the grand scheme of things. With Doc Rogers and Joe in his pocket, he flew under the radar for years, but we're pretty sure he has ties to the big guys. Daphne, it's out of my hands."

"Yeah, but the FBI is going to prosecute, right?"

"It's out of my hands," he repeated. "I'll do my part here to cooperate with them and see that we uncover as much as we can about his operation. But if prosecutors decide to give him a deal in order to go after someone bigger..." He lifted his hands helplessly.

I sat back, the wind knocked out of me. I had never imagined it might end like this. I knew the truth, and for that, I was grateful. But it wasn't up to me to get justice after all. That was in the hands of someone else, and there was nothing I could do about it.

Fiona came over and put a hand on my shoulder. "We know the truth," she said quietly. "You did right by your mama. Everyone knows the truth about why she did what she did now, that she didn't take her own life. She gave it up to protect you. Even if Marco gets some kind of deal, his life will never be the same. It's over for him, Daphne. He doesn't rule this town anymore. And that's something to be proud of."

"You should also be proud of saving Christie's life," Greg added. "We would never have found her if you hadn't told us where to look. Marco may have been planning to let her live, but the life he had in mind for her was no life at all." Based on the look on his face, I didn't even want to ask.

I shook my head in disbelief. "He seemed so concerned about her when I was investigating Don's murder. He had me so fooled. I thought he and Sophia genuinely cared about her. They seemed like just a sweet older couple, acting as honorary godparents to her and her baby. I mean, they took her in when she had no place to go!"

Greg nodded. "In Marco's mind, as Don's mistress, she was part of the family, especially since she was carrying Don's baby. Remember, Don had become an important member of the organization, and that baby was blood family to Don. So they were both protected."

"Protected," I said, shaking my head. "Protected until he kidnapped her."

Greg sighed. "Marco has his own sense of morals, and family is his number-one priority. But when Christie became a threat to him, he put her in her place. He offered her a deal first. Gave her a chance to become a mistress for one of the other members of the family. She was shocked, of course, having been totally blind to the truth of who Don and Marco were. The idea of becoming a mistress repulsed her. It was one thing when it was Don, someone she thought she was in love with. The idea of being a kept woman by a man she barely knew was a different story, and she told him what he could do with it. So he was going to, in his words, educate her."

I shuddered. "I'm so glad she's okay."

"She's okay because of you," Greg repeated, pressing the point. "What you've done here is important. I don't want you to ever forget that."

"But it's also my fault she was in danger to begin with," I said. "I'm the one who told Joe she had the cell phone."

Greg shook his head. "I don't think Joe told Marco. I'm guessing if you gave him the phone, he would have added it to his collection of evidence and told you he couldn't trace it. Christie told us she brought the phone to work and confided in Sophia about the whole thing. Sophia told Marco, and you know the rest."

Emerson walked over and took my hand, bringing it to his lips for a kiss. "They're right, sweetheart. You can't blame yourself for what happened. Christie trusted the wrong people repeatedly. You saved her life. Don't get down because you can't control what's going to happen now. You should be proud of what you've done."

I suddenly remembered something else. "When Marco told Luke to kill us, he asked if Luke could do it himself or if he needed to bring in Billy. Was he talking about Bill Brinksley's son?"

Greg shot me a strange look. "I don't know. We haven't come across a Billy yet. But we'll look into it."

"Okay." I sat back again and breathed.

They were right. There was nothing else I could do now. I had come to Rosemary Mountain to find the truth about what happened to my mother, and I had succeeded. Nobody would ever again say she killed herself. And like Fiona had said, it was over for Marco. He would no longer rule this town. It might not be the justice he deserved, but there was justice there, just the same.

I looked at the table and saw the beautiful bouquet of spring flowers sitting on it. "This is a beautiful party," I said, "and I'm so grateful you all came. I can't wait to put all of this to bed and celebrate the future with you. But there's one thing I need to do first."

Emerson looked at me questioningly.

"I think I know," Fiona said quietly. She took the bouquet of flowers and handed them to me. "Load her back up in the truck, Emerson. I'll give you directions."

We pulled up to the tiny graveyard. I had avoided it the whole time I had lived here. I had been afraid of what I would feel—or maybe afraid I might feel nothing at all. But it was time.

Emerson helped me out of the truck and back into the wheelchair, then he pushed it down the pathway, following Fiona's directions. Toward the back of the cemetery, underneath an oak tree, was a small tombstone. *Eileen Sullivan. Beloved wife and mother.*

The tears started falling as I read the words. I gave the flowers to Emerson, who placed them at the foot of the little stone. I closed my eyes, wondering if I could feel her here.

But I couldn't feel anything different here at all. And suddenly, I realized that was okay. Because she wasn't here, waiting for me. She had been with me all along, watching over me.

She always would be.

We returned to the party and celebrated the future with our friends —our chosen family. As the party finally dispersed, with the sun setting behind the trees, a light rain began falling over Rosemary Mountain. I leaned against Emerson, his hand on my shoulder, and sighed. It felt like a cleansing rain. A fresh start for us—and for the town we both loved.

At that moment, a rainbow appeared in the sky and I knew everything was really going to be okay.

Epilogue
One Year Later...

"Almost there now," Fiona's voice came, soothing me even in this state.

"I can't do it anymore," I begged.

"Yes, you can. You're the strongest person I know. Emerson, tell her."

My husband looked down at me, his deep-brown eyes meeting mine with a love so fierce, so deep, it eased the pain racking through my body.

"You've got this," he said, squeezing my hand. "Almost there."

I nodded, gaining strength from his.

"That's right!" Fiona called out. "Just one more push, girly, and I think we'll be done!"

So I pushed. With everything I had left within me, I pushed. And just when I thought I couldn't take another fraction of a second, the world changed.

"Well, lookie there!" Fiona cried. "It's a girl!"

Fiona quickly brought the baby to me and laid her on my chest. She was the tiniest thing I had ever seen, so pale and small, with a shocking head of red hair. I immediately laughed, pain forgotten, as I stroked my daughter's cheek.

"A girl. A girl with red hair." I looked up at Emerson, my eyes twinkling. "Two of us. You're in trouble now."

But there was no thought of trouble in Emerson's eyes. He stared down at his daughter in awe, already obviously in love. Yes, this sweet girl would have her daddy wrapped around her little fingers in no time.

He looked from her to me, tears in his eyes. "I love you," he said.

"I love you, too." My heart was so full of love I felt it might burst.

"Can I... Can I see her?" Mom's voice came from across the room, small and timid, as if she wasn't sure she was welcome.

"Of course," I said.

Mom came over and the four of us all stared down at this gorgeous little wonder, this sweet gift from heaven.

"Have you thought of a name yet?" Fiona asked.

I looked at Emerson. He nodded, confirming.

"We have," I said softly. "Mom, Fiona... I'd like you to meet our daughter, Fiona Eileen Jones. We're going to call her Eileen."

"Sullivan-Jones," Emerson corrected.

I looked up at him, questioning.

"There should be an Eileen Sullivan in the world," he said.

My eyes filled with happy tears, and as I looked at Mom, I saw hers were teary too. She smiled at me, then quickly ducked away and grabbed a tissue, while Fiona beamed at us all.

We were a family. All five of us. And as I gazed down at my precious daughter, I had the overwhelming conviction that the best was yet to come.

ACKNOWLEDGMENTS

This book was written for everyone who took a chance on a new author, read *Secrets in the Cottage,* and fell in love with Rosemary Mountain the way I did. Putting a book out into the world is a scary thing, and your encouragement and excitement mean absolutely everything to me. I can never thank you enough for how you've changed my life. I hope this chapter of Daphne's story was everything you wanted it to be.

As always, I owe a great debt to my husband, Brandon. Thank you for being my biggest supporter, an invaluable life partner, my best friend, and my soulmate. I could not do this without you.

I would also like to thank my children, who continue to support me on this journey. I cherish our "coffeeshop writing dates" and movie nights. You're my world and I love you so much!

Special thanks to my sister Jessica for being the best secret beta reader ever. I'm thrilled you loved the book, and appreciate your feedback and help.

I would also like to thank Mickey Reed, my new editor, for her exceptional work on this book. Thanks also to Brooke Passmore of BY THE BROOKE DESIGNS for another beautiful Rosemary Mountain Mystery cover. I'm grateful to have such a great team!

Special thanks also goes to Hollye A., who lent her expertise in social work and law enforcement to assist with a particular plot point. I appreciate you answering my questions and explaining so much to me!

I would also like to thank my friends Krysten S., Julia P., and Whitney S., for keeping me encouraged through the writing process. Your support means the world, and I cherish every single "Rosemary Mountain" surprise gift you've sent me!

Special thanks also to Juniper Tree Meadery and Weber's Book House, both in Paragould, Arkansas, for supporting this local author! If you're ever traveling through Paragould, both places are worth a stop. They are incredible family-run businesses that truly embrace the local movement.

Finally, a big thank you to my friends, family, and community as a whole. You have all shown me so much encouragement through this, and I cannot thank you enough.

About the Author

Nicole Gardner lives in NE Arkansas with her husband, their two sons, and their two crazy dogs. If she's not at her desk, you'll likely find her either in the garden, or creating teas and tinctures in the kitchen.

Nicole's background is in psychology. This fascination with human behavior and relationship dynamics plays a significant role in her writing and the way she shapes her characters.

www.nicolegardnerbooks.com